DEAD SEA

DEAD SEA

A Richard Mariner Adventure

Peter Tonkin

severn House

This first world edition published 2012
in Great Britain and 2013 in the USA by
SEVERN HOUSE PUBLISHERS LTD of
19 Cedar Road, Sutton, Surrey, England, SM2 5DA.

British Library Cataloguing in Publication Data

Tonkin, Peter.
  Dead sea.
  1. Mariner, Richard (Fictitious character)--Fiction.
  2. Mariner, Robin (Fictitious character)--Fiction.
  3. Lottery tickets--Fiction. 4. Marine pollution--
  Fiction. 5. Pacific Ocean--Fiction. 6. Suspense fiction.
  I. Title
  823.9'2-dc23

ISBN-13: 978-0-7278-8231-8 (cased)

All Severn House titles are printed on acid-free paper.

Severn House Publishers support The Forest Stewardship Council [FSC],
the leading international forest certification organisation. All our titles that
are printed on Greenpeace-approved FSC-certified paper carry the FSC logo.

Typeset by Palimpsest Book Production Ltd.,
Falkirk, Stirlingshire, Scotland.
Printed and bound in Great Britain by
MPG Books Ltd., Bodmin, Cornwall.

For Cham, Guy and Mark,
As always.

And to the staff and students of Combe Bank School,
many of whom helped with the creation of this story
and some of whom are in it.

Acknowledgements

Dead Sea began when I joined *The Ecologist* and was sent a copy of Mark Lynas' *High Tide*. This sparked interest in the Pacific and in Tuvalu. Interest which was piqued by reports of 'The Great Pacific Garbage Patch' that began to surface at once. I turned immediately to Brian Dunning's essential Skeptoid website which explained the actual state of the so called 'garbage patch'. My son, Guy, completing a dissertation on the effect of ecological writing on current American literature, then recommended Alan Weisman's *The World Without Us*. Both Mr Lynas and Professor Weisman were kind enough to answer my contacts and their work has influenced the story as it has turned out; though the 'garbage patch' as it appears in the closing chapters, and what happens to it in the end, are based on my brother Simon's experiences as RAF press-liaison officer during the Piper Alpha disaster.

The 'garbage' question was made more interesting by the news reports of wreckage from the Japanese earthquake and tsunami of 2011 still drifting across the North Pacific, and, in particular, of the fate of the *Ryou-Un Maru*. Other books that influenced the final outcome of *Dead Sea* were Paul Brown's *Global Warming*, and Donovan Hohn's *Moby-Duck*, the latter particularly because Mr Hohn sailed from Hawaii to the area and dived in it, searching for the garbage.

For once I did not need to approach the Chart and Pilot division of Kelvin Hughes – a long-term standby in nautical matters – for I had the relevant pilots as well as the Rough Guides to all the land-based sections of the story. And I had the Internet. Google Earth allowed me to research every location from Tuvalu to French Frigate Shoals in the finest detail. Detail only rivalled by Mary Gostelow's Girlahead website which took me into the most exclusive recesses of the Mandarin Oriental, Tokyo, and, through 'The Gal's' experiences, allowed me to learn how to get a PhD in Sushi. Once again, 'The Gal' was kind enough to reply to my contact and her adventures became Richard's.

Liberty's vessel *Flint* is based on *Plastiki,* a vessel made of plastic bottles which has actually sailed across the North Pacific. Liberty herself, as with one or two other characters, has been constructed during a series of negotiations with students at Combe Bank School as part of a project to show how literature can be interactive as well as the result of an individual view. I must also thank two advisors to whom I turn when I need hands-on advice about sailing. Thank you Mike Higgins and Peter Halsor. Every tack and gybe the girls make correctly is down to you. Every mistake is down to me. Finally I must thank my brother Simon and my wife Cham who read and advised at every stage of writing. I really could not have done it without you.

Peter Tonkin, Tunbridge Wells and Sharm El Sheikh

Challenger

Heritage Mariner's exploration vessel *Poseidon* sat at three one point three degrees north and one four five point zero degrees east in the sweltering heat of a North Pacific midsummer noon. The adapted corvette was precisely positioned, facing eastwards, her slim cutwater slicing through the lazy swells, eighteen hundred miles due east of her last port of call, Shanghai, and four miles vertically above the northernmost reach of the Marianas Trench.

For the moment, the Pacific was living up to its name. Long deep-water rollers surged gently westwards and perhaps only a master mariner like Richard Mariner himself would have noted the slight steepening of the westward-rolling waves as they came counter to the relentless swirl of the currents just below them, where the North Equatorial Current turned back on itself and joined the Kuroshio Current which flowed up the coasts of China and Japan before turning and running east.

Richard, or his captain, Captain Chang, had orders to hold her command dead-still at the confluence of these restlessly conflicting forces, while *Poseidon*'s owners went about the business which had brought them here.

Poseidon could have been Coleridge's painted ship idling upon a painted ocean. Given only that a modern artist would have had to add to the picture a number of twenty-first-century details. The bustle of the scientific teams on the foredeck between the gantries that reached out over the ocean to port and starboard. The group of ethnic Han seamen standing listlessly, angling off the square stern in the diminishing shadow of the helicopter up on its landing pad, waiting for the watch to change. And, perhaps most importantly, the fact that their fishing lines reached down into the lazily departing waves past a widespread slick of partially decomposing plastic junk.

It was this slowly disintegrating rubbish, among other things, which had brought Richard east from Heritage House in London.

This, and the thick, poisonous, plastic soup that lay trapped in the currents beneath. For the foredeck gantries – and the groups of scientists and engineers busy between them – had carried two of the most advanced deep-water exploration vessels on the planet and the powerful men who owned them. And lowered them over the side two hours ago on a mission to discover how deep this deadly Sargasso of rotting detritus sank.

The air was so still that even the tattered plastic bags, decaying bottles, silver-sided chip and crisp packets lay at rest among the speckles of oil tar and little drifts of Styrofoam bobbing against *Poseidon*'s cutwater, and the Heritage Mariner house colours drooped at the jackstaff on the forepeak, almost covering the Greenbaum International pennant hanging just below. Both colours were flying not only because the deep-sea exploration vessel was one of several cooperatively funded by both huge business enterprises, but because the men who controlled those enterprises were both aboard. Not only Richard Mariner but also Nic Greenbaum. *Well*, thought Richard, as the slight rocking movement of *Poseidon*'s hull was transmitted to him through the back and seat of the control chair into which he was wedged, not strictly *aboard*, perhaps. Certainly not mentally. Mentally, Richard was down in the experimental remote exploration vehicle *Neptune*, while his old friend and associate Nic Greenbaum was in control of *Salacia*, *Neptune*'s even more experimental sister. *Neptune* and *Salacia* were easing themselves side by side down towards the upper reaches of the abyssal trench, three miles beneath *Poseidon*'s hull. The broad beams of the lights with which the vehicles were festooned probed the inky darkness of the deepest ocean reaches. At the moment, they illuminated little besides each other for, from the surface down, it seemed that this part of the ocean was as dead and deserted as the still sky above it. Every flash of early colour and later movement had turned out to be some shard of rubbish, some sliver of plastic, trapped at the confluence of the mighty currents swirling purposefully around them.

During the two hours of the dive so far, the sunlight in the upper waters and the halogen lights further down had shown far less life and far more rubbish than either Richard or Nic had expected. One or two schools of lean tuna, three or four cruising sharks, but all around, sloping down the sunbeams, seemingly endless curtains of plastic fragments, undulating lazily like the flakes in a world-sized Christmas snow globe.

Richard half-expected to see Santa or a Snowman towering somewhere behind the restless blizzard. But as they had explored deeper and deeper, with no apparent lessening of the glittering whiteout, his festive thoughts had darkened and his open face had folded into an ever-deepening frown. Even at a thousand metres down, *Salacia* seemed to come and go as the polluted water thickened and thinned around her. Things had not improved, in fact, until the vessels hit the real deeps more than two thousand metres down, where the icy waters set up thermal barriers as impenetrable as strata layers in rock formations, and the currents of the upper ocean became irrelevant.

While Richard knew the workaday outlines of the crablike *Neptune* perfectly, he was constantly struck by the futuristic beauty of her younger sister. *Salacia* was an elongated teardrop of the most indestructible crystals, toughened glasses and tempered alloys available. Where *Neptune* gathered her lights, arms, cameras and propulsion systems all beneath a roughly circular carapace designed to protect her more delicate parts from the unimaginable pressures of the deep, *Salacia* appeared to have the gossamer vulnerability of a jellyfish. Her bow section seemed to be one big drop of unbreakable crystal; the rest of her – lights, arms, propulsion and all – arrayed around and behind that one unwinking, silvery eye, like the tendrils of a Portuguese Man of War.

And yet, as Richard was well aware, the appearance of fragility was utterly misleading. *Salacia* was an extension of the Chinese *Jialong* deep-sea exploration programme which had already sent men more than seven thousand metres deep. She was designed to go where even *Neptune* could not venture – down to the bottom of the Challenger Deep. A place visited by very few: by Piccard and Walsh in 1960, and by James Cameron in 2012. A place apparently as dead at seven miles down as the plastic poisoned surface was above.

And somewhere in between the two marine deserts sat the two deep-sea exploration vessels with almost nothing to observe except each other. The screens in front of Richard showed much more than *Salacia*'s picture etched against the glittering blackness all around her. They gave full-spectrum analysis of everything anywhere near *Neptune* herself – thermal imaging; 3D broad-spectrum sonar modelling of the ocean bed towards which they were easing so carefully, temperatures, pressures, and, crucially, depths. 'Just coming past four thousand metres now,' Richard rumbled, his gaze flickering steadily over the range of familiar readouts. He lifted his right hand briefly off the control to adjust the micro-mic at his throat and ease the earphones slightly. 'Seabed another thirty-five hundred metres below . . .'

'Three thousand, four hundred and thirty-seven,' observed Nic's precise Boston tones in Richard's head. 'Yes, I see. I think *Salacia*'s readouts are more accurate than yours.'

'I was just rounding up,' countered Richard easily. 'The seabed immediately below us is only the upper edge of a cliff in any case. The cliff foot is another . . .'

'One thousand, six hundred and nine metres down. Yes. I see,' drawled Nic. 'Five thousand and forty-six metres to the ocean bed itself. Looks like we're just under halfway there . . .' Like Richard, the tenser things got, the slower he talked and the faster he thought.

'And that's only the start of the trench,' observed Richard. 'It gets deeper pretty quickly the further south you go.'

'The gates of hell. Yeah. "Abandon hope all ye . . ."'

'*What's that?*' Richard interrupted his friend's quotation, his voice suddenly showing some of the tension that he actually felt.

Out of the blackness swam the largest jellyfish Richard had ever seen. It arrived unannounced because it was so diaphanous that the sonar pulses passed right through it as though it was made of the water that surrounded it. None of the other systems registered it either. It was so much a thing of the element it inhabited that it registered no movement, showed no heat signature, gave out no light signal. It may well have had sections or patterns of luminosity, as many deep-water life forms did, but they had been overwhelmed by the glare of the two deep-sea vessels' lights. It suddenly appeared, therefore, disturbingly abruptly, ghostlike, and almost shockingly identical to *Salacia*.

The huge silvery bell of its body must measure almost three

metres across, thought Richard. And the tentacles trailing after it must reach nearly forty metres back, though the shadow behind it made accuracy difficult. 'You registering this?' he asked Nic.

'Yup.'

With a weary pulse of its enormous body, the gigantic jellyfish pulled itself closer to *Salacia*, as though hoping it had found a companion in the midst of this massive emptiness.

'I think she likes you,' Richard observed. He swung *Neptune* easily inwards, closer to the cruising monster.

'Don't disturb her,' ordered Nic. 'It's our first date. We're just getting acquainted . . .'

Richard glanced up at the series of monitors above *Neptune*'s display, which gave *Salacia*'s point of view. It was exactly as though Nic's vessel was staring into a looking glass, he thought. Then he eased back as Nic pushed *Salacia* forward gently, the two colossal silvery bubbles – one of strengthened glass and the other of watery jelly – seeming to close towards each other like reflections coming together in a massive mirror. The pressure down here was passing four thousand atmospheres, he thought, double-checking the read-outs. How could a life form apparently as fragile as spun glass possibly exist?

'You any idea what she is?' enquired Nic.

'Looks like a Lion's Mane to me,' Richard answered. 'Lion's Mane jellyfish are supposed to be the biggest and I can't imagine anything much bigger than this. But I thought they stayed up in the Arctic. It's pretty rare to see one this far south. Maybe . . .' His voice tailed off as he became lost in thought.

'Yeah?' prompted Nic. 'Maybe . . .?'

'The north polar icecap is still melting, even if the Antarctic seems to be gaining ice again,' said Richard slowly. 'Maybe the meltwater from the Arctic Ocean is pushing creatures like this one further south. Setting up new currents in the deep ocean . . .'

'It's a theory.' Nic didn't sound particularly convinced but he fell silent and Richard eased *Neptune* closer to the jellyfish. Her lights probed the darkness behind the huge creature, showing a forest of trailing tendrils reaching away into blue-black shadow. And more. Richard was suddenly frowning almost thunderously and swearing under his breath. For tangled in the huge creature's tentacles was a massive section of drift net. Orange cable – an indestructible mixture of polypropylene and Kevlar – led to two big orange plastic floats separated by fat tubes of Styrofoam. The orange balloons squashed flat by the pressure, but the Styrofoam somehow still holding its shape. Behind this billowed the better part of sixty square metres of indestructible orange fishing net – complete with the rotting corpses and skeletons of whatever the net had been set to catch. No wonder the huge jellyfish seemed to be pulling itself so wearily through the water.

With hardly a second thought, Richard sent *Neptune* further back along the huge creature's tentacles, already unfolding the mechanical arms, calculating the most effective way of cutting the netting free. He had no idea whether the jellyfish could feel any pain near its extremities, and if so how it would react to even a well-intentioned attempt to cut the jetsam free. At worst it would simply make a run for it. But *Neptune* and *Salacia* could both outrun it easily. So, with any luck . . .

As Nic held the bubble-bow of his vessel face-to-face with the jellyfish – seemingly communicating on some alien level, the English business magnate focused his own thoughts and actions on the central tangle of tendril and cable. As delicately as a surgeon placing a stent in a blocked artery, he reached *Neptune*'s longest arm forward until the crab-claw clipper at the end of it could cut the mare's nest of dead and living fibres apart. He extended a second arm equipped with pincers, and gently took hold of one end of the cable. Only when he had a firm grip did he start cutting the tangle of netting free.

The huge jellyfish whirled into motion at the first touch. Like a fisherman at the end of a line, Richard seemed to feel the power of the creature's reaction. *Neptune*'s head jerked down. The gripping pincers slid back along the cable as the jellyfish fought to escape. Like some kind of massive kite on the windiest of days, it heaved again and again. Richard's concentration remained focused upon the Gordian knot of palp and plastic he was cutting. A third incision coincided with a fourth huge downward heave. The net tore free and the jellyfish was gone, its speed enhanced immeasurably by the fact that *Neptune* was now holding the putrid sea anchor which had been slowing it down so terribly.

But even as it did so, *Salacia*'s warning systems kicked in. *Neptune*'s sonar started acting up, going haywire. As Richard looked at the monitors, trying to work out what on earth was going on now, Nic's voice drawled through his headset: 'Hey, Richard, looks like there's something really big down there just below us. And it's coming up towards us pretty damn fast. Far too fast for comfort, in fact . . .'

Deep

'*It's coming up!*'
'Can you see it? See what it is?'
'Not yet. But I think it's pretty big! Yes. I'm sure it's big!'
Sudden excitement at *Poseidon*'s stern filled the last moments before the eight bells sounded for the noon watch. Crewman Ironwrist Wan had managed to hook something at long last and now he was wrestling his fishing rod as though trying to land a whale. His mate, Fatfist Wu, was jumping in ungainly leaps around him, calculating whether Ironwrist would get his catch aboard before First Lieutenant Straightline Jiang called them on to duty, which he would do the instant the bell sounded or Captain Mongol Chang would be down on him like a ton of bricks. His nickname 'Straightline' referred to his preferred navigating technique. Her nickname, 'Mongol' referred to her leadership style – reminiscent of Genghis Khan's on a bad day – rather than to her appearance or ethnicity, though she was notoriously ugly, in the opinion of her adoring crew.

The thought of time running out prompted Ironwrist to depart from his much-vaunted artistry as the ship's master angler and simply jerk his catch out of the littered sea. A sizeable tuna soared up out of the water and on to the deck where it landed with a considerable *whack!* to lie writhing in the last shade under the ship's Changhe CA109 helicopter. The men gathered round it and Ironwrist shouldered his way through until he was crouching over it. He tried to get the hook out of its mouth but the fish seemed intent on biting off his fingers; so, aware of the speed with which noon was approaching, he whacked it over the head with the handle of his rod until it lay still. As soon as he was certain it was dead, he pulled out the gutting knife he had wheedled out of the ship's cook on the promise of giving his catch over to be added to the pot for dinner.

But somehow the fish didn't look all that appetizing. It was well over a metre in length, and bore all the usual familiar markings of a Pacific Bluefin tuna. But where the body between head and tail should have been rounded, full-packed, almost like a shell for a twenty-five-millimetre gun, there were only lean flanks, dull grey sides, and a strangely distended grey-white belly.

'That's a sorry-looking specimen,' said Staightline Jiang, arriving to stir up his watch before eight bells called them to their various duties.

'Yes,' agreed Fatfist. 'It looks like one of those pictures of starving African kids. All skin and bone and swollen belly.'

Ironwrist just grunted and slit the fish open. Its stomach burst all over the deck, disgorging handfuls of brightly coloured plastic splinters. 'Shit,' said the ship's master angler in disgust. 'Would you look at that? This poor creature must have gorged itself to bursting on that crap. And the more it filled its belly, the more it starved to death!' The others nodded silently in disgusted agreement. The sea heaved wearily. The ship rocked. The rubbish on the surface whispered against her sides. Eight bells tolled.

'No wonder it was after your fingers, then!' laughed Fatfist. 'They'd have been its first square meal in ages.'

'That's enough. Get it over the side with the rest of the rubbish,' ordered Straightline. 'And get to your watch stations. Now!'

'That's the afternoon watch,' said Richard as the bells rang through *Poseidon*. 'It's our signal to come up.' Less than ten seconds had elapsed since Nic's alarm warned of that massive, mysterious movement below and it was still sounding. *Neptune* was still holding the big square of netting cut from the Lion's Mane jellyfish, but at least the sonar seemed to be settling down.

'Good timing,' observed Nic. 'And weren't we supposed to be testing the emergency surfacing routines?'

Both men hit the switches designed to release compressed air into the variable buoyancy tanks forcing out the water which had allowed them to explore at this depth. *Neptune* and *Salacia* began to head for the surface, still side by side, like a couple of steel and crystal bubbles. As soon as they did so, *Salacia*'s alarm fell silent. *Neptune*'s sonar returned to normal. The tension eased. It had taken them three hours to get down – it would take them the better part of twenty minutes to return to the surface. Richard decided that clearing the deep of one more piece of dangerous rubbish was more important than winning Nic's race, so he kept hold of the net and didn't push for full buoyancy yet, though the submersible's burden was slowing *Neptune* as effectively as it had slowed the jellyfish.

Richard kept his eyes glued to the screens that showed what both of the vessels were experiencing as *Salacia* began to pull ahead. *Neptune*'s equipment was designed to look all around. Light, sonar – everything reached out in a sphere around the vessel, presenting as many facts as could be gleaned, warning of as many dangers. *Salacia*'s more advanced systems were designed to do the same, but were sensitive to a much higher degree.

Nic's systems might well be oversensitive, thought Richard hopefully, as fifteen minutes passed and everything on his monitors continued to read clear and safe while the two vessels raced on up towards the two-thousand-metre mark, the better part of ten metres apart now. Perhaps *Salacia* had misinterpreted a shoal of fish as one great entity. Or a deep-water current which had been given added weight by temperature, compression or salinity.

To be fair, compression was unlikely, Richard allowed. Even at these depths and under this pressure, water compressed only fractionally. But an unexpected wall of dense, salty water might explain the disturbance to *Neptune*'s sonar too. Especially if the thoughts about escaping Arctic abyssal streams he had shared with Nic earlier were anywhere near the truth. Could the Oyashio Current, flowing south through the Bering Strait between Russia and Alaska, be gaining enough force to push further south than ever, its water less salty than the Pacific Ocean's, perhaps – but so much colder. Settling unsuspected into the lower depths, full of displaced Arctic life forms. Something must have brought that enormous Lion's Mane jellyfish down here. The jellyfish and God alone knew what else . . .

Which was precisely where Richard had reached in his thoughts when the giant sperm whale attacked.

Richard's first warning was that his sonar suddenly went wild again. His next was that *Salacia*'s warning system kicked in, flashing on to the monitors arranged above *Neptune*'s immediately in front of him. And his third was when the creature's great square head came out of the shadows, heading across the video screens towards Nic's vessel at breathtaking speed. At first, Richard thought the two underwater research vessels were being attacked by a submarine. All he could see was a great square steely-grey shape heading in at flank speed. Then he registered a trail of silvery bubbles rising from the upper edge of the cliff-like bow. A long, narrow jaw that gaped, lined with tusklike teeth. And a tiny eye caught the light, glinting.

Richard thought, *My God! It's Moby Dick!* 'Nic!' he bellowed. 'Look out!'

The whale went for *Salacia* first, apparently because she was bigger, brighter and in the lead. But in fact *Neptune* was closer to the massive cetacean. Richard had only been holding the compressed-air controls at three-quarters. He jammed them both full open now, and watched *Neptune* gather speed and buoyancy in the readouts as she raced to the protection of her threatened sister.

Providentially, *Neptune* still held the square of netting, and so the quick-thinking Richard was able to pull it across the whale's face like a remote-controlled underwater toreador flirting his cape at a charging bull. The whale's sonar – which, Richard realized, must have been interfering with his own – failed to read netting and the great square face charged straight into the bright strands which obligingly wrapped themselves around it, the lower end swinging into the gape of its mouth. Richard's hands flew across the control console, making sure *Neptune* kept firm hold of the net while at the same time reversing the pressure so the vessel stopped rising and hung there, like a bright yellow bumblebee hovering beside a steel-grey locomotive.

'Nic,' ordered Richard, his deep voice regaining a matter-of-fact calm as his hands worked feverishly, 'get up and out as fast as you can.'

Even as he spoke, the door behind him opened and he felt rather than saw Captain Chang step into the control room. 'I see this on bridge monitor,' she snapped angrily, as though Richard and Nic were playing with the whale simply to irritate her. 'I do not believe what I see. You catching a *whale* there, Captain Mariner? You mad?'

Richard would have answered her, especially as he understood the unspoken message – *you bring that monster near my command and there will be BIG trouble, gwailo!* – but there was never any realistic chance.

Because the instant the net tightened, *Neptune* was off on a wild ride. Richard watched the readouts unreeling with dizzying speed as *Neptune* rode the leviathan down, then he frowned and began to ease air back into the buoyancy tanks, playing the whale in a way that *Poseidon*'s master angler Ironwrist Wan might have done. But seeking to distract the monster, keep it in play until *Salacia* was safe with no real thought of actually landing the thing. He was no mad Captain Ahab, after all, seeking to revenge the loss of his leg. And he had no intention of pulling the net off the Lion's Mane jellyfish simply to leave it wrapped around a sperm whale if he could help it.

Within moments Richard had lost sight of *Salacia* and was only able to track his companion using *Neptune*'s GPS system. His cameras showed only darkness above and below. More darkness off to the right. And on the left, the heaving flank of the massive creature he was lashed to. There was a brownish-grey wall of flesh, beginning to fold into wrinkles like elephant's skin. The creature's right eye. Then the readouts were going haywire as the whale reversed its run at two-and-a-half-thousand metres and started heading for the surface. He glanced up at the timer. The mad ride had lasted five minutes so far. *Salacia* would be up in ten minutes. 'You'd better get ready to retrieve *Salacia*,' he said to Chang.

'I stay,' snapped captain Chang. 'I make sure. *Pessonarry!*' He might own the vessels, said her angry tone. But she was in command and responsible. And after years of working with her, he was more than happy with her decision.

The two signatures on the GPS were moving well apart now. And *Neptune*'s signature was well clear of *Poseidon*'s position too. Which was just as well, because it looked from *Neptune*'s depth gauge as though the whale *Neptune* was attached to was heading full-speed for the surface. What the fearsome pressure changes were doing to the deep-sea vehicle's more delicate elements as the pair of them hurled up through the water, he hesitated to guess. How that damage would be compounded by a short flight through the lower air, he didn't even want to think about. But somewhere in the back of his mind he began to compose a very interesting letter to his insurers at Lloyd's of London.

Suddenly the cameras facing away from the massive grey flank were showing the deepest indigo colour. Ink-dark water was speckled with that blizzard of plastic, as though the whale were dragging *Neptune* through the heart of the Milky Way. The first sunbeams stabbed down like silvery blades, but still there were only blues – the blues of the sky at a frosty dawn – no reds or yellows yet. Richard switched off all the lights and the net went from orange to brown at once. But moments later, the first yellow wavelengths got through and the nearly indestructible plastic began to return to its accustomed colour.

An instant later, the whale tore through the surface and *Neptune* was in flight. The huge square head jerked one way and then another. The momentum of the heavy little explorer simply tore the net free of that huge rocklike cliff face of dark grey flesh and, trailing the bright plastic after it, *Neptune* tumbled across the lower sky and plunged back into the water.

As the silvery surface closed over *Neptune* once again, *Salacia*'s cameras showed the surface opening as she came up at more or less the same spot as Ironwrist's tuna. Richard fought to regain control of his vessel, at the same time scanning the readouts for warning of the whale's return. But all was calm and quiet. 'Could you call Ironwrist down to relieve me?' he asked Captain Chang. 'He can bring *Neptune* home. I want to go up and see *Salacia* aboard.'

Ten minutes later, Richard was up on the foredeck, watching as *Salacia* was winched up into her place. Then he stood beside the deckhand, whose duty was to loosen the bolts and open the vessel's main hatch. He reached in and helped Nic step unsteadily out on to the deck. 'Wild ride,' he observed as he helped his friend down on to the stretcher that would carry him to the decompression chamber – just in case the atmosphere in the experimental bathyscaphe had varied enough to pump nitrogen into his blood.

'*From hell's heart I stab at thee*,' answered Nic wearily but with a half grin as he lowered himself on to the stretcher. '*For hate's sake I spit my last breath at thee . . .*'

'Is that Ahab from *Moby Dick*?' asked Richard, walking across to the decompression chamber beside his friend at the heart of a group of scientists and physicians. 'Or Khan from *Star Trek*?'

'I'll count my legs and get back to you,' promised Nic as the door of the decompression chamber clanged shut behind him.

Richard slapped the top of the metal canister with a laugh, then walked on down the length of the ship, past the bridge house and the Changhe helicopter, past the wet patch on the deck that was still littered with plastic from the tuna's belly and down to the aft rail. He leaned against this, narrow-eyed, looking away west towards Japan, watching for the first sight of the returning *Neptune*.

The high sun abruptly vanished behind a low overcast and a squally shower came whipping across the water towards him, carrying in its skirts a storm of decomposing bags and packets, setting the half-rotted bottles, cups, wrappers and plastic can-rings bobbing and dancing on the polluted water.

'We have to do something about this,' Richard said to himself. 'Before it's too late. If it isn't too late already . . .'

Bottle

Richard Mariner was probably the tallest person standing on the south side pavement of the Route Fifty Road Bridge overlooking the Arakawa River to the north of Tokyo a year later. He was certainly the wettest. Even his wife, Robin, who stood by his side, was holding an umbrella – supplied by the Mandarin Oriental Hotel together with the Rolls-Royce waiting to whisk them back across town into the warmth and dryness of their suite when the ceremony was over. Everyone nearby held an umbrella. Even Dr Tanaka – who also held the big plastic bottle which had once contained a grape-flavoured Cheerio soft drink that he was proposing to throw into the foaming water. And the TV crews who were going to film him doing it.

Only Richard refused to arm himself against the thunderous downpour, preferring to rely on the double cape of his Burberry trench coat and the collar that turned up as high as his steely blue eyes, almost hiding the white line along his cheekbone, which resembled a Prussian aristocrat's duelling scar. A scar caused by the typhoon Straightline Jiang had taken *Poseidon* straight through some years earlier, brought into unusual prominence this evening by the cold, the blinding lights of the local representatives of the World's press and the deafening, penetrating deluge.

During the year since Richard had stood at *Poseidon*'s after-rail and decided to do something about the pollution in the north Pacific, it seemed never to have stopped raining. Everywhere around the Pacific rim had seen biblical deluges leading to catastrophic flooding. And yet the threatened rise in overall sea levels had not been so apparent; not even in Tuvalu, the tiny mid-Pacific island nation so famously at risk. In the mid-Pacific archipelagos, in fact, there had been falling water levels and fearsome drought instead. And to make things worse, it looked as though this year was going to be a particularly powerful La Nina year; with the threat of more torrential rainfall and further flooding in many of the already sodden areas, combined with drought and falling water levels in the islands.

But Dr Tanaka had a theory to explain all of these things – one that he was going to test during the next few months. With the help of Heritage Mariner, Greenbaum International, Richard, Nic, Richard's wife and business partner, Robin and Nic's daughter, Liberty – and the big plastic Cheerio bottle. 'As Greenbaum International Fellow of Sustainable Energy and Climate Change at Tokyo University, it has been my task to study what is currently happening to the climate of the Pacific Basin and to predict its likely results,' Dr Tanaka was explaining to the earnest young woman from Nippon News, his voice carrying over the roaring of the waters above and below to the umbrella-sheltered teams from Kyodo News, Radio Japan NHK, CNN, NewsCorp and the BBC. 'And as the first major test of the theory I have formulated, I propose to place this bottle in the river here.'

'What is the point of adding more rubbish to an already littered waterway?' wondered the Nippon News reporter. Her cameraman swung round to point his lens at the foaming torrent of the Arakawa's surface just beneath the trembling bridge. The river's slick brown back was littered with a range of flotsam whirling down towards Tokyo Bay at a dizzying velocity.

'You will be aware, I am sure, that trash such as this, especially plastic trash, has been sucked out of rivers and off coastal landfills by a combination of wind and rain all around the Pacific Rim during the last decade and more – then swirled away into what has become known as the Great North Pacific Garbage Patch, where it has broken down into small pieces some of which have entered the food chain, with extremely disturbing results.'

'That's not new,' persisted the young woman. 'Everyone knows about the garbage patch twice the size of Texas . . .'

'But you can't see it,' explained Tanaka. 'It's there, but it's not visible on Google Earth . . . Perhaps, Captain Mariner, you would explain. You have been closer to the actuality of it than anyone else here . . .'

Richard looked down into the camera and started to explain. 'The length of time the plastic takes to get from all round the North Pacific Rim into the middle of the ocean means that a combination of sun and saltwater can break down its structure. By the time the plastic reaches the relatively slow-moving circular swirl at the centre of the currents, beneath the light winds at the heart of the ocean, only a small percentage of it is recognizable as bottles, can-rings, bags and so forth. The rest has half dissolved into the water. It's a weird kind of inedible soup – deadly to the creatures that try to eat it, and yet not thick enough to constitute a hazard to shipping. Not that there's much shipping out there, in any case. My work with Mr Greenbaum aboard our co-funded deep-water explorer *Poseidon* has established that all the pollution is under the surface except for some particularly hard-wearing bottles, bags and crisp packets. Or has been until very recently.'

Richard's ice-blue eyes narrowed as he stared unflinchingly down into the lens of the camera behind the young reporter's shoulder. 'Until the last few months at least, it hasn't been visible from space at all – unlike the wreckage from the terrible tsunami of March 2011, for instance, that's still apparently drifting across the Pacific from Japan to British Columbia in a kind of floating island. That is quite astonishing given the simple size of the area affected – some estimates suggest half a million square miles.' His long, lean face folded into a frown. 'But Doctor Tanaka's work has proved that things are beginning to change. And not for the better.'

'It is my basic contention,' inserted the doctor, smoothly reclaiming the attention of the reporter and the millions of her audience, 'that the unprecedented rise in precipitation around the Pacific Rim is beginning to accelerate the currents that swirl around the edges of the ocean. This rise in mean speed – if we can prove it exists and then measure it – might well explain the rise in sea level here, in Western America, Queensland and Indonesia that we have seen. It might also explain the fall in sea level in the middle of the Pacific. The physics are simple – and may be observed every time water flows out of a shower stall, bath or hand basin in a vortex that raises the outer edges and lowers the central area. But of course there is no plughole in the centre of the Pacific. Instead, what we have is a case of greatly accelerated speeds along major currents like the Kuroshio Current and the California Current – and these could well have disastrous side effects even beyond raising water levels at the edges of the gyre or vortex while lowering them at the centre. Such as sucking water out of the Arctic Ocean, for instance, as some of the work done by Mr Greenbaum and Captain Mariner might suggest. Also, moving plastic waste from Eastern Asia and Western America into the 'Garbage Patch' area swiftly enough to bypass the destructive action of sunlight and seawater which has broken down their structure in the past – and to create a solid island – a *plastic Sargasso*, if you will, substantial enough to become a genuine hazard to commercial shipping . . .'

'As well as a fatal hazard to wild life of all sorts . . .' added Richard, 'as Mr Greenbaum and I have already proved beyond doubt. Though we're just another couple among hundreds flagging up the danger . . .'

'But not an average "couple"!' said the young reporter. 'You and Mr Greenbaum represent enormous power and influence. It is almost as though British Petroleum had joined forces with Microsoft to bring the world's attention to the problem. After all, that is why we are here today, is it not? There is more to this than Doctor Tanaka and his plastic bottle!'

'If the doctor is correct,' Richard observed drily, 'that will become the most famous plastic bottle on the planet.'

'It already has a fan club,' interjected the doctor, holding the clear two-litre Grape-flavour Cheerio container up under the camera lights. Beneath the tightly sealed silver-coloured cap and the solar-powered waterproof transmitter immediately underneath it, the bottle was packed tight with slips of paper. 'My students and I have purchased tickets for the Jumbo Lottery and put them in here,' he announced. 'The bottle is packed with several hundred of them, in fact. At about the time I expect the bottle to arrive – unscathed and showing no signs of decomposition at all – in the middle of the North Pacific Gyre, in mid-August, the lottery will have been drawn. And the winning ticket will be worth in excess of one-hundred-million US dollars!'

There was a hiss of shock loud enough to overcome the drumming of the rain as the impact of his words ran through the crowd on the bridge.

'But what happens if the winning ticket is in the bottle?' demanded the reporter, horrified. 'It could well be lost forever; even if you can track the bottle's location, how would anyone ever reach it? Recover it?'

'Then the first of the two vessels racing to pick it up will be able to bring it home,' answered Richard.

Robin stepped forward then, apparently oblivious to the cascade that rolled like a mini Niagara off her umbrella and into her beloved husband's handmade footwear. And, indeed, over the blue picture of a boat set into the sidewalk beneath the exclusive leather of their soles. 'I will be captaining Heritage Mariner's Fastnet-winning multihull *Katapult*,' she announced brusquely as the beam of the camera lights gleamed on the riot of her golden curls and the still grey breadth of her eyes. 'And Mr Greenbaum's daughter, Liberty, who is already an America's Cup winner with her team from Stanford University – where she is this year's student commodore of the Graduate Business School's sailing club and president of the MBA association – will be captaining Greenbaum International's experimental vessel *Flint*, which is made entirely out of reclaimed polystyrene.'

Robin held their attention with the same calm, experienced authority that Richard had exercised. 'Ms Greenbaum and I will be running a kind of twin Transpac. *Flint* will sail from Vancouver, British Columbia, and *Katapult* will sail from Tuvalu. We will set sail on the first of August, each racing flat out for the other's point of departure, on reciprocal headings. And we are planning to meet in the middle of the North Pacific Gyre formed by the ocean currents ten days later, at about the same time as Doctor Tanaka's bottle gets there. We will have satellite tracking equipment aboard which will let us observe its progress at all times.'

'That sounds dangerous,' observed the reporter roundly. 'Two experimental yachts commanded by women, sailing into the middle of an oceanic desert the size of the Empty Quarter in the Sahara – where there are likely to be no currents, no winds, and the possibility of a sea of solid plastic flotsam the size of Texas.'

'And there in the middle of it,' added Robin cheerfully, 'Doctor Tanaka's bottle, which could well be worth one-hundred-million dollars. A risk worth taking in all sorts of ways, I'd say. And not just for the publicity.'

'Talking of which,' added the good doctor triumphantly, 'it is Zero Hour! Time to get this show on the road. Wish the good ship *Cheerio* luck!' And with that, he crossed to the railing in three determined strides and dropped the bottle into the foaming water.

Under the pool of camera lights the bottle sank out of sight, and the crowd straining against the south-side railing held its breath until the silver cap bobbed up again surprisingly far downstream. The moment that it did so, there was a ragged, spontaneous cheer that grew and grew in confidence as the bottle whirled away.

'Now that's what I call publicity,' said Richard an hour later as he came out of the en suite bathroom still steaming from his shower, and stepped into the master bedroom of the Mandarin Oriental's Presidential Suite. Robin was sprawled across the king-sized bed, and in spite of the views that the suite commanded of Tokyo Bay, The Imperial Palace and Mount Fuji in the distance, she was looking at her laptop. On the wall above her was a thirty-seven-inch LCD TV, and through in the lounge beyond, between the doors into the private dining suite and the study, there was a fifty-two-inch big brother. Both were showing how wise Richard had been to refuse an umbrella. The TV lights illuminating him during the interview shone upward slightly, etching his angular face memorably against the stormy sky, emphasizing the hook of his nose, the lines of his cheekbones, the brutal line of the duelling scar, the wild blue dazzle of his eyes. The powerful authority of his words. The TVs' sound was on mute, but Richard could read his own lips well enough.

'Then the first of the two vessels racing to pick it up will be able to bring it home,' he was saying.

The camera lights swung round on to Robin and at once she seemed smaller in comparison. Her face at first invisible behind a wall of silver raindrops cascading like a waterfall in front of her. Then constricted, somehow diminished by the makeshift shelter of the Oriental's canvas umbrella – a green tent above the guinea gold of her hair. Her wide grey eyes seemingly reflecting the stormy sky she was sheltering from as she looked earnestly out of the twin TV pictures. Her silent lips moved. *'I will be captaining Heritage Mariner's Fastnet-winning multihull* Katapult.'

Richard sat down beside her, still towelling the black waves of his hair, wondering what could be distracting her from the breathtaking views, from her own TV interview. The laptop's seventeen-inch screen was filled with a Google Earth picture of Tokyo. And there, superimposed upon it, was the readout from the GPS locator system showing the Cheerio bottle's current location. 'My God!' he breathed, suddenly understanding – sharing – her fascination. The red dot that showed the bottle's location was out in the bay already, some vagrant current of the regimented river's outflow swirling it eastwards along the city coastline as though it was eager to join the mighty Kuroshio Current immediately – or perhaps it just wanted to catch a glimpse of Tokyo Disneyland before it set out on its long, lonely voyage.

'That's a Le Mans start if ever I saw one!' he joked, patting the snow-white terry-towelling hillock of her bottom. 'Maybe you'd be better in *Marilyn* than in *Katapult* . . .' *Marilyn*, his bright red cigarette go-faster launch could reach speeds approaching seventy-five miles per hour. *Katapult* could only sail at forty-five – and that on a good, breezy day.

'Very funny,' she answered, her voice preoccupied. 'You know Liberty would never talk to either of us ever again if we pulled a stunt like that. And the gorgeous Miss Greenbaum is your godchild, after all.'

'But still and all,' he said, 'Doctor Tanaka's bottle is moving at one hell of a speed.'

'I Skyped Liberty while you were in the shower,' said Robin. 'She's offline at the moment but she sends her love. And we've agreed to upgrade the bottle. She is now a ship. The good ship *Cheerio*, in fact. And yes. She is moving at quite a lick. She'll bear some close watching during the next couple of months.'

'But it's far too soon to get fixated on her now,' Richard decided. 'We've far more important things to consider in the meantime.'

'Like what?' asked Robin innocently.

'Like are you feeling hungry?' he asked by way of answer. 'They've set out a cold buffet. Or I can order up something hot. Even the room-service menu has more Michelin stars than there are chairs in our private dining room.'

She closed the laptop and slid it on the bedside table. 'Maybe later,' she said, squirming sensuously over on to her side. Like Richard, she had warmed herself up since their return, but she had been in the Jacuzzi and her skin was glowing pink, hot to the touch. Like him, she was wearing nothing more than a huge white towel and the Chanel perfume another Marilyn entirely famously wore to bed. The towel opened conveniently beneath his hand. The fragrance of No. 5 filled the massive master suite so powerfully that even the air conditioning was powerless against it.

'Maybe later,' he agreed. 'In the meantime, it occurs to me that we haven't christened this bed yet. And, now I come to think of it,' he added, loosening the towel round his own slim waist, 'there are beds in two other rooms in this suite alone. So we'd better get busy, my love . . .'

Liberty

L iberty Greenbaum paused for a moment in her progress across Jericho Park, Vancouver, and swept the weight of her hair back as she squinted across the dull grey chop of English Bay trying to catch a glimpse of *Flint*. Like her godfather Richard Mariner on the road bridge in Tokyo three months earlier, she wasn't letting the weather worry her. Even though she had simply shrugged a navy Helly Hansen three-quarter-length rigging coat over her Carven trouser suit and strode out on to the six hundred metres of park-front shoreline separating the yacht club from the sailing centre, thus ruining several thousand dollars' worth of grand couture and a pair of Jimmy Choos almost as expensive as Richard's handmade Lobb Oxfords. But there had been a bunch of students out here waiting to walk with her and she wasn't the kind of woman to ignore her friends – or her fans.

The crowd of University of British Columbia students behind her paused also, straining, like her, to catch a glimpse of her vessel *Flint*, as she sailed across from the Royal Vancouver Yacht Club to the Jericho Sailing Centre ready for 'the off'. It was the first of August and coming up to high water. Liberty had a lot to do and not much time left, as anyone watching her recent broadcast from the grand reception at the Royal Yacht Club would have been very well aware. But *Flint* was hidden beyond the grey veils of torrential rain. This despite Liberty's command being more than thirty-five metres of bright white Styrofoam from stem to stern with a beam of fifteen metres and a foremast as tall as the hull was long, and with a triangular mainsail the shape and colour of a snow-covered Alp 210 metres square.

Liberty was frustrated that her mate Maya MacArthur was at the helm while she had been trapped into lunching in comfort and giving TV interviews instead of sailing her baby across the bay. But she had known for all of her twenty-five years that these little frustrations just came with the territory. And this race against Robin in *Katapult* was, after all, all about publicity.

Although, at twenty-five, Liberty was a graduate student now, she still fitted in well with the UBC undergrads who had waited like fans after a rock concert outside the Royal Yacht Club while she did lunch and interviews. Except that she was taller, wiser and far more experienced than any of them. Together with her still-youthful potential, Liberty was blessed with an aristocratic beauty. Coupled with smoky-blue eyes and an extravagance of honey-coloured hair, this made it all too easy for her to get her face on the front of magazines as widely separated as *Vanity Fair* and *Forbes* in the States, *Elle* and *The Economist* in the UK – and *Yachting Monthly* all over the world. Not that Liberty ever stopped for long enough to think about herself as a celebrity, let alone a pin-up. To think much about herself at all, in fact. She was usually far too wrapped up in whatever she was doing. And in her time she seemed to have done quite a lot. Under normal circumstances, she hardly ever thought about her past, but the speeches she had just sat through had brought half-forgotten details into unusually sharp focus.

Liberty's earliest memories were a footloose mixture of maids and nannies, hotels and houses all over the world as she had followed her parents while they took over the reins of Greenbaum Oil, expanding it into Greenbaum Petrochemical and then Greenbaum International. An itinerant childhood centred on her grandparents' rambling old mansion in Hyannis Port, because it was here that Grandpa Greenbaum had taught her to sail in the long, lazy summer vacations she had enjoyed with him. At the ripe age of five she had skippered her first vessel – a tiny skiff – out on the seeming vastness of Nantucket Sound.

By the age of seven, the reed-thin, iron-willed Liberty was at Amberley, an exclusive little private school in the south of England. England, because her parents were now settled in Mayfair, where they oversaw the rapid expansion of the Greenbaum International into Europe and all points east. At Amberley she first met William and Mary, the Mariner twins, immediate friends though some years her junior. And, through William and Mary, she gained access to the Heritage Mariner facilities in Southampton where, over the years on the Solent, her grandfather's lessons in distant Nantucket had been expanded exponentially as first Doc Weary then his daughter Florence had taken her up from dinghies through Lasers to keelboats and yachts. Single, double and multihull. From simple little inshore sloops to ocean-going schooners.

By the time Liberty left Amberley for Hunter College High on E94th Street, New York, aged thirteen, she had crewed *Katapult* on her Fastnet trials around the Isle of Wight and risen from a pampered mascot to a valued team member. And she had sprouted from five feet in her socks to five foot eight with muscles as unyielding as her determination. Her progress had brought the Mariner and Greenbaum families and business empires together. She had also captained the school hockey team, the fencing team and the debating team during their most successful year in Amberley's history. But she had had enough of pampered private school life. She wanted to try a new mix of academic excellence and broad-based acquaintance. Her mother had been unhappy, but her father talked her round. Something he could not have managed with Liberty herself.

At Hunter College High, Liberty rose through Sophomore to Senior – from five-eight to a whisker under six feet tall – at the head of her class, captaining the girls' lacrosse and fencing teams and the mixed debating team, easily holding her own against the boys. She fitted in with all sorts of ethnicities and backgrounds easily as a United Nations rep. On the side, she joined the Manhattan Sailing Club and continued to work her way up through the sailing classes and responsibilities towards keelboat skipper. Her academic studies in science, maths, languages and English were outstanding. But they paled beside her grasp of economics and business concepts examined in the social studies programmes, and in the summer schools she tried to fit into her busy schedule. And her SATs scores were simply phenomenal. She seemed destined to follow Meryl Streep to Vassar, Katherine Hepburn to Bryn Mawr or Elizabeth Arden and Oprah Winfrey to Harvard.

But no. The irresistibly headstrong Liberty vanished eastwards once again to the London Business School, then ranked first in the world. Here, studying in classrooms overlooking Regent's Park and safely bedded down in the familiar Greenbaum

International company flat in Mayfair, the tall, slim bundle of Yankee energy enlivened her studies by starting the Americas Club, then joining the acting, business, wine and women's touch rugby clubs. In the absence of an LBS fencing club, she joined the Central London Fencing Club in Westminster, where she polished up her skills with foil, epee and sabre. And she joined the LBS sailing club, thus reacquainting herself with the Solent and the Heritage Mariner facilities – and vessels – nearby. With Doc and with Florence. And with *Katapult*.

Liberty graduated from the London Business School top of her class as usual, with grades that almost embarrassed her tutors. Consequently, she would have been welcome to take her MBA anywhere in the world – let alone anywhere in the States. But The Leland Stanford Junior University of Palo Alto, California, had always been part of the plan because of the sailing there. And also because, in the interim, Stanford had just pipped LBS to the position of top grad school for business in the world.

Even had Liberty not been something of a legend, now, after whipping the Navy into second place and lifting the Rose Bowl last January, it would have been no trouble for her to make links between the Stanford and UBC Sailing Clubs, as the troupe of faithful UBC undergrads around her proved clearly enough. She hadn't even needed to call on Greenbaum International's Vancouver headquarters for help. In many of the circles she moved in now, her name carried more weight than her father's.

But, she had admitted during her speech to the Royal Yacht Club – and the media – that she felt she hadn't done much since arriving in Vancouver. Nothing, in fact, beyond fitting and supplying *Flint*, shaking her down and pulling the four-woman crew into shape. Not that the crew had needed much pulling. Maya MacArthur was in the Stanford sailing club with her; Emma Toda and Bella Chung-Wolf were old adversaries from USC who knew their sailing inside out from fighting them through regatta after regatta, mostly across San Francisco Bay. But the fitting and supplying, chandlering and victualling had been slow work. In spite of all the careful pre-preparation, the chandleries, ships' stores and supermarkets had fought to supply not so much what she needed, but what she needed in the quantity, size and weight required to ballast her temperamental command.

Flint was unique. Her name arose out of the fact that her hull was made of specially strengthened and treated polystyrene. Like her famous precursor *Plastiki*, a twenty-metre, two-masted, three-man ketch with a hull made of plastic bottles, her name was to be a play on words. In *Plastiki*'s case an elision of Plastic Kontiki. In *Flint*'s case, the emphasis on POLYstyrene. And the most famous nautical polly the team could think of was Long John Silver's parrot Captain Flint in R.L. Stevenson's *Treasure Island*. So *Captain Flint* she had become. Then plain *Flint* for short. But her hull needed vary careful weighting and packing, for it was as buoyant as a Styrofoam coffee cup. And, when her sails were full, as unsteady.

The weather had been bad enough to slow things further, and it showed no sign of easing now. But at least they were nearly at the Jericho Sailing Club. Liberty came striding past the tennis courts and round on to the sailing centre, with the bedraggled but buoyant students trooping after her. And as the crowd of youngsters came down through the centre itself towards the long single finger of the jetty, two things happened at once.

Flint came in out of the grey misty rain, materializing like a ghost ship as she slid silently towards the outer end of the quay, the flapping of her big white mainsail lost beneath the cheer that the students gave now they had sight of her at last. And the familiar, world-famous figure of Nic Greenbaum materialized, equally ghostly, at the inner end of the pier. Liberty was distracted from the breathtaking sight of her command for the instant it took him to sweep her into his icy, sodden embrace. His short grey beard scraped comfortably against her cheek. 'Hiya, Daddy,' she said, her eyes suddenly prickling with an intensity of emotion she had not thought to feel.

'You don't think I'd have missed this?' he teased, releasing her and twirling her round to slip a long arm over her shoulder.

'I was beginning to wonder. Wouldn't you have been happier at the Royal Yacht Club?' She glanced back across Jericho Park to the distant golden glimmer of the building she had just left.

'Naaw . . .' He drew the negative out lazily. 'This isn't about the glad-handing and the publicity. You've taken care of that in spades. This is just about a proud Poppa wanting to wave bye-bye to his little girl. Mom sends her love. Sent this too . . .' He hefted a case that looked promisingly nautical and practical. 'Just what you need to slip under your Helly Hansen, I'd say.'

As he spoke, Nic was hurrying his daughter down the quay towards the sailing boat as she swung against her mooring line, waiting for her skipper and high water. Ten minutes later she was aboard, having stopped off in the little quayside shower facility to empty the bag of the matched set of Helly Hansen sailing gear – several layers of it – and fill it with sodden haute couture and mud-smeared leopard-skin leather.

'You on a *Yachting Monthly* photoshoot?' asked Maya, as she scrambled aboard into the cockpit, almost as expensively attired here as she had been in the Royal Yacht Club.

'Mother,' explained Liberty, embarrassed. 'But we could all be on some kind of photoshoot. I don't trust my dad at all . . .'

'We could cast off now and slip away,' tempted Maya as she handed over the big yachting helm. 'We're all rigged and ready.'

'That'd be cheating . . .' Liberty hesitated uncharacteristically.

'Too late anyway,' chimed in Bella Chung-Wolf, calling up from her electronic equipment console down in the cabin. 'We're at high water now.'

'Off we go, then!' ordered Liberty with no further ado. Emma Toda cast off at the bows and Maya ratcheted the mainsail tight. The squall coming in past the Royal Yacht Club took *Flint* at once and the wheel kicked into life under Liberty's hands while the kids on the Jericho pier cheered her away.

Flint was maybe half a mile out into English Bay with Bella calling up headings, when the first of the press-packed Greenbaum International helicopters came swooping down into camera range.

Tuvalu

The helicopters thundered in low enough to make Richard look up from the shallow cavity of *Katapult*'s cockpit, where he was adjusting the aft anchors to hold her in the natural dock just deep enough to accommodate her three keels. 'Now that,' he called to Robin, 'is what I call *high water* . . .'

'Very funny,' Robin retorted from the needle sharp bow of the central hull. She shaded her eyes with her right hand and looked up past the white tube of the tight-furled foresail, following his gaze up towards the New Zealand Air Force choppers which were laden with fresh water for the drought-stricken island.

'NOT,' added Florence Weary, also calling back from the slim, smooth whaleback of the forecastle, her gaze also reaching up past the tall main mast with its cross-trees etched against the hard blue of the clear, hot sky. 'The guys on the islands are dying of thirst, you know? It's not a joking matter, Richard.'

'Well it looks like the closest to high water we'll get,' Richard riposted cheerfully, if hardly sensitively, moving back beneath the light awning he had rigged as a sunshade earlier and gesturing over the side at Te Namo Lagoon which occupied the centre of the tiny island nation's principal atoll. 'If this water was any lower we could run the world land speed championships here instead of the flats at Salt Lake.'

Rohini Verma looked up from the computer console to the right of the main cabin six steps down, behind and beneath the watertight doors that were designed to close below the main navigating position when the vessel was under full sail. She pushed her glasses back up her long nose and dabbed at the sweat beading her upper lip. The fitful breeze that cooled Richard and made the awning flap occasionally didn't reach down there. 'You know very well that high water will come. It is a tidal thing. Nothing to do with global warming or Doctor Tanaka's plughole effect. To do with the *moon*.'

'It's the *sun* that's worrying me now,' riposted Richard from the safety of the awning's wind-cooled shadow. 'What's the temperature down there with you, Rohini? Forty-five Celsius? Goodness knows what it must be out on the beach there.'

'Hot enough to cook shrimp,' called Flo feelingly from the unshaded bow. 'Without the barbie.'

'Then I'm surprised it isn't barbecuing Akelita's toes,' concluded Richard. 'Because she's strolling out across it now.'

The fourth and last member of the all-woman crew approached almost lazily, carrying a palm-frond bag full of goodies from the Jimmy Store on Tuvalu Street. Like the town it supplied it sat well behind the crest of the golden slope behind her, invisible from here.

'She's a local girl,' observed Robin enviously, watching her wade out into the lagoon, scarcely more than paddling out to where the multihull sat restlessly, ready to sail at high water. 'Acclimatized. *You're* the one I'm worried about, Richard. Did you bring sandals with you when you came aboard this morning? We cast off when Rohini calls high tide and you're not coming with us.'

'I have my O'Neills,' he assured her. 'Wet or dry they'll see me through. And it isn't that far up to town.'

Katapult was anchored on the lagoon side of Fongafale Island, largest of the circular chain of islets that comprised Tuvalu atoll. Beyond the white sand slope of the beach, there was a fringe of vivid green palms, then a short, shaded walk between beachside shacks and houses through to Fongafale Street, followed by a slightly longer stroll past the banana plantation to Tuvalu Street, and, on the ocean side of that, the buildings at the start of the International Airport runway, the Matagigali Bar and JY's Ocean restaurant.

Halfway down the runway on the ocean side were the airport buildings themselves – where the NZ Air Force chopper boys would be signing in, Richard suspected, before unloading their precious freshwater cargo and heading up towards the Matagigali for a different sort of liquid refreshment entirely. And on the lagoon side of the runway opposite the Airport buildings, south of the banana plantation, stood the National Bank, post office with its new cell phone mast and the government and municipal buildings beside it. There was a hospital, a couple of schools and the Vaiaku Lagi Hotel, one of whose wonderful upstairs double rooms currently contained what little was left of the Mariners' luggage now that Robin had moved what she needed for a thirty-day cruise into her skipper's accommodation aboard *Katapult*.

As Richard reached this point in his thoughts, Akelita climbed aboard, mounting the aft ladder like Venus rising from a shallow ocean, one-handed, with the palm-frond bag on her shoulder. She stepped lithely down into the afterdeck well, beside Richard, filling his nostrils with the heady scents of sea salt, coconut – and of the foo yung she had purchased for the crew's last dirtside lunch.

Akelita heard Richard's tummy rumbling. 'Not for you,' she warned severely. 'For girls only. You eat ashore, Capting.' Then she relented with a dazzling Polynesian smile. 'They expecting you in three-quarter hour. They make extra, with special fried rice. *Man-size*.' Then she disappeared below, squeezing past Rohini and her equipment. 'Lunch!' she called. 'Eight bells. Noon watch!'

It hit Richard then. The immediacy of his parting with the beautiful vessel, her lovely crew and her beloved skipper. He squared his jaw. 'How long to the top of the water, Rohini?' he asked, his voice quiet and his tone serious at last.

'Thirty-three minutes,' she answered.

Richard nodded once and reached into his shorts for his cell phone. 'Better get ready, Willy,' he said as soon as contact was made.

Like Nic Greenbaum, Richard had the publicity planned both for maximum impact and for minimum intrusion. The cutting edge of media here was Willy, the lead reporter for Radio Tuvalu. But Willy was more than just a small island radio hack. As well as a pencil and reporter's pad, a microphone and a recorder, he had a top of the line digital video camera. And he had an adapter that plugged his camera straight into the most powerful computer at the Motolalu Internet Cafe less than fifty metres from Richard's hotel.

Today the Motolalu, thought Richard, *tomorrow the world*. In this case, literally. Richard had called in a range of favours everywhere from NewsCorp to the BBC and once it was uploaded on to the Internet, Willy's footage was due to be out worldwide within hours of *Katapult*'s departure. Running in tandem, in fact, with Nic Greenbaum's much more in-your-face plans for coverage of *Flint*'s departure from Vancouver.

These thoughts filled the mere seconds between Akelita's call and the arrival of the hungry women. Had Richard felt sentimental before at the thought of parting from *Katapult*, her crew and his wife, he felt positively isolated now. Underfoot indeed, as Robin and Flo shoved rudely past him, all too well aware that foo yung does not hold its heat for long. And that a fresher, larger batch would be waiting for him as they tacked across the lagoon and out through the Te Ava Tepuka Vili channel immediately south of Tepuka Island at the north-west of the atoll itself, in an hour

or so's time. 'Right,' said Robin as she heaved past him as though
he no longer existed, 'we've just got time for a final briefing as
we eat. We need to get ready for a slow start, I'm afraid . . .'

The winds were light and variable, thought Richard, frowning.
They would in all probability get a much less decisive start than
Flint in stormy Vancouver. But they would stick to the rules and
use what wind they had. Certainly, they would not use *Katapult*'s
motors in anything less than an emergency. Especially as, if Dr
Tanaka was correct, they might well need their motors in ten
days' time when they hit the Sargasso of plastic he predicted
would be accumulating around the good vessel *Cheerio* in the
middle of the Great North Pacific Gyre.

Richard looked down into the fragrant darkness of *Katapult*'s
cabin where Robin was already leading the brisk discussion and
decided it was time for him to go ashore. He and Robin had said
'goodbye' in their favourite fashion last night, christening yet
another bed in the process. There was nothing to be gained from
fond farewells now, he thought. If there was anything important
Robin needed to say, there was the ship-to-shore. That would
have to do, no matter how intimate the message. Privacy, in any
case, would be a happy dream for the next thirty days. For Robin
and her crew at least. Just as he had been something between a
diversion and a hindrance all morning, he would only be a distraction now. He stepped up on to the transom above the well of the
afterdeck, placing his foot on to the wet patch left by Akelita as
she stepped aboard. The cool on his left sole reminded him about
his O'Neills and he stooped to grab them before he swung himself
outboard and climbed down the ladder into the surprisingly warm
and welcoming water.

Richard was in the shallows at the derisory surf line, hopping
on one leg as he pulled his O'Neills on when Willy arrived. 'Are
they ready to set sail?'

Richard consulted his Rolex Oyster Perpetual Yachtmaster.
'Fifteen minutes,' he said. 'They'll want to set the sails and get
everything ship shape first.'

'That should make good copy,' said Willy eagerly, unfolding
the side-section of his camera to get the beautiful vessel in frame.
'What are they doing now?'

Richard decided that foo yung would not make good copy. 'They'll be having a final briefing,' he explained shortly, coming erect with his feet now sand-proof.

Satisfied that he could get a newsworthy picture of *Katapult*, Willy pulled a digital sound recorder out of his pocket and connected it to the camera's built-in sound system. 'This is Willy Fatato, reporting for the Tuvalu Media Corporation,' he announced. 'I'm talking to Captain Richard Mariner as his wife, Captain Robin Mariner, prepares to set sail on the race across the Northern Pacific which has gripped the news channels worldwide during the last few days. Captain Mariner,' he said, full-voice and formal, 'can you explain to the audience what precisely is going on aboard *Katapult* during the final moments before she sets sail on her epic voyage?'

Although Willy's camera was clearly pointing at *Katapult* once more, Richard automatically drew his hand back over his wind-tousled hair. 'The skipper, Captain Robin Mariner, will be giving the crew their final briefing,' he answered formally. 'As well as crucial details about race strategy, she will be discussing how best to get a good start, given the current conditions. Captain Mariner will no doubt be aware of the need to tack across Te Namo Lagoon with the utmost care and precision if she hopes to exit northwards as planned through the Te Ava Tepuka Vili channel, which is extremely narrow. It is a series of manoeuvres that would test the most seasoned skipper and crew . . .'

Richard paused. There was an instant of silence. Then, from *Katapult* there came a sharp report, as though someone had fired a pistol shot. A tiny black object flew out from under the white canvas awning he had rigged that morning and performed a perfect parabola into the water, where it bobbed like a cork. Because, he realized, it *was* a cork.

'And, of course,' he continued without missing a beat, 'the captain will be following the naval tradition of blessing the voyage with a glass of champagne . . .'

'*Naval tradition*,' said Willy, highly amused, an hour later. 'That was impressive.'

'Years of practise,' answered Richard round a mouthful of foo yung. 'I could bullshit for Great Britain at the next Olympics.'

The camera lay between them on a table in the Chinese restaurant, its side panel open to reveal the vivid picture of *Katapult* vanishing northwards across the lagoon towards Te Ava Tepuka Vili channel under full sail. 'Captain Mariner could skipper *Katapult* for Great Britain at the next Olympics,' observed Willy. 'I thought you said she'll find it hard to tack straight through the channel south of Tepuka . . .'

'I know,' said Richard, laying aside his chopsticks in favour of a spoon. 'She went out like a ferret down a drainpipe. I never cease to underestimate her.'

His cell phone purred. He slid it out and pressed it to his ear. 'You got any footage left on that?' he asked after a moment or two of attentive silence.

'Half an hour or so,' answered Willy. 'Why?'

'Something I want you to see. More news, maybe – though something for later, when the heat's gone out of the *Katapult* story.'

Half an hour later still, Willy and Richard were at the north end of the airport runway, looking west away over the breathtaking Lake Tarasal towards the eastern horizon. And here, as though by some massive magic trick, a supertanker had appeared. Willy could see the name *Prometheus* on her forecastle, and Heritage Mariner colours at her masthead and on her funnel. Behind him, the New Zealand Air Force choppers began to thunder up into the afternoon air.

'What's this?' asked Willy, confused, bellowing to get his voice over the thrumming rotors. 'An oil tanker?'

'A supertanker, yes,' answered Richard. 'But in this case not an *oil* tanker.'

'Then what?' demanded Willy, pulling out his camera as the first of the choppers began to settle away across the South Pacific towards the massive vessel like a dragonfly dipping towards a lily pad.

'Well,' began Richard, satisfyingly aware that, just as he had underestimated Robin's seamanship, so she had underestimated him. 'What you're actually looking at there is a quarter of a million barrels of fresh, clean drinking water.'

Fears

Richard had no trouble hitching a lift on one of the RNZAF choppers and was back at their base in Ohakea, North Island, a couple of days later, all too well aware that he was heading in exactly the opposite direction to the woman he loved. But he had little time to mope or to indulge the lively fears that peopled his nightmares during the few restless hours of sleep he achieved in the interim. The guys at Ohakea were happy to drop him down to the nearest international airport, but only after he agreed to be guest of honour for dinner at the station's mess.

Another all but sleepless night of travel twenty-four hours after the mess night put him on the six ten a.m. BA flight from Wellington to Heathrow, and he touched down, nearly five thousand dollars poorer, frazzled and full of unreasoning fears – even after thirty-five hours in the pampered calm of first class – at five fifty BST on a cold and overcast morning at the beginning of the second week of August. He took a taxi to the company flat the Mariners kept at Heritage House on the corner of Leadenhall Street in the City of London – using the opportunity of a hold-up at seven a.m. as they crawled past Heston services to phone ahead and warn the twenty-four-hour people at Crewfinders that he was on his way home. And so he heaved himself in through the private entrance and stepped into the lift a little before eight thirty.

He stepped out, feeling himself relax amid the homely familiarity of the place thirty seconds later still, at eight thirty on the dot. There were fresh flowers in the reception. In the bedroom, beyond the freshly made bed he had a wardrobe full of pressed coats and suits. Cupboards full of shoes. Drawers full of socks and underwear. Shelves of shirts. Ties, cufflinks – everything he could wish for. En suite, a bathroom stocked with his preferred shaving equipment, soaps and fragrances. Across the sitting room, a kitchen groaning with his favourite foodstuffs. And, in the garage far below, both his Bentley Continental and his classic E-Type Jaguar. What more could a man require? He just had to be careful not to open the wrong door or to slide out the wrong drawer or look in the wrong cabinet – or he would find himself face-to-face with Robin's stuff. Head to head with her absence once again. And the fears it brought, no matter how much faith he had in her.

Fighting off his preoccupation, he showered, shaved, checked messages, found there were none from Robin or about her, ordered a wake-up call for ten o'clock and tucked down for a slightly longer power nap than Lady Thatcher had preferred, feeling very much at home. Having decided, in fact, that this would be his home for the duration. With the twins safely in the hands of irresistibly indulgent grandparents in the South of France until the academic year began in October, he had every intention of staying in the flat until Robin returned. He loved Ashenden, their great old house on the south coast, but simply could not face the thought of spending the month there alone. And in any case, staying in the London flat would put him right at the heart of the action. Not to mention, of course, that he had a world-class business to run.

But, he had to admit to himself as he rose in response to his wake-up call, that he was hardly slumming it. He shrugged a brand-new cotton shirt over his broad shoulders, buttoned it, slipped his favourite cufflinks through the double cuffs, then stepped into midnight-blue pinstripe suit trousers. Tightening the belt around his trim waist, he strolled through to the kitchen and made himself a sandwich of crisp dry-cure smoky bacon and wholewheat toast. A cup of his favourite Blue Mountain high roast Arabica coffee, black, no sugar, and a glance at the *Financial Times* he found nestling in the wire cage behind the letterbox, then he was ready. Ten minutes later, he stepped out of the flat's front door, every inch the leading British businessman dressed for a busy day, turned right and right again, then slid his security card into the slot beside the interconnecting door that led him through into the Heritage Mariner offices. 'Now that,' he said to himself, suddenly almost buoyant, 'is what I call commuting!'

Throughout a packed schedule of meetings, he made sure he was kept as fully abreast of the progress made by *Katapult* and

Flint as he was of the fluctuations in market prices, of shipping schedules, of project progress, of panics; grist to the mill of Heritage Mariner. But there was nothing substantial to report on the two yachts until a conference call came through from San Francisco at seven p.m. London time. It was Nic. 'How's it going, old buddy?' the American demanded, bright-eyed and ebullient as ever. It was ten a.m. PST.

'Fine.' Richard growled. 'Any news of the girls?'

'Nothing you won't be on top of. But I wondered if you'd seen the Fox Special? They've edited it all together in record time, so I hear. I'd guessed they'd run it by your guys if they haven't run it by mine.'

'No.' Richard sat up, frowning. 'Nobody here has said anything about it. When's it going out?'

'Part of their package in the *One O'Clock News* programme.'

'If that's Eastern Standard Time, then that's now,' said Richard. He reached over and grabbed the TV remote. He flipped through the Sky channels until he hit Fox International.

Suddenly it was as though Richard was looking into a mirror. His face half filled the screen. And Robin was sitting beside him. 'Of course we have fears,' she was saying. 'We'd be stupid not to see the risks.' The camera panned across to Liberty, scanning over a line of vital young female faces as it swept past the two crews. On the big photo wall behind them were pictures of the girls in younger days. The earnest young adventurers answering the questions were revealed in a range of attractive but alluring beachwear.

'*Flint* is almost invisible, for example,' said Liberty, her face serious; the picture behind her showing her in seemingly skintight fencing whites. 'A polystyrene hull doesn't give much of an image on radar after all. We've had to put extra radar reflectors aboard so that nearby shipping can make us out. We'll be sailing through some pretty busy waters, certainly to begin with . . .'

'And how will you all get along, cooped up together for a month and more?' asked the interviewer.

'Yes, that's another fear,' Liberty admitted. The camera lingered first on her, then on the other members of her crew as she spoke. Each of the others seemed – in younger, less sensible days – to have been beach bunnies and wannabe *Playboy* pin-ups.

'Maya and I are old shipmates, but Emma and Bella have only sailed with us during the training and the short shakedown voyages.'

Liberty looked across towards Robin. 'I've actually done more sailing hours with Robin and Flo Weary than I have with them. But I'm sure it'll all be fine . . .'

'And what about your crew, Captain Mariner?'

'The same,' answered Robin shortly. 'We've trained together. But only Flo and I have done all that many hours together.' The pictures behind her were like something out of a beachwear catalogue. Or a lingerie directory. Nothing really in criminally bad taste, but enough to raise Richard's eyebrows. 'But you have to understand, there was an exhaustive selection and profiling process. Catfights are the least of our worries,' insisted Robin seriously.

'What other worries do you have, then Captain? What fears?' probed the interviewer. And Richard realized. The beachwear backdrop was not designed to make the girls seem sexy. It was to emphasize their vulnerability. And it was doing a good job.

'Well, obviously, there's communication. We can't just pick up a cell phone and call for help if the radio crashes or the computer goes down. And in many ways the North Pacific is more remote than the Amazon rainforest or the African jungle. But I'm experienced with navigation of course, and, like Maya over there, Flo is one of the leading yachts women of her generation. As is Rohini here, in fact. And Akelita has been sailing Oceania since she was born.' The backdrop changed abruptly. Bikinis were replaced by sailing kit. Suddenly the women looked as competent as they sounded. But still the subtext lingered. Eight girls going out into the great unknown – their lives at the least at risk . . .

'You getting this?' Richard asked Nic.

'Yup. Scary stuff.'

'It would be,' Richard agreed, 'except that they're all first-rate yachtswomen as Robin says. Even if things get a bit hairy, they can handle it.' He emphasized the words, not because he needed to convince Nic but because he wished to counteract the message given out by the programme itself.

'I hope so. Liberty's mom is worried . . .'

'But you're OK yourself?'

'As calm as I was the day her grandfather celebrated her fifth birthday by letting her sail out alone across Nantucket Bay. Comes with the territory. Father of boys – *you worry*. Father of girls—'

'*You pray*. Yes. I get that. So do husbands.'

'Some husbands. Some wives. Some prayers, I guess . . .' A light flashed beside Nic. Communication failed abruptly.

The Fox programme had cut to footage Richard had not seen before. Shots of *Katapult* sailing like a white gull across the deep blue of Te Namo Lagoon from Willy's digital camera; others of *Flint* being whirled like a snowflake across the stormy grey of English Bay.

And this cut to a big, bright map of the Pacific Ocean. All sixty-four million square miles of it. Three bright red spots gave the current positions of the yachts and of their objective. Richard strained to get some kind of accurate fix from the display, but with no success. The spots were too small; the map was too big. He sat back, his frown deeper still. He'd check up more closely on his own laptop later. In the meantime he wanted to listen.

'And you can see at once,' said the voiceover from the invisible commentator, 'that *Katapult* has made little progress so far. She is all but becalmed there a little north and east of Tuvalu, well south and west of Hawaii, in the middle of that huge, featureless, mid-Pacific wilderness. Whereas *Flint,* on the contrary, is sailing almost at the limit of her design speed and seems to have covered a great deal of distance. Just not quite in the right direction so far! She has been pushed well off course by the storm system above her – though she could hardly be sailing any faster, as I say. And Doctor Tanaka's bottle, the famous good ship *Cheerio* has also made surprising progress – and is very nearly at the spot he predicted it will have reached in seven days' time from now!'

It was just after two a.m. in Manila but the man who occupied the equivalent flat to Richard's at the top of the huge building that housed the main offices of Luzon Logging in the heart of Quezon City rarely slept. He too was watching the Fox Network programme, but unlike Richard he was not bothered with the excited tones of the voiceover. He had turned the sound off and was watching the subtitles instead. He slept little and was careful how he listened because of the terrible damage done to his ears. His head was long, lined, bald. His nose was pronounced. Hooked. His chin was broad and square. He had been a striking man given the mixed heritage from Dutch/Indonesian parents that had left his skin the colour of old ivory. Now he was simply memorable because of the great black boxes that clamped to either side of his skull like the jaws of a vice. If he took them off – loosened them, even, he was profoundly, helplessly deaf. His ears and much of the delicate bone structure immediately within them had been catastrophically shattered by an uncontrolled plunge from high in the air to the bottom of a deep river.

A disastrous fall for which the deaf man blamed Richard Mariner.

The long, dark Indonesian eyes watched the screen intently. Then, when the programme was finished, an unsteady hand rewound it so that the intent gaze could observe the bikini-clad forms of the eight contestants once again.

Like Richard, he recognized that the message here was one of vulnerability, not of sexual availability. But the problem was that this man was excited by power. And he most enjoyed exercising it over people who were vulnerable. It was the exploitation of vulnerability, the pressure he could bring to bear on his victims towards helplessness and humiliation that most excited him. It was a pleasure that he practised in private on the rare occasions that the desire overcame him. And those few victims whose helplessness he enjoyed to the full never survived to tell the tale.

And now his greatest enemy seemed to have sent eight of his most attractively vulnerable associates in two almost laughably fragile craft into the vastness of the North Pacific. Into the deaf man's playground. And, as with the ridiculous Japanese doctor's pointless bottle of Cheerio, the women's vessels were fitted with tracking devices so he would know at any time of the day or night exactly where they were. Exactly where he could get his hands on them, when the desire to do so became too strong to control any longer.

The phone began to ring but he did not hear it. And such was his concentration on the defenceless bodies frozen on the screen that he did not even see the warning light flashing in time to the urgent sound.

It was just after three in the morning in Tokyo, but Dr Reona Tanaka still found it impossible to sleep. A man of lifelong abstinence, he was on his third bottle of Sake. A man of strict propriety, he had nevertheless spent an evening of extremely improper, unprofessional abandon in the arms of one of his most beautiful colleagues. A man of almost monastic self-denial, he now found that the sight of his new-found love returning naked from the bathroom of his tiny university flat made him ready for action again – for the fourth time since he had realized the truth.

Seeing how ready he was once more, Dr Aika Rei stepped delicately astride him and prepared to lower herself. 'You're sure?' she teased again, taking him gently in hand. 'You're *certain*?'

'I have the number written down. There can be no mistake. I have the winning ticket.'

Satisfied, she settled into place once more and leaned forward until her hair formed a fragrant tent around his face. 'And where have you put it? Where is the ticket itself?' she whispered.

And the realization cut through the euphoria then. Through the euphoria, the sake and the sensuality. He felt himself begin to soften as he looked up at her with simple horror.

'I put it in the bottle with all the others,' he whispered soberly. 'It's in the good ship *Cheerio* somewhere out in the middle of the ocean. All one-hundred-and-ten-million US dollars' worth of it.'

Calm

'Look,' shouted Liberty, raising her voice only just above the relentless storm to reach Maya down in the communications and navigation area – *the snug,* as they called it now. Maya, like the rest of them, was dressed in orange oilskins as though they were sailing at the North Pole instead of British

Columbia. 'We just have to stay calm. This won't last, and at least its swinging us round so we're almost back on course. Think how far we've come already!'

'Yeah. More than a thousand miles. Mostly in the wrong direction.'

Liberty closed her eyes for a moment and tried not to get distracted as the wind inflated her hood like a beach ball, almost literally making her light-headed. Thank God she had abandoned the idea of live camera coverage almost immediately, she thought. What they lost in publicity value they would gain by protecting their reputations. 'Oh, come on, Maya! Where's the grit you showed in your last scheduled contact with *Katapult*? *Flint* is streets ahead of *her*. All we have to do is stay calm, keep going and try not to weaken.'

'But three days. Three whole days and then some. We're coming up for eighty hours! Watch on watch. And for what?!'

Liberty had split the crew into two watches. It had been the last thing she did on camera. But even that had been a bit of a challenge. Should she keep Maya with her and make it seem like Stanford versus USC? Or should she head one watch and let Maya head the other – as though the Stanford students couldn't trust the Southern Californians to do it on their own. There was the potential for a downside either way. Especially when time and tiredness took their toll.

In the end she decided to keep Maya with her because her fellow Stanford student could be so negative, though Liberty had kept this motivation strictly to herself. She did not want the world to know what a pain she thought her watch-mate could be at times. At times such as the present, in fact. But Liberty could see Maya's point. The last three days had been hellish. With the best will in the world they couldn't have filmed any of it. They had trouble enough keeping up with their scheduled contacts – with *Katapult*, with the back-up teams ashore.

But in the face of it all, *Flint* had held together. And the storm-bound run to the south of their planned course had at least kept them too close to land to make the really big seas a threat no matter how squally the wind became down to the south of Portland. But the girls had all become seasick with morale-destroying regularity. Nelson's ailment and the relentless cold were really

beginning to sap their strength now. To use up the very last of
Maya's very limited supply of good nature. Especially as she was
beginning to suspect that the USC watch was pulling a good deal
less than their weight.

In consultation with Robin, on camera for the world to see,
Liberty had worked out a watch schedule designed to let the
teams she finally selected get a reasonable amount of rest – under
the right circumstances. Given her English training, it had seemed
an uncomfortable liberty to take with a tradition almost as old
as the age of sail, but she and Robin had decided that if they
allowed two seven-hour night watches – from nine p.m. to four
a.m., then four a.m. to eleven, the rest of the day would split
conveniently into five two-hour watches. So team A would get
the nine to four night watch on the first night and the four to
eleven a.m. one the next day, and so in rotation, day after day
as necessary, with everybody up and about from eleven a.m. to
nine p.m., notionally taking charge watch by watch in two-hour
blocks as the daylight hours passed.

It had looked OK on paper – but, like everything else they
had planned, it had all gone to hell in a handcart in the face of
the relentless storms. Now it was just past eleven a.m. Watch A,
the Stanford girls, should have been relieved the better part of
ten minutes ago. The USC Watch B girls were still asleep –
militantly so – almost *mutinously* so, said Maya venomously,
thoroughly disgruntled.

'Look,' she snarled, pulling herself erect, trying not to let too
much moisture get on to the electrical equipment beside her.
'Why don't I go and shake a leg for them, Libby? Roll them out
and up? Someone has to run this boat right no matter what!'

Liberty swung the helm over hard enough to make her watch-
mate sit down again. Sit down painfully hard, in fact. Water
sloshed across the afterdeck and cascaded into the sea. '*You* look,'
she snarled. 'First, I'm the skipper. I run the boat. I say who
shakes a leg and when – and who rolls who out. Secondly, it's
Liberty, not Libby. *Never* Libby. Thirdly, you signed on for this.
Come hell or high water, come what may. There was no clause
saying, "When the going gets tough, Maya gets going *home*".
There wasn't even a codicil saying, "When the going gets tough,
Maya starts bitching"! Fourthly . . .'

But they never found out what 'fourthly' might have been because just at that moment, the driving squall-mist to port of them was parted by the cutwater of a ship. A cutwater at least twice as tall as *Flint*'s main mast, its forepeak leaning out and almost over them at once, so steep was the rake of the bow. And the whole thing was coming directly towards *Flint* at what seemed like supersonic speed. Liberty got a horrified glimpse of a sheer, sharp steel blade rising and spreading like a black metal awning above her from an avalanche of white foam at its oncoming forefoot to a broad forecastle high enough to be wreathed in low clouds above. A wide, wide forecastle with, of all things, *Walt Disney* written in gold across it – as though the man himself had come down from heaven as a gigantic spirit with a gargantuan autograph pen full of golden ink.

A siren bellowed like the last trump, so loud it seemed to be sounding inside Liberty's head. She screamed, really believing for a second that the overwhelming noise had burst her eardrums. But even as she screamed, Liberty was spinning the wheel hard over, tearing the muscles in her shoulders and back, looking up though tear-bright eyes to see the storm-reefed mainsail slam hard over, tight as a drumskin and straining fit to burst. Maya was thrown further back into her seat. The whole hull tilted hard over – so hard, in fact, that the equipment Maya was using began to slide down on top of her. There was a muffled scream as the B watch were actually rolled out of their bunks.

Liberty found the breath to articulate her terror and her rage. 'I will NOT,' she screamed at the oncoming monster, 'I will NOT be run down and beaten by MICKEY FUCKING MOUSE . . .'

Robin looked up from *Katapult*'s wheel at the listless sag of her mainsail. The sunlight glinted on her golden curls, hazy but still strong. 'Four days,' she said to herself, quietly but dejectedly. 'What was that song? 'Don't say there's nothing to do in the Doldrums'. Four days of almost total calm. And how far have we come?'

Rohini Verma the Indian sailboat champion and companion on the A watch looked up. Her brown eyes widened slightly and her forehead gathered into a thoughtful frown between her straight black brows and her severely swept-back hair. 'Just on two hundred miles according to the GPS,' she answered. 'That's—'

'About two knots mean speed,' answered Robin. 'And when I think that *Katapult* can pull nearly forty-five under full sail . . .'

'It's frustrating,' Flo Weary said, picking up the conversation as the B watch came up at eleven a.m. on the dot, straightening to sweep back her mahogany red mane and stretch her long, lithe body after the constriction of seven hours in a narrow bunk. 'But it's not the end of the world.'

'We might as well be at the end of the world,' said Robin, uncharacteristically glum. 'We're at the heart of a dead calm surrounded by a combination of mist and heat haze you could cut with a knife. If the world ended a couple of hundred metres ahead we'd sail right over the edge and never know it.'

'Naaaw,' said Flo with an irrepressible chuckle, coming up past Rohini at the console, stepping up into the well of the after-deck and up again to stand beside Robin at the multihull's big wheel. 'We'd all have died of old age long before *Katapult* sailed another couple of hundred metres.'

'Look on the bright side,' insisted Akelita, as she relieved Rohini at the communications console. 'We could be aboard *Flint*!' She shivered as she spoke, and her silky skin rose in goosebumps.

Robin looked down as the island girl shivered, looking very much like she had in the photos Fox had got hold of – wearing nothing more than a micro-kini and mega tan. And coconut-scented sun oil. Flo was dressed much like Akelita – as were the others. Robin emphasized her age and seniority by simply slinging a scarf around her waist and knotting it at her right hip to serve as a short skirt. But her shoulders and the upper slopes of her breasts were as brown and freckled as everyone else's aboard. And as thoughtlessly on display. They were due to film another half hour of lively footage at noon, she thought wearily. But unless the girls covered up, it would only be suitable for the adult channels.

'Yes,' added Rohini. '*Flint*'s travelled nearly twelve hundred miles, running down the coast past Portland almost as far as San Francisco, then back up and out towards her planned course. Twelve hundred. That would be hard sailing even without the weather they're having. Maya MacArthur checked in at eight and boy did she sound pissed.'

'Sick and tired,' added Robin. 'Literally.'

'Yeah,' agreed Rohini. 'They've not been putting in the news footage as agreed because they've been too busy. Can we do extra? I mean . . .' She looked around her nearly naked companions, her speaking gaze seeming to echo Robin's thoughts. Too little news; too much adult content.

'What was the name of that English girl?' asked Flo, apparently apropos of nothing. 'The one who told the papers she sometimes sailed in the nude when she was single-handing? Now that's what I call publicity . . .'

A short silence fell then.

B Watch had relieved A Watch. Flo was beside Robin at the big wheel and Akelita beside Rohini at the multihull's massive bank of computer equipment, but nothing had really changed. Nothing much had changed for eighty hours except that sunlight and moonlight had succeeded each other beyond the haze of the high, hot sky.

The sail flapped.

Robin felt a tiny caress on her cheek. The mist ahead seemed to stir. The ocean beneath them heaved gently, a deep-water roller going almost invisibly from one part of the sixty-five million square miles of vacancy surrounding them to another.

Robin drew in breath to tell her crew it was time to get decently dressed for the noon broadcast, but paused. The ghostly caress on her cheek was strangely reborn as a fluttering right at the back of her throat. She began to frown, all thoughts of filming or communicating whipping straight out of her mind.

The mainsail flapped. And the sound seemed to trick off something in her head. There was the deepest, quietest, rumbling sound seeming to come from the writhing mist all around her. For just one heart-stoppingly superstitious instant, she actually wondered whether *Katapult* was just about to sail blindly over the edge of the world as she had said.

'Can . . .' she said. She intended to ask, *can you guys hear that?* But she stopped at that one word because what she was hearing suddenly seemed less important than what she was seeing. The mist ahead of them began to darken incredibly rapidly and as it did so, it became strangely agitated. *Katapult* pitched strongly enough to make the women stagger.

'Hey,' said Rohini. 'What on earth . . .'

And a fish fell out of the sky. A sizeable, fat-flanked fish. It landed on the well of the afterdeck and bounced, twisting, down the steps to land at Akelita's feet. 'Is that a flying fish?' asked Rohini.

'No,' said Akelita. 'It's a mackerel. A jack . . .'

And another jack mackerel smashed into the well deck, narrowly missing Flo. Then, incredibly, it was raining fish. 'What the hell . . .' said Akelita, her voice almost lost in the roaring of the finny deluge. In the roaring of something ahead. Something monstrous – something that sounded every bit as dangerous as the end of the world itself.

'Sails in,' ordered Robin. 'Get the sails in. Start the motor. *MOVE!*'

Robin had been watching the darkening, writhing mist ahead, more and more acutely aware of the gathering rumble. Even before the fish started falling from the sky in simply biblical numbers.

Suddenly the mist was whipped away entirely, like a magician's cloak off a spectacular illusion. And there, dead ahead and lazily approaching, was a towering black-headed, dark-hearted waterspout.

Rage

Reona Tanaka had never been as far south as the Yokosuka dock complex before. Indeed, once the taxi passed through the Kawasaki Ward, except for a distant glimpse of the familiar buildings at Kanto Gakuin University, he was effectively as lost as if he had been on the moon. Or rather on Mercury, he thought angrily. On Mercury it never stopped raining, which gave the planet a lot in common with Tokyo this summer. Seething, he looked out of the streaming windows at the districts the taxi was speeding through. He would never have ventured into an area such as this had he not been desperate. And the fact that he was desperate enough to do so now simply filled him with a boiling sense of outrage.

Had not the far more intrepid Dr Aika Rei not agreed to accompany him? Even at this unnaturally late hour and on a night such as this. Just as it was she who had convinced him that he should keep his good news secret even from his friends at the university; even from his ultimate employers Mr Greenbaum and Captain Mariner. But at least she was willing to help him. And it was she who had made the discreetest possible enquiries about how on earth they could get to the priceless bottle before anyone else could do so. But even her presence was hardly proving to be reliable armour against a seething childish sense that life was being spectacularly unfair to him at the moment.

Reona kept an eye on the taxi's meter, watching the price of this unnerving excursion clock up relentlessly. It made his mind fill with bitter amusement that he, a US dollar millionaire one-hundred-and-ten times over, should be forced to watch his yen so carefully. Particularly as the yen stood at eighty to the dollar this morning. And a mathematical mind such as Dr Tanaka's had no trouble in calculating that he was a Japanese yen millionaire eight thousand, eight hundred million times over. That made him a billionaire in anybody's language. A multi-billionaire, if such a thing existed. A multi-billionaire who could not get his hands on his multi-billions.

A thought that Aika Rei clearly shared. Had she snuggled against him any more tightly, their bodies would have melted through the layers of clothing separating skin from skin. The erotic idea was far more appealing than thoughts about what Mr Greenbaum or Captain Mariner would do when they discovered his perfidy; or about the meteorology of Mercury – or the destination they were heading for. And so he allowed it to linger as the taxi sped through the terrible weather further and further down towards the docks. 'Where are we now?' he enquired for perhaps the tenth time since they had left the university.

'Natsuchimacho,' came the not very helpful reply.

Not very helpful to Reona, at any rate. 'Nearly there,' whispered Aika Rei. 'If we look out carefully we'll see some really hot cars. They do a lot of drifting down here in the docks.'

'Drifting?' he asked, intrigued.

'Like in the movies,' Aika Rei explained. '*Tokyo Drift.*'

Which left him none the wiser.

She had clearly ventured far further out of her ivory tower than the Greenbaum Professor had. A fact proved by her sexual technique as much as by her breadth of contacts – and her urban cultural knowledge.

'Do you know what to do?' she demanded abruptly.

'Act casual,' he answered uneasily. 'Be vague. We're honeymooners looking for a bit of an adventure . . .'

In the four days since he realized the enormity of what had happened to him, it was the best that they could come up with. Though to be fair, in an attempt at maintaining normality in the face of the increasingly rabid media hunt for the owner of the winning lottery ticket – definitely worth $110 million according to the publicity – they had both worked their normal hours as usual and only really got to make plans during their brief sleeping time together. When, one way and another, not a lot of sleeping had been done. And, he thought in an angry panic now, as the taxi slowed, nowhere near enough planning either.

The taxi coasted to a halt. 'Here we are,' whispered Aika Rei.

Grimacing against the brief brightness of the taxi's interior light, Reona handed over the fare and climbed out. With Aika Rei at his side guiding him with her body, he hurried through the shadowy downpour towards the door of a bar illuminated by a bright red neon sign. He glanced up as the pair of them stumbled in.

The place was called RAGE.

How apt.

Half-blinded by the bar's dim atmosphere, Reona was just able to make out a short, shiny bar backed with glass shelves laden with bottles of every colour he could imagine. Behind the counter a tall, slim young man was mixing a cocktail with all the theatrical bravura of a sushi chef. The bar was busy but not packed; half-a-dozen tables in the middle, all but empty. A dozen private booths around the walls, all full of couples. Every head turned as they stumbled in and hardly surprisingly. Aika Rei was the only woman in the place.

But at least that fact speeded things up. A tall man in immaculate uniform stood up and beckoned them to a nearby booth.

Close-to, his face seemed to belie the neatness of his turnout. It had a battered, almost brutal quality and seemed to be set in a perpetual frown.

'I am Sakai Inazo, first officer of the freighter *Dagupan Maru*.' He introduced himself formally, bowing from the waist.

'Reona . . .' began Reona, only to stop in simple horror that he had almost given his real name.

'Reona *Gakuin*,' chimed in Aika Rei smoothly. She too had noticed the university buildings earlier. 'Mr and Mrs Reona Gakuin. Newly married,' she tittered as though shy.

'I understand you are seeking passage?' continued Lieutenant Sakai, sitting down and gesturing them to do the same.

'We are considering it,' answered Aika Rei, as Reona fought to get his brain in gear. 'It is our honeymoon.'

'You had better think quickly, then,' advised the officer, studying his hands thoughtfully. 'We sail tomorrow for Vancouver. Captain Yamamoto is old fashioned. We sail with the tide.'

'What is your cargo?' asked Reona, still enraged by his amateurish error – unable to think of anything else.

'The officer's long dark eyes rested on him, seeming to notice him for the first time. 'Timber,' he answered non-committally. Reona noticed that his hands were big, brutal and battered. As he talked, he kept closing them into fists.

'Do you carry a lot of wood?' asked Reona fatuously.

'The hull's owned by an Indonesian consortium. Luzon Logging,' growled Sakai as though that explained everything. His eyes flickered down to his fists. They closed as though he was strangling an invisible enemy.

'The cargo's not important,' snapped Aika Rei. 'Can you accommodate us?'

'The captain's usually happy to make a little extra on the side.' The big fists opened. 'If you can afford the passage, then you'll be welcome aboard.'

'And you'll be going straight across the North Pacific,' said Reona, pulling a printout from an inner pocket. 'Past this position here?'

The sailor took the piece of paper, spread it on the table top and looked at it. 'This isn't a chart,' he observed, as though mildly surprised by the fact.

'But the position is given very accurately,' answered Reona, pointing with overeager emphasis. 'You can see it there. Northings and eastings to three decimal places . . .'

The brutal face looked up. The edges of the eyes crinkled just as though Lieutenant Sakai was smiling. 'Yes,' said the sailor decisively. 'We go right past there.'

'Then we'd like to book passage with you,' Aika Rei concluded, equally decisively. 'How much will it be, when do we need to come aboard and what documentation do we need to bring?'

The first officer of the *Dagupan Maru* looked at her silently. 'You seem pretty eager,' he observed after a heartbeat.

'It's our honeymoon . . .' insisted Reona weakly.

'OK,' decided Sakai. 'We have a deal subject to the captain's agreement. Leave me a contact and I'll get back to you within six hours. High tide is just before midnight tomorrow night. We'll be sailing on that.' He looked at his watch. 'Twenty-six hours. Plenty of time.'

While Aika Rei gave contact details, Reona Tanaka asked the barman to call them a taxi – but he just gestured to a business card beside a payphone. Still, the taxi turned up five minutes after Reona called, and the pair of college doctors were heading north towards civilization again within fifteen minutes of the deal being struck. Reona was so relieved to be getting out of the place that he forgot to reclaim his printout.

Half an hour later, the printout was lying on the chart desk in the chart room of Luzon Logging's freighter *Dagupan Maru*. Navigating officer Sakai had marked on the chart of their voyage the precise location of the dot marked on it – northings and eastings to three decimal points. Captain Yamamoto stood beside him, looking down with a frown. The battered old freighter stirred as the tide swept up towards the flood. Her holds full of priceless timber – the ruins of a palace, in fact. Rain thundered out of the low sky, but the harbour watch officer hadn't bothered to switch on the clearview wipers so the whole bridge seemed like something from a submarine. The grumble of the generators was lost beneath the thunder of the deluge. Captain Yamamoto would normally have been in his bunk – especially on the night before setting sail – but Sakai had got him up and about. 'You're certain, Number One?' he demanded harshly.

'As certain as I can be. The man is Doctor Reona Tanaka. He even let slip his first name. And his face has been all over the media for months. I guess you can get to be a doctor these days without being too bright at all. I have no idea who the woman is.'

'But she's in charge?' probed the captain thoughtfully.

'Decidedly.' Sakai shrugged.

'Very well. What is the next step in your thinking?'

'The chart reference he gave was the most recent location of his famous bottle. The Cheerio. That's according to Nippon News.' Sakai nodded towards the screen of a laptop he had tuned to the station's online broadcast. An animated young woman reporter was talking silently in front of a vast map of the Pacific – like a forecaster in front of tomorrow's weather chart.

'Very well,' allowed the captain. 'Then?'

Sakai pressed a button on the laptop's keyboard and a recording replaced the live broadcast. The big blue chart with its telltale three dots was replaced by Tanaka's streaming face, and the Cheerio bottle he was holding up beside it. The railings of a bridge were visible in the background, and, beyond, the surface of a river in full spate. A set of figures in the lower right corner gave a time and a date the better part of three months back. '*It already has a fan club*,' bellowed Dr Tanaka over the thunder of the downpour, nodding at the bottle. '*My students and I have purchased tickets for the Jumbo Lottery and put them in here. The bottle is packed with several hundred of them, in fact. At about the time I expect the bottle to arrive – unscathed and showing no signs of decomposition at all – in the middle of the North Pacific Gyre, in mid-August, the lottery will have been drawn. And the winning ticket will be worth in excess of 100 million US dollars!*'

'You think that's it?' demanded Yamamoto. 'You think one of those tickets hit the jackpot?'

'I think that's the guy I just talked to in Rage,' answered Sakai. 'I think he wants to get to where that bottle is. I think he wants to do it in secret. And I think every news service in Japan is trying to work out who did win the grand lottery jackpot.'

'But how in hell's name do they think they're going to get the bottle even if we do sail right past it?'

'I think they think they'll think of something. They have one-hundred-and-ten-million US reasons to do so, after all. Shit. If it came right down to it, they could promise every man aboard the *Dagupan* a million US dollars to help – and still walk away with one hell of a fortune!'

Captain Yamamoto nodded. 'OK,' he decided. 'You tell them it's all fine. Just enough cash up front, paperwork and bullshit so she doesn't get suspicious. But I want them both aboard this time tomorrow night. Meanwhile, I'll refer this all upstairs.' He glanced at the chronometers above the vacant helm. The high tide he planned to sail on would be here in twenty-two-and-three-quarter hours' time. It was one a.m. precisely, Japan Standard Time.

At one a.m. Philippines Time, one hour later, the deaf man in his office on top of the Luzon Logging Building in Quezon City Manila was watching the latest broadcast from *Katapult*. He was uncertain how to react to the almost arrogant display of flesh, but every now and then one of the younger women would turn and flaunt herself with a brazen arrogance that made him shake with suppressed rage. The Indonesian girl seemed to be sporting little more than underwear. It pushed her breasts into a prominence that almost infuriated him. It emphasized her thighs and posterior in a manner that made him shudder with indignation. The Indian woman and the Australian were hardly wearing anything more. They were as alluring as a lingerie catalogue. And such things were not at all to his taste. The unthinking display of oiled skin was not something that appealed to him in the slightest. And yet, every now and then, he found himself shouting insults at them as though they were the most common street harlots from the red light districts down by the docks.

On the other hand, he found himself straining to see through the far more modest covering worn by the English skipper. The turquoise wrap covering her loins would go transparent in certain lights allowing his eager eyes to invade her modesty as far as to the convex V of cotton covering her private parts. The wind – what there was of it – would flirt every now and then with the

exciting curls of her hair, seeming to suck her nipples into prominence through the thin stuff of her bikini top. And she seemed
unaware of what she was occasionally revealing, which added a
frisson of voyeurism to his sensuous contemplation of her. A
frisson of pleasure extended almost unbearably by the fact that
he actually knew the woman in question. Had met her, and his
enemy – her husband. Had touched her, felt the firm grip of that
hand upon his own. Where he shouted insults at the others, he
whispered endearments to her. Which, had anyone been there to
hear him, would have been far more unsettlingly sinister than
the shouting.

But the deaf man's nature was by no means simple. He was
no thug, no back-alley assassin. Those who had damaged him
– and there were a good few across Indonesia and beyond – had
not yet met unexpected, lingering and agonizing ends. Had he
been, like his adversary Richard Mariner, an aficionado of *Star
Trek*, he might have agreed with the villainous, cloned super-
being Khan Noonien Singh and the Klingon authorities he cited
that *revenge is a dish best served cold.* That indeed was the way
in which Professor Satang S. Sittart, Chief Executive Officer of
Luzon Logging, among many less legitimate concerns, certainly
preferred it, and how he planned to serve it should the chance
arise.

As, it seemed, the chance might soon, in fact, arise.

He continued to study the TV picture of Robin Mariner, trying,
with only limited success, to see right through her skimpy
clothing. Imagining what he might take lingering pleasure in
doing, should the body he was observing so avidly ever come
within his reach once more. Beginning to feel his way towards
plans which might in fact ensure that it would do so. Increasingly
enraptured at the prospect.

But this time when the phone beside him started to ring and
flash, he registered the fact. He dragged his eyes away from
Robin's bikini bottoms and flicked the audio switch. 'Yes?' he
barked.

'Professor Sittart,' came a nervous voice on the far end of the
connection. 'It seems that there is a situation aboard Luzon
Logging's freighter *Dagupan Maru*, due to depart Tokyo docks
tomorrow night, which might be worthy of your interest . . .'

Run

The captain of the Walt Disney cruise liner would have no chance of turning aside. Liberty could see that. He had no option other than to do what he was doing. Honking his horn and hoping. The siren sounded again; the decibels hitting her ears like something solid.

Liberty, on the other hand, could do something. If *Flint* stayed still the liner would hit her midships on the port side, break her in two, ride over what was left of her and kill her. If she just ran forward under reefed sails she might make it clear by the skin of her teeth but that huge bow wave would come in over her low stern and flood her – she would still go down, literally pooped, and probably still roll over as well. It seemed to Liberty that her all too vulnerable command's only hope was to control the angle at which the yacht's hull met that deadly wave, always assuming she could stay clear of the massive hull which was creating it.

Liberty was holding *Flint*'s big wheel over to port as hard as it would go, and watching through narrow, streaming eyes as the huge bow wave rolled towards her like a tsunami and she swung her frail vessel's head round to meet it.

'Are you mad?' bellowed Maya in the moment of relative silence between the second and third warning blasts. 'My God, are you turning *towards* the liner? Are you flaming *mad* . . .'

'Probably,' answered Liberty through gritted teeth, dropping her voice slightly. Very slightly, given the storm wind, the torrential downpour, the howls of protest from B Watch in the cabin and the avalanche of water bearing down on them. 'I want whatever hits us to come in on the bows, not the side. I want *Flint* up and over that bow wave – not rolled on to her beam ends, pitch-poled or pooped. But we're leaning too far over into the turn. I don't want my mainmast smashed to kindling either. Start the motors, would you?'

The motors were a blessed addition; the result of an indulgent father and godfather worrying about the safety of their child and godchild. Liberty had discussed mechanical propulsion at some length with Richard, Robin and Flo's father, revolutionary ship designer Doc Weary. Then they had all talked their discussions over with Dad's design team, who had been told to spare no expense. The result was a pair of specially adapted Mercury 1350s which combined maximum propulsion with carefully calculated ballast weight and negligible environmental impact. They were actually positioned beneath the cabin and right above the centreboard where they could steady the hull as well as powering the vessel.

The minute Maya hit the start button, the massive motors exploded into action, spinning the propshafts in parallel and making the twin screws thrash into motion almost as swiftly and effectively as those beneath the counter of Richard's flame-red go-faster Cigarette Top Gun launch *Marilyn*. And she could reach seventy knots from a standing start in a little over five minutes.

Flint didn't have anything like five minutes, of course, Liberty calculated, her mind chilled by the immediacy of violent action, like Richard's which always acted coldly under pressure. She certainly didn't have *Marilyn*'s sleek, slim-hipped carbon-fibre hull either. But then she didn't actually have to get up to seventy knots. She just had to thrust her head round hard against the irresistible dictates of her tiller, so that all the power beneath her stern could swing the slim bows at her other end those few degrees further to port before the wilderness of foam and water tumbling massively ahead of the liner hit *Flint*'s vulnerable beam and rolled her under as fatally as a pyroclastic flow roaring down the side of an erupting volcano.

As soon as Liberty felt the massive surge of power beneath her feet she began to let *Flint*'s head ease off fractionally. The super-buoyant polystyrene hull was swinging swiftly in an arc that threatened to bring her on to a reciprocal with the liner. From sitting across the big ship's path like the cross on a capital T, *Flint* would soon be in danger of meeting her head to head. And ramming the Disney vessel was by no means part of Liberty's plan either.

As *Flint* felt the pressure ease, and her hull came to rely on the twin Mercuries rather than the squall wind, so she began to come upright, her mast heads swinging away from the black-painted, gold-signed flare of the liner's bow. And as she did so, the bow wave hit. A wall of foam came washing up over *Flint*'s port forequarter and solid green water went thundering across her foredeck, twisting the vessel over, shrugging her aside, sitting her further upright even as it pushed her away until the masts were penduluming out towards the starboard like the fingers of a metronome and the deck was rolling back the other way.

Under Liberty's iron grip, the hull slid sideways down the great surf along the liner's flank, as the bow wave rolled over into wake at the point where the next great wave was born. And still *Flint* held doggedly upright as the wake simply carried her further and further from the black cliff of her side. Heading for safety, even though the angle of the water meant that foam came rumbling aboard over the uphill port side even as it flooded in over the downhill starboard and met in the middle like the Red Sea closing behind Moses.

But *Flint* simply refused to roll, and her skipper held her steady through it all. Her head went down until the white water exploded against the arrowhead of her raised bridge house. But then she tossed her head up, thrusting the deadly water away like a white whale breaching.

It was only when the huge, square stern swept past, thirty metres from their port side, and *Flint* swung back upright once more, bobbing safely over the crest of that great wake wave and down into the first trough, that Liberty at last swung the wheel over the other way, sending her command skipping nimbly back and away out to starboard, safely under control again.

'You can kill the motors now, Maya,' said Liberty breathlessly. 'Check the B Watch and look for damage below. Then see if you can raise Mickey Mouse on the two-way. That rodent and I need to talk.'

'Yes, Skipper,' said Maya.

And suddenly there was no more doubt about who was in command of *Flint*.

The wind faltered so unexpectedly that Liberty looked up, wondering whether it was another trick of the liner's massive hull. As though it could be followed by a wind shadow as well as by a wake. But no. The clouds thinned suddenly. The sun came out high in the eastern sky as though it was going to shine exclusively on Portland or Vancouver. A rainbow appeared in the west and Liberty turned *Flint* hard over and ran for the foot of it like a leprechaun seeking her pot of gold.

By the time Maya and the B Watch came up out of the cabin to report everything shipshape and secure below, the rain had eased to a drizzle and *Flint* was running steadily under clearing skies across a brisk north-easterly that sent her racing back on to the course Liberty had planned for her.

Then, while Maya checked the electrical equipment and raised the Disney liner's radio officer, who swiftly passed the irate skipper on to an extremely shaken captain, Emma Toda and Bella Chung-Wolf trimmed the sails so that *Flint* could settle down and accelerate smoothly towards the top speed of her design spec in the precise direction she needed to be sailing. Within twelve hours they had picked up a westerly-flowing outrider of the great Alaska Current and that great liquid travelator grasped the yacht's solid keel, working in tandem with the breeze, allowing *Flint* to run steady and true towards the convergence zone, the garbage patch and the telltale red dot of the locator in Dr Tanaka's Cheerio bottle.

And that was a situation which was to last the better part of the next three days.

Robin had faced waterspouts before. But none as big as this one, and never in a vessel as small or fragile as *Katapult*. 'I need power, Flo,' she ordered. 'B Watch, get below and break out the life jackets!' As she spoke, the last of the deluge of mackerel fell on to the deck and bounced back into the sea from where they had been sucked by the spout. Except for the ones trapped in the well deck below her. Which would make a nice fresh supper for *Katapult*'s crew – if they weren't feeding the fish themselves by suppertime.

Katapult's design meant that the foresail could be wrapped around a line running up from the forepeak to the top of the single mast. And that the mainsail wound around a matching spindle inside the aerodynamic body of the mast itself. Under most conditions these actions would be hand-cranked by the crew. In an emergency they could be controlled by the computer. This was an emergency. *Katapult* went from full sail to bare sticks in fifteen seconds, even as her motors kicked in.

The multihull's propulsion system was nowhere near as powerful as *Flint*'s but it was responsive and potent enough to give the beautiful vessel a solid boot up the backside. On the other hand, Liberty only had her masts and hull to worry about. Robin had the two sleek outriders that sat on the end of computer-controlled gull-wings and steadied the vessel without the need for a centreboard or keel that could slow her down in races by dragging through the water below. But Robin didn't want the outriders torn off. Didn't want the articulated gull-wings damaged. So, though the circumstances were vastly different, Robin's reaction was the same as Liberty's had been. She put the big wheel of the helm hard over to port.

The foot of the spout hit the surface of the ocean about half a mile in front of *Katapult*. It was hard to be more precise than that because the point of impact was shrouded in a cone of spray that spread out in a whirling grey-white mist around it and bounced back up past thirty metres. The main column of the thing writhed sinuously above this into the low cloud that had given birth to it and Robin had an instantaneous impression of a storm front that cut the sky in half with unnerving precision. The leading edge of it seemed to be drawn across the sky with a gigantic ruler. An edge that passed immediately above her head.

On Robin's left it was a bright, sunny morning. On her right it was almost as dark as night. Beneath the absolute blanket of cumulus, a solid-looking wall of rain reached down to the sea like grey concrete. But that was still miles distant. The spout stood on the leading edge of the front, and Robin could swear that there were others, further away behind it, stretching into the distance like columns in a temple. As their furious activity sucked away the last of the mist, they made the air along the huge storm front absolutely crystal clear. The day had gone from blindingly claustrophobic to magisterially vast. The sea went from indigo on the left-hand horizon, through vivid green dead ahead to white-streaked elephant grey beneath the equally distant downpour away to her right.

It was an instant of clarity that Robin had never experienced before and was never likely to experience again. The entire enormity of it burned itself indelibly into her subconscious. Then the reality slammed back into place as the icy air was in

motion around her. Suddenly very actively indeed. A squall
wind hit her shoulder like a rugby forward tackling high. A
heartbeat later it was as though she and *Katapult* were trapped
in a wind tunnel.

But Robin was by no means standing idle as she took that one
startled glance. The whole of her attention was claimed by the
monster lazily sweeping in towards her. The wind on her back
like a living force. The race to get *Katapult* out into the light.
With the helm hard over, she gunned the motors to maximum,
feeling *Katapult* struggling to answer the conflicting dictates of
the forces unleashed within and around her. The motors turned
a pair of racing propellers seeking to thrust her full ahead. The
rudder sought to swing the three points of her bow hard over to
the left. The wind howling through what little rigging she
possessed was trying to blow her to the right, into the grip of
the waterspout which – counter-intuitively – was sailing relentlessly towards her, dead against the wind itself. But of course it
was creating the wind by sucking air into the enormous gyre at
its heart. The harder it inhaled, the stronger the wind blew, the
faster the spout approached, drawing the atmosphere relentlessly
into itself. Spewing it up, like the mackerel, into the wildly
writhing storm cloud above.

Had *Katapult* possessed a keel like *Flint*, that might have
steadied her, made the water cling to her in spite of the wind
– but she had outriggers instead. And the starboard outrigger was
porpoising increasingly deeply into the water as the triple hull
fought to turn away from the spout while the wind pulled the
masts towards it. Robin slammed her left hand off the wheel,
overrode the computer control system and pushed both outriggers
down into the water, feeling the skittish hull steady beneath her
widespread feet, though the wheel began to turn back relentlessly
against her one-handed grip. Immediately, a wall of spray whipped
up the wind and slapped painfully into her face as though the
spout was angered by her action. It was the outer edge of the
inverted cone at the foot of the thing. Robin was deluged with
water in an instant. Water that felt shockingly warm except that
the wind chill of the relentless gale turned it icy at once. Robin
realized inconsequentially how little she was wearing – and that
made her feel more vulnerable still.

For a heart-stopping moment, Robin found herself inside the cone of spray, trapped for an instant between the buffeting curtain of waterdrops made dazzlingly bright by the sunlight of the half day beyond. As though a jewel box full of diamonds and sapphires had been caught in a tornado. And, on her left, less than a hundred metres distant, the foot of the spout itself. The surface of the water in between was fizzing as though the ocean had become champagne. The sound of rushing water, foaming bubbles and screaming wind made an already dizzying experience almost hallucinatory. She saw the great white trunk of the thing lift off the water with a slow majesty she had never expected. It settled back again, then lifted once more, unexpectedly fine, almost diaphanous.

The wind howling past her seemed to hesitate for an instant. She slammed the rudder back hard over. *Katapult*'s screaming motors pulled her left at last – smashed her back through the gemstone wall, which immediately lost its diamond and sapphire brightness, turning instantly as dark and threatening as the low, writhing sky.

But that moment, that one flaw in the wind, that instant of hesitation by the monstrous spout, made all the difference. *Katapult* began to gather way, turning obediently on to her new heading, pulling out of the twister's clutches like a knight breaking free from a witch's spell in a fairy tale. And, as though the breaking of its spell could lead to the undoing of its power, the waterspout began to falter. When Robin glanced over her shoulder for the first time a couple of seconds later, the trunk had lifted once again, and the cone wall was thinning, slowing, falling back into the restless water. The fierceness began to fade from that relentless headwind, hitting her now in the face instead of the back. And, perhaps most weirdly of all, the day ahead of her was as bright, blue and sunshiny as any she had enjoyed on Tuvalu. It was only when she looked back, like Lot's wife in the Bible, that she saw the bright day's exact opposite still treading at her heels.

And that was what Flo saw first as she came up out of the cabin wearing a starkly impractical combination tiny bikini and bulky lifebelt. 'Jesus,' she said forthrightly, 'that looks nasty.'

'But at least the spout seems to have gone,' answered Robin

breathlessly. 'I think we can stow the emergency equipment and get rigged – and dressed – for some stormy weather.'

Flo gave a grin. 'That's just what this baby was built for.' She patted *Katapult* with sisterly pride. 'You don't win the Fastnet in anything less than a gale.'

'True enough,' agreed Robin. 'And you don't win it in a bikini either.'

Rohini and Akelita appeared a moment later, both more sensibly clad in shorts and shirts. Robin handed over the wheel, then she and Flo changed and tidied up below.

Robin found that she was moving like a very old lady indeed, her arms, shoulders and back all stiff and sore. But the pain she felt was as nothing compared to the shock she got when she looked in a mirror and saw what the wind had done to her hair.

The storm front had closed over the sky by mid-afternoon and the lazy, misty calm was replaced by a brisk wet south-westerly which *Katapult* approved of very much indeed. She filled her sails, kicked up her heels, and headed towards the forty-five-knot top speed she was famously capable of delivering. At the same time she seemed to settle to work, her central hull sitting steadily in the water leaning only a few degrees off the vertical even in the strongest gusts, as the outriggers aquaplaned on or below the surface, holding her steadier than even *Flint*'s keel could ever have done. Holding her steady enough to allow Robin to light the LPG hob on the cooker in their tiny galley so that she could fry the fish presented to them by the waterspout that morning.

Fish in such abundance, indeed, that they were still eating it three days later when their long fast run came to an abrupt end.

News

Communications with *Katapult*, thought Richard wryly, were a little like London buses. You waited ages for a message, and then . . .

The first call came through a little after four a.m. London time. It came through on Richard's bedside phone and he sat up at the first ring, his heart racing, wrenched out of a nightmare involving Robin, sharks and, of all things, a giant octopus. He grabbed the handset and slammed it to his ear, fearing the worst. 'Yes?' he grated, his throat dry and rusty.

'It's Audrey at the Crewfinders twenty-four-hour desk, Captain Mariner . . .'

'Yes?' he repeated. Audrey was only about thirty metres away from him in the Crewfinders office which, with the company flat, occupied the top floor of Heritage House. Crewfinders was always on the alert. Its famous promise was to replace any crew member on any vessel, anywhere in the world within twenty-four hours. There was a team in that office waiting to send sailors from one place to another twenty-four seven. High days and holidays as well. Particularly then, for it was at the traditional celebration times that people got tipsy or careless – or both – and accidents started to happen. Therefore all the Heritage Mariner news came to the twenty-four-hour desk first.

'I'm sorry to disturb you so late, Captain,' Audrey apologized gently. *Not bad news then*, thought Richard. No emergency. Something routine.

'Yes?' he repeated, his voice still rough.

'*Katapult* has just put in a routine status report on the ship-to-shore radio. It went to the coastguards at Falmouth but we're monitoring the wavelength. It goes into a little more detail than is usual in such contacts so I thought it might be of interest. Shall I play it for you?'

'Please . . .'

There was a click, a brief burst of static, and then Robin's voice, a scratchy, distant whisper. 'I say again *Katapult* . . . It is sixteen hundred hours precisely, local time. Our current time is Tuvalu Standard minus one hour. All is well. We are making good progress now. Everyone aboard fit and healthy. We crossed the equator four hours ago and are currently at: nought point four eight degrees north and one seven six point three eight degrees west. Howland Island is immediately to our starboard and we are proceeding at thirty knots along a heading of nought point five nought degrees magnetic. We have come over one thousand miles since departing Tuvalu and expect to reach Johnston Atoll at one six point seven degrees north, one six nine

point nought five degrees west in a little over thirty-six hours if
the wind persists. We will have to vary our headings depending
on precisely where the locator beacon shows the bottle actually
to be four days or so from now. And, come to that, what state
we find the Great Pacific Garbage Patch to be in when we get
to the edge of it – let alone to the middle.' Robin's voice came
and went during the next few minutes as she reported wind and
weather, then formally confirmed their position, course and
heading once again. Then it whispered away into crackling
silence.

'That's all we have, Captain,' announced Audrey, her voice in
contrast to Robin's loud enough to make Richard jump.

'That's fine, thanks, Audrey. It's enough to put my mind at
rest, at any rate.' Even as he spoke the polite lie he wondered
why he still felt so tense. He was still in the grip of whatever
chemicals the nightmare had released into his system, of course
– but it was more than that. It was something to do with the fact
that Robin was out there adventuring and he was stuck here as
little more than her audience. He longed to be doing something.
Anything.

'I'm pleased to hear that, Captain,' said Audrey, over the top
of these thoughts. 'I'll alert you if anything else comes in from
them. Goodnight.'

Richard settled down, closed his eyes and called to mind a
chart of the Pacific, mentally tracing *Katapult*'s course from
Tuvalu past Howland Island a thousand miles to the north-east,
then on to the Johnston Atoll, one of the remotest places on earth,
twelve hundred miles north-east again, a thousand miles west of
Hawaii. Then on once again into the massive, empty vastness
between Hawaii and Midway, a channel nearly fifteen hundred
miles wide which only really ended with the Aleutian Islands,
the Bering Strait and the south coast of Alaska. With no islands
or atolls anywhere in between at all, except French Frigate Shoals,
the last of the way-stations they had planned along the way.

But even the ones he could call to mind were islands and atolls
in name, but nothing more than specks of coral in fact. The only
fact he could remember about Howland Island was that it had
been the destination the intrepid aerial explorer Amelia Earhart
never reached on her solo round-the-world flight when she

vanished into that vastness in the nineteen thirties. Johnston Atoll was utterly deserted. Hardly surprisingly: it had been a nuclear test ground in the fifties and sixties before it became a dumping ground for all the chemical weapons that the US refused to admit they ever possessed. It was where the Americans had disposed of their Agent Orange poison after the Vietnam War. The girls would need to be desperate indeed to go ashore there. If they ever got that far. Beyond that, the Shoals named for the French Frigates that had only survived their encounter with the deadly coral heads by an amazing stroke of luck. And, after French Frigate Shoal, there was nothing except empty ocean and the accumulating mass of floating rubbish that lay trapped at the heart of it.

He dosed off into another haunted slumber in which he was face-to-face with the octopus again – but this time it had a vaguely familiar human face. With a hooked nose. Long, dark eyes. Something strangely wrong with its ears. And it was holding Robin in one of its massive tentacles. It was a relief when her choking screams became a familiar ringtone and he woke to find that his cell phone was sounding.

This time it was a courtesy call from the Falmouth Coastguard bringing him up to date with Robin's latest report. At least their reception was clearer than Audrey's had been. But the information was, of course, just the same. After he broke contact, he heaved himself out of bed and went to make a coffee. His Rolex informed him that it was coming up to six in any case and his day tended to start at six when he was ashore – just halfway through the morning watch.

He switched on his radio and as he stood in the shower, the *Today Programme* on BBC Radio 4 informed him that Liberty Greenbaum had reported in as well. The news report was briefer, but it gave him everything he really wanted to know. *Flint* was over a thousand miles out of Vancouver heading along her planned south-westerly course now. There were no islands and precious few vessels anywhere near her. But all aboard were fit and well. Progress was precisely as planned and they too hoped to reach the rendezvous point north of Hawaii at the same time as *Katapult* and Professor Tanaka's Cheerio bottle.

The familiar voice of the regular anchorman added a further

tag to the story, '*And, according to this morning's* Times, *there is still no sign of the lucky winner of the Japanese Lottery. One-hundred-and-ten-million United States dollars – or their equivalent in Yen – are waiting to be claimed, apparently, but no one knows who holds the winning ticket . . .*'

His interest piqued, Richard wrapped a bath towel round his waist and padded through to the sitting room, towelling his short black hair dry with a hand towel as he went. He flipped up his laptop and clicked through to the live broadcast from *Japan Today*. The lunchtime news was just finishing as two p.m. Tokyo time clicked up. The newscaster was reporting a story in such a flood of enthusiasm that Richard stood no chance at all of following what she was saying. But the English subtitles explained that she, like BBC Radio 4, was speculating about the identity of the mysterious lottery winner. 'The winning ticket was purchased from an outlet in the Bunkyo District,' she was saying. 'And this has led some people to guess that the winner may be a student at the university. However, Bunkyo is one of the most heavily populated areas of the city with more than two-hundred-thousand people registered as residing in the ward, let alone the great number of people who come into the area on a regular basis to visit attractions such as the Tokyo Dome, the cathedral and the gardens . . .'

Frowning, Richard pulled up a chair and sat, leaning forward a little to read the rapidly changing script. As he did so, however, he noticed that the Skype logo was flashing and he clicked on it without thinking.

The screen cleared at once to a picture of a hazy blue horizon at whose shadowy centre lay a long golden heave of land, just tall enough to rise above a wall-to-wall vista of ocean and catch some brightness from a westering sun. Lazy waves gathered themselves from the bottom of the screen and rolled gently away until they smashed into white surf on the pale flank of beach. The whole picture heaved dizzyingly and the familiar lines of *Katapult*'s cockpit and after-rail came and went at weird angles. Then, disorientatingly, almost shockingly, a pair of breasts in a skimpy bikini top were all but pressed against the screen. He half expected a giant green tentacle to appear from the restless water and wrap itself around the golden body at the far end of the Skype contact. Then, at last, Robin's sunburned face appeared amid a wild riot of wind-blown hair. There were freckles across the bridge of her nose. Her eyes were wide and grey. And her glowing face split into the most enormous grin.

'Hello, sailor,' she said. 'You're a sight for sore eyes. Lucky it's me and not one of the other girls getting an eyeful!'

And he remembered with a start how little he was wearing.

'Shall I get dressed?' he asked.

'Don't you dare!' she chuckled. 'I want to remember you just the way you are. It'll give me something to liven up my dreams.'

'OK,' he answered easily. 'I'm never one to disappoint a lady.' He draped his hand towel round his shoulders and leaned back. 'If that's still Howland Island behind you then you've done better than Amelia Earhart.'

'Ah. Someone forwarded my report to the coastguards . . .' The smile deepened. She was having a whale of a time, he realized with a pang of jealousy.

'A couple of people,' he nodded. 'It sounds as though you have the bit between your teeth now . . .'

'And then some. We've been going like the clappers. There's a perfect wind behind us and *Katapult* is really in her element. The only down side has been the fact that we've found it all but impossible to get a decent signal in or out.'

'Looks like you're all right now. *Flint*'s OK as well, by all accounts.'

'I know. We've been in contact with her. And we've uploaded some good footage that we took during the run up here. Some excellent close-ups of a waterspout, for instance. And a storm front like you wouldn't believe. We should be all over the TV news by teatime. Teatime *your time*. It's teatime *our time* already . . . Now, quickly, while whatever satellite up there continues to smile upon us, how are the kids?'

Richard was still bringing Robin up to speed with family and business news when the connection faltered then failed. He sat looking at the screen thoughtfully for a moment or two, wondering what on earth Robin had been doing to get close-up pictures of a waterspout. Then, still deep in thought he rose, turned and walked back through to his dressing room. He had no memory of hitting the back button on his laptop, but he must have done, because, as he opened his underwear drawer, he was suddenly treated to another diatribe of excited Japanese.

He gave a dry chuckle and dropped the towel round his waist. He stepped into his underwear then hopped from foot to foot pulling on his socks. He chose a white cotton shirt and a mid-grey suit. He had tightened the belt and was standing in front of the mirror perfecting his half-Windsor knot in a gold-patterned silk tie when one of the words in the Japanese broadcast caused him to stop.

'. . . Tanaka . . .' it said, quite clearly.

Frowning, Richard walked back through into the sitting room.

The same excitable news anchor from *Japan Today* had her head and shoulders framed on the screen. Behind her there was a picture of Professor Reona Tanaka, full face in close-up. No sooner were the familiar features there than they were gone. And the photograph of a young woman replaced them.

Also missing is his colleague, Dr Aika Rei, said the translation across the bottom of the screen. *Neither she nor Professor Tanaka have been seen for several days and the Tokyo Police have begun a manhunt.*

Richard was walking towards the laptop, shaking his head in simple surprise, when his cell phone started to ring again. He glanced at its screen as he picked it up. Nic Greenbaum's picture looked back at him.

'Mariner,' he said, putting it to his ear. 'You're up late, Nic. Is it about Tanaka?'

'Yeah,' came Nic's familiar voice, his usual laid-back California drawl absent. 'But it's not as late as you think. I'm at a meeting in Las Vegas just in from the glad-handing and the floor show. Only eight hours behind you, Buddy. Still, Tanaka's chosen one hell of a time to go awol.'

'You think something's up?' demanded Richard at once. 'Something beyond some kind of a runaway romance?'

'I don't know, Richard. I mean, the guy seemed pretty level-headed to me.'

'And to me,' agreed Richard thoughtfully. 'Far too sensible to walk out on a lifelong career at the pinnacle of his ambition, only ten days away from becoming the pin-up boy of the environmental lobby, if this Cheerio thing goes right.'

'On the other hand . . .' temporized Nic.

'Yeah. He probably didn't get out much. This woman could have turned his head, I suppose. God knows it's happened before.'

'No way of knowing. But the sixty-four-thousand-dollar question is . . .'

'Where does his disappearance leave us?' Richard completed Nic's thought. 'And *Katapult* and *Flint*, come to that?'

'Both Libby and Robin seem to be bang on course,' said Nic. 'And as far as I know, the bottle's still there. Still bleeping out its little tracker signal.'

'So what part of our plans will be messed up if Professor Tanaka doesn't reappear in time?' mused Richard. 'And what do we need to do in the way of damage limitation?'

'The next thing Professor Tanaka was due to be part of was the Tokyo reception to celebrate the recovery of the bottle. Preparations for that are well in hand, and building up nicely as *Katapult* and *Flint* close in – and the signal from that damn bottle stays loud and clear.'

'We're both due to be there for that,' said Richard. 'It's all set to be the climax of the whole thing. I suppose we could cover for him to a certain extent if he hasn't shown up again by then.'

'Everything except the science, you mean.'

'I suppose so. But it seems a bit cold-blooded. Look. Heritage Mariner have associates in Ōsaki district. How is Greenbaum International placed?'

'Business centre just down the road from you. You think I should get some of our people busy on looking for poor old Reona?'

'Not so much of the '*poor old Reona*'. Have you seen a picture of the girl he's supposed to have gone off with?'

'Hot, huh?'

'And then some. But yes. I do feel we should at least ask around. I mean, I know he's more Greenbaum International than Heritage Mariner, but even so, he's—'

'Family . . .' said Nic thoughtfully. 'The kind of *family* they used to have here in Vegas.' He was speaking in a mock-mafioso accent and he paused for a moment so that Richard could get the message.

'Yes. Well put. Family. And for all we know, he could be in trouble.'

'Look,' said Nic suddenly. 'I tell you what. My desk is pretty clear now that this meeting is over and done with, what with seeing Libby off and just planning to pass through the LA office on my way to Tokyo. How's your desk fixed?'

'Like yours. I have a good team well briefed. I've really just been touching base on my way through too.'

'Then let's go for it. You and me both. The distance from Vegas is about the same as from London, give or take a couple of hundred miles. I'll bet you dinner at the winner's choice of menu and location that my guys at GI can get me to the Tokyo Hilton faster than your guys at HM can get you there.'

'Except that I'd be heading for the Mandarin Oriental, you've got a bet. Menu and restaurant, winner's choice.'

Richard broke contact on his phone with his right hand even as he picked up the receiver of the internal phone with his left. Within five seconds he was talking to Audrey at Crewfinders once again, his heart racing; but not with worry this time. With excitement. 'Audrey, I'd like you to get me to Tokyo as fast as you can,' he said crisply. 'And book me a suite at the Mandarin from tomorrow afternoon. Check-in time's from two p.m., if I remember right.'

Flight

'The next flight out is the Etihad Airways A308 departing Heathrow Terminal Five at nine fifteen this morning,' said Audrey. 'Arrives at Tokyo Narita at one p.m. local time tomorrow.'

'Book me on it,' said Richard. 'I'll pick up any paperwork for the flight at the check-in desk. All my Japan documentation is current. I just have to get to Heathrow inside an hour.' He looked at his Rolex and hesitated. 'What's the next one after the Etihad flight?'

'BA to Tokyo Hadena International an hour later. Same terminal. Flight Number 007 direct. New service.'

'Haneda's thirty miles nearer the city centre. What's the flight time?'

'Fifteen hours. You should touch down before ten a.m. local. And you know your cell won't work in Japan. You'll have to pick up a local one.'

'That's OK, I'll take my laptop. Email works. Book me a seat on that one too. I'll decide when I get to Terminal Five.'

'You want me to call for the chopper, Captain?'

'No, thanks, Audrey. I think I know a quicker way.'

'If you're thinking what I think you're thinking, the code for your satellite navigation system is TW6 2GA.'

'Got it. Thanks, Audrey. But I know the way like the back of my hand. I'll be in touch when I get there.'

Fizzing with excitement, Richard ran through to the bedroom once again. In a specially adapted section of his wardrobe, he kept a travelling case that was always packed with his essentials – even his passport and his Kindle – so that he could grab and go at a moment's notice. It was designed for use when some great ship somewhere on a vast and distant ocean suddenly found itself without a captain or a senior navigating officer and Richard had to get from Heritage House to its command bridge in the shortest possible time. But the system was just as effective when it came to winning crazy wagers with old friends. It was a neat, efficient piece of kit and simply hefting it out of the wardrobe gave Richard an extra buzz of excitement.

He pulled the case out with gleeful exuberance, therefore, threw it on the tumbled bed, ran back for his laptop and charger, pulling on the jacket to his charcoal-grey suit as he went, slid them into the special compartment, grabbed his cell phone and dropped that into his jacket pocket, slipped on his shoes and hit the front door. He grabbed a light Aquascutum off the coat stand on the way through – Tokyo would be hot and damp, he guessed. Thirty degrees Celsius, with an unseasonable amount of rain forecast for August. Finally, he caught up the keys to his Bentley Continental, which was sitting beside his E-Type Jaguar in the garage below, and tossed them gleefully into the air as he kicked the door closed behind him.

In the lift on the way down, he ran through the familiar checklist in his head. He could rely on Audrey to update everyone who needed to know that he had gone. Heritage Mariner's senior board were used to Richard and Robin appearing and disappearing at odd times. While the Mariners were increasingly the public faces of the company, they had been careful to put in place teams of executives who were more than capable of running things in their absence.

But the first calls Audrey would make, Richard suspected, would be to finish making his reservation on the Etihad A380 confirming ticket and seat, with maximum legroom possible. Alerting the Mandarin to his flight arrival time, confirming his suite – an open-ended booking. Confirming with Heathrow that he would be occupying the secure slot that Heritage Mariner kept in the Terminal Five Business Car Park – as well as at all the others – for emergencies such as this. Then getting on to BA with his back-up plan and warning the Mandarin that things might change a little in an hour or so's time.

But high on the list, he knew, would be a quick call to Grimaud in the South of France to update his parents and his children on his latest hare-brained scheme. Then, no doubt, she would see if she could get hold of *Katapult* or *Flint*.

With these thoughts tumbling through his mind, he stepped out of the lift into the company car park beneath Heritage House. A few purposeful strides took him to the sleek rear of his matt black Bentley, almost invisible in the shadows. He pressed the remote, unlocked the deadlocks, popped the boot and slid his case in, folded the raincoat and suit jacket in on top of it, closed the cool black metal and all but ran to the driver's door.

He eased into the red-stitched black leather driver's seat and felt it adjusting automatically to him as he slid his custom key into the dash. He rolled up his shirtsleeves, popped up the cover, punched in the key code and pushed the starter. The whole car purred into life like a sleepy panther beginning to come awake. He slid his seat belt home, flicked the paddle gearshift into reverse and eased back into the turning area, feeling the car settle on to its haunches, ready to spring forward. It was all he could do not to make the tyres squeal as he let her roll forward, feeling his lips curl into an excited smile and thinking *free at last, free at last . . .*

A moment later, the sleek black bonnet with its signature winged B came prowling up from the underground car park and out into Cornhill swinging smoothly down towards Mansion House Street like a big cat hunting gazelle. The alarm sounded quietly, reminding him that he was in the Congestion Charging Zone. Audrey would take care of that, he thought, as he tapped the paddle gearshift and eased his foot down on the accelerator. Thirty seconds later he was turning past the Grecian temple frontages of The Bank of England and the Mansion House opposite, and on to Queen Victoria Street. At six fifteen a.m. there was hardly anything else on the road except for delivery vans. Too early for buses or taxis yet; all those millions of tourists still tucked up in bed. Half of them, of course, Japanese. The thought made him chuckle out loud.

Forty seconds later, he had eased carefully past the Central London Magistrates' Court, and was heading along the all but empty Queen Victoria Street for White Lion Hill. The sun had been up in a clear blue sky for a little over forty minutes, but he was heading west so its brightness only dazzled occasionally in his rear-view, glinting off the windows of the taller buildings ahead. He felt a heady possessiveness as he guided his beloved car through the familiar thoroughfares, past some of the most important and historic buildings in London. This was *his* city, he felt. He had lived and worked all over the world; owned houses on the Scottish Borders, on the Norfolk coast and just along from the White Cliffs overlooking the Channel; but nevertheless he found himself singing in his best imitation Sinatra voice, '*It's my kind of town . . .*'

The Bentley rumbled down White Lion Hill into the sudden neon gloom of the Blackfriars Underpass, and for three minutes the bellow of the engine was contained within the tunnel, then Richard sent her – exactly on the speed-limit – out on to the Victoria Embankment. With the Thames on his left at full-flood, brown and golden in the morning light and the Temple Gardens, Somerset House and The Savoy speeding past on his right, he eased past the gilded thrust of Cleopatra's needle snarled beneath the end of Hungerford Bridge then turned right at the lights on to Northumberland Avenue.

Moments later still, the black panther of the Bentley was

grumbling past Charing Cross Station, only just coming alive as the first commuters arrived and meandered, dazzled, out into the still-clear morning. Then, easing past the end of Whitehall under Nelson's stony gaze – and the somnolent, almost kindred regard of Landseer's lions, Richard entered the great roundabout of Trafalgar Square. He glanced up at the famous carvings and then he signalled left, sweeping through the gathering traffic and swinging beneath Admiralty Arch.

Then, with a wiggle of her panther hips he eased the Continental into The Mall, giving a mental prayer of thanks that it was too early for the Changing of the Guard. The dusty pink perfection of The Mall led straight as a die through St James's Park to the roundabout outside Buckingham Palace. Nelson's gaze was replaced by that of Victoria, Queen Empress, also guarded by regal lions, as he swung round the fountain and past the front of Buckingham Palace itself and on to Constitution Hill.

With the trees of Green Park on the one hand and Buckingham Palace Gardens behind the security wall on the other, he pushed the speed limit for another thirty seconds before swinging left into Duke of Wellington Place, with the Duke of Wellington Arch seeming to wheel around on his right. Then he bore right into Grosvenor Place and almost immediately left on to Knightsbridge.

Easing the pedal down a fraction more, Richard sped past The Sheraton on his left with the Mandarin Oriental Hyde Park almost opposite, past Harvey Nicholls and then, moments later, past Harrods as Knightsbridge became the Brompton Road. Ten minutes later the A4 had metamorphosed through Thurloe Place to the Cromwell Road to the Talgarth Road and leaped up on to the Hammersmith Flyover.

Within half an hour of leaving Heritage House Richard was easing the Bentley through Hogarth Lane and down on to the M4 Motorway with the traffic beginning to thicken around him. A couple of quick flips of the gear-paddle and the Bentley had leaped up from forty mph to eighty, roaring with satisfaction as the little aerodynamic fin rose behind her rear window. Five minutes and seven miles later, he was purring past the slip road signposted Heathrow Terminals One, Two and Three. The six forty-five Virgin Jumbo eased itself into the air above him, heading for New York. He held steady until he reached the M25 turnoff, then disorientatingly followed the signpost to Gatwick, growling down the steep left curve on to the busy southbound motorway. Four minutes later still, he was swinging left again into the lane marked Terminal Five.

Richard parked the Bentley at ten past seven and hefted his kit out of the back before turning down his shirt cuffs, slipping on his jacket, setting the deadlocks and strolling down to the pod stop. He checked the time on his cell phone rather than his Rolex because he was calling Audrey as he waited. The pod rolled up at seven fifteen on the dot, just as he made contact.

'The Etihad flight was overbooked,' she announced apologetically as he folded himself with some difficulty into the little remote vehicle, pushing his case and coat on to the seat opposite, thankful that he was the only passenger. 'But I've got you on the BA flight at ten thirty. First class. I take it this is company business because the flight isn't what you'd call cheap.'

'First class never is,' he answered shortly. 'And yes. I'm going early but I'd still have had to go sometime.'

'But, on the plus side,' she answered more gently, 'there's the Concorde Lounge for you to wait in.'

Five minutes later, Richard unfolded himself from the pod like a large hermit crab coming out of a small shell outside Terminal Five. He strolled down the length of Departures and arrived at the BA first-class check-in desk at seven thirty on the dot. All his paperwork was waiting for him and he was happy to scan it in, check in the suitcase and sling his laptop bag over one shoulder while the Aquascutum went over the other, before he strolled on through Fast Track Security to the Concorde Lounge.

The steel-haired receptionist on the Concorde Lounge desk checked his documents rather more thoroughly than the man at security had done before she grudgingly permitted him to enter her lair. But once he was past her, he was pleasantly surprised by the spacious brightness of the Concorde Lounge. The floor was of honey-coloured wood overlain with plain chocolate carpets. The ceiling was high and one whole wall appeared to be a series of tall windows opening out on to an exclusive covered balcony. Down the wall at ninety degrees to this there was a bar. On the other side the area opened further into a restaurant with further sections for work and rest beyond. There was even what appeared to be a large shower and spa section. Massage and foot spa were apparently available.

But so, more to the point, was breakfast.

The girl in the restaurant was more approachable than the woman on reception and Richard was able to parlay the mid-Atlantic cuisine offering BLT, organic sausages and scrambled egg with salmon into something approaching a full English breakfast that was beautifully cooked, artfully presented – and it tasted fantastic. It was accompanied by freshly squeezed orange juice and a cafetière of Blue Mountain high roast coffee.

He finished the second cup at eight and wandered through to the work area. Once he had found a plug for his laptop he used the Wi-Fi facility to access the electronic work desk at Heritage Mariner. He spent the next hour scanning and saving to the laptop's hard drive – and then to a couple of thirty-two gigabyte USB memory sticks that he kept handy for just such emergencies.

All in all, by the time his flight was called he had stored more than enough work in one place or another to keep him going through most of the time he proposed to spend in Tokyo – let alone the time it was going to take him to get there. But he was reckoning on working non-stop on the flight – without the need for Internet access in the air – and then he would email everything he had done back to the office from the Mandarin Oriental – if he had time before Nic took him out to dinner in Tokyo's best restaurant tomorrow evening. He had heard great things of Akira Kurosawa – as restaurateur as well as film director – but hadn't got across town to his legendary eatery *Kurosawa* in Chiyoda district on his last visit. Maybe now was the time . . .

The BA Airbus lifted off at ten thirty on the dot and Richard worked for twelve solid hours with only short breaks for a light and excellent luncheon followed four hours later by an equally excellent dinner. By that time the battery on his laptop was running out of power and his own energy was beginning to diminish as well. In his head it was ten thirty in the evening but outside it was coming up for five, and at 30,000 feet it was already dawn.

A two-hour power nap set Richard up as effectively as a full night's sleep – and would do so for several nights in a row, he knew – but only if he got a chance to catch up somewhere further down the road. So he was able to spend the last hour filling in the required security documentation, which was a good deal less than he had to complete on his visits to Sharm el Sheikh in Egypt or to Benin la Bas in West Africa, and catching up with his Kindle edition of a couple of adventure thrillers by Clive Cussler and Wilbur Smith.

BA flight 007 whispered on to Tokyo International's main runway at a little after ten a.m. local time. Richard was in Hadena's main building by ten thirty and was walking through security with his suitcase before eleven, pausing only at the International Exchange to top up his supply of Yen.

The Airport Express was easy to find and he settled into a seat with Wi-Fi access, opened his laptop and paid the excess for connection. The run to Tokyo station was twenty minutes and before the first five had passed he was in contact with the Mandarin, confirming his booking and arrival time, and arranging for a car to collect him from the Yaesu South exit.

He stepped out of the back of the Mandarin's limo on Ninobashi and ran up between the columns that might have graced the Bank of England into the Mandarin Oriental at midday on the dot. He strode across towards the reception, fizzing with excitement, only to stop, simply flabbergasted. For there, leaning nonchalantly with an elbow on the polished desktop, deep in conversation with Christian Hassang the manager, was Nic Greenbaum.

And even as Richard stood hesitating in the middle of the bustling lobby, the American swung round with gleeful theatricality. 'Hey, Richard! Here you are at last!' he drawled. 'What kept you, Buddy?'

Dock

'Five minutes,' admitted Nic with a laugh.

'Less,' emphasized Christian Hassang. 'Mr Greenbaum hardly had time to draw breath before you arrived.'

'Still, you made it before I did,' said Richard, shaking his head in wonder.

'Courtesy of Richard Branson,' shrugged Nic, still smiling. 'Virgin all the way. Must be just about the *only* virgin in Vegas, I guess.'

'Probably why they were so keen to get out of the place,' joked Richard, beginning to relax. 'You must have started in the middle of the night.'

'Four a.m. red-eye and lucky to get aboard. Thought I was going to have to bribe my way on at the departures gate. But I ended up winning the seat on a bet! The flip of a silver dollar, just like that! First class too. Rockstar Treatment and all. Offered to pay up after I won but the guy said, "No – a bet's a bet!" Only in Vegas, I tell you! Lifted off bang on time. One-hour layover in LA and straight over the Pacific, sleeping like a baby. I was down in Narita just before ten local – good tailwind so I'm told. N'Ex first-class green car to Tokyo station in fifty minutes and Christian here was waiting for me himself. We pulled up just ahead of you.'

'I thought you were going for the Hilton.'

'Seemed silly when I thought of it – splitting our forces like that. We're both here on the same mission, looking for the same guy. The same gal, maybe. Seems logical to stay together if we can.'

'As long as we're not sharing a room,' answered Richard, glancing at Christian as he spoke.

'Adjoining suites,' said the general manager. 'And you're booked in to Sora on our thirty-eighth floor for the eight-thirty sitting this evening. It is, I flatter myself, the finest sushi restaurant in Tokyo, perhaps in the world. You were fortunate there was a cancellation. But it seems to be Mr Greenbaum's lucky day.'

'Perhaps I should buy a lottery ticket,' suggested Nic cheerfully. 'They're apparently thinking of going for a rollover on that one-hundred-and-ten-million-dollar jackpot if the original winner doesn't show up soon!'

'That's something we can think about on our way downtown,' said Richard. 'The first thing I want to do is to find out how the search for Tanaka is proceeding.'

'You have an appointment with one of the investigating officers later this afternoon at the Metropolitan Police Department headquarters at the Keishicho building,' said Christian briskly. 'But now let us get you signed in and you can go to your suites and freshen up. Perhaps think about lunch or late breakfast, according to where your body clocks are at present. Captain Mariner, I have the local cell phones you and Mr Greenbaum will require. They are fully charged, topped up with credit and pre-programmed as you requested. And a limousine will take you to the Keishicho in good time.'

They ate in K'shiki on the thirty-eighth floor, which was still serving Western-style breakfast on request, even though they were pushing it a little. Both of them had checked in with head office and updated everyone who needed to know where they were and what they were doing as they freshened up. So they made plans for the day as they ate. They would see the police officer together and then take their search for Tanaka from there. It seemed logical that they should split up if they went back to the university. Nic could find out quite a bit as the sponsor of Tanaka's department and Richard would try and exercise his charm on anyone who knew the lovely Dr Aika Rei. After the publicity surrounding the launch of the *Cheerio*, Richard's face was as familiar around the Tokyo University Science campus as Nic's was and neither of them thought there would be much trouble in making some general enquiries.

Their limousine drew up outside the big grey wedge-shaped Keishicho police headquarters at ten to four, and at four precisely they were shown into the office of Police Officer Sato Ozawa. The office was not large – and neither was Officer Ozawa. Richard felt as though he and Nic had been pushed into one of the laser-guided car park pods at Heathrow. Ozawa mistook his concern about bumping his head on the low ceiling for a more formal greeting and rose to bow in return, before waving his overpowering visitors to a pair of worryingly flimsy chairs.

He arranged a pile of papers a little fussily, nodding the bald egg of his head thoughtfully. His body was also egg-shaped, Richard noted; a bantam egg, maybe. The buttons of his uniform still strained across both chest and paunch. 'I understand you are here to ask how the enquiry into the disappearance of Professor Tanaka and Doctor Rei is progressing,' he said after a thoughtful pause. He spoke quietly in American-accented English which sounded strange with the formality of his diction, making him seem pompous.

'Greenbaum International sponsors his department and research,' said Nic.

'And Heritage Mariner is co-sponsoring his current experiment with climate change,' added Richard. 'He is an important man to both of us.'

'I have seen the publicity,' nodded Ozawa courteously. 'And of course both yourselves and your businesses are familiar to me. I understand your concern. However, I regret to say that I can only be of limited help. We have interviewed many of his colleagues whose general opinion seems to be that his disappearance might well have been caused by the stress that the very publicity you talk of was putting him under.'

'But if that were the case,' probed Richard, frowning, 'why would Doctor Rei disappear with him?'

'At first we considered her disappearance to be coincidence,' said the officer. 'We do not jump to conclusions until we have proof. However, a taxi driver did admit that he had driven a couple matching their description from the university to a bar in the dock area the night before the disappearance. He said they behaved like lovers in his cab.'

Richard raised an eyebrow.

Officer Ozawa frowned. 'No impropriety is intended by this phrase. They embraced and whispered, that is all. Another cab driver, whose company services the same bar admitted to taking what we presume to be the same couple back to the university area later that same evening. He observed that they were intimate – whispering – and seemed excited. We have of course made enquiries at the bar itself but have made no progress there. It is not, I must admit, the sort of place a man of Professor Tanaka's standing or reputation would be likely to frequent. It is popular with passing sailors and illegal drifters. That is about all.'

'Drifters?' asked Nic.

'Illegal car racers. It is a popular pastime with young undesirables. Perhaps you have heard of the Hollywood movie. *Fast and Furious . . .*'

'. . . *Tokyo Drift.* I've heard of it,' said Richard. 'But there's no possibility that Tanaka was involved in illegal car racing, surely?'

Ozawa shrugged. 'It is as conceivable or as inconceivable as anything else. We have nothing solid enough to support further speculation. We have not been able to find a cab driver who will admit to transporting the missing couple anywhere on the morning that they were first reported missing. We can discover nothing of their movements then or subsequently; our best guess remains that they have run away together. But the point I am making' – Ozawa leaned forward to emphasize the point he was making – 'is that there is no question of kidnap or foul play. And it is not illegal for two consenting adults to run away together, even if they don't bother warning their friends, family or employers of their intention.'

'So, if there is no illegal act, then there is no case for the police to look into,' Richard concluded.

'Indeed,' nodded Officer Ozawa, leaning back lugubriously. 'I regret to say that you understand the situation perfectly. Unless a body – or two – or a ransom note of some kind turns up, the case is closed.'

'So, there's nothing else you can tell us that might help,' said Nic.

'No.' The egg-shaped head shook regretfully. 'There is, I am afraid, nothing further.'

'Except,' said Richard, leaning forward until his chair creaked dangerously, 'for the name of the bar they visited on the evening before they vanished.'

'*Sore Thumbs R Us*,' observed Richard.

'What?' asked Nic, looking round, frowning.

'We stick out a bit . . .'

'Yeah. You could say . . .' They were the only Westerners in Rage. They were dressed in a trench coat and an Aquascutum, surrounded by clients in black leather and navy donkey jackets. From the general reaction to their arrival, they were the first of their ethnic, social and financial groupings to visit in quite a while. More than that, they were a good deal older than at least half of the dockside bar's clientele and taller than all of them by quite a way.

'Well, I don't drink,' said Richard, 'and I know sod-all about drifting. So I'll start with the sailors, shall I?' Without another word, he strolled across to the nearest table not surrounded by stylish teenagers and produced Tanaka's picture. 'Gentlemen,' he rumbled. 'Any of you recognize this?'

He might have been speaking to statues.

'This?' he tried, unabashed. Dr Rei's attractive face joined her colleague's. One of the sailors blinked. Another licked his lips.

'They probably don't speak English,' offered Nic from the bar. 'This guy apparently doesn't.'

'Not convinced,' answered Richard cheerfully. 'English is still the language of the sea. English and cash. Perhaps you recognize this, then, gentlemen?' Suddenly, beside Tanaka's picture there was a hundred-dollar bill.

Now there was a stir of interest round the table. Through the bar, indeed. Richard eased back. Let everyone have a good look. Leaned forward over the sailors' table again.

'All we want to know is who they talked to. If they were talking to seafarers then they'll all be long gone. We know that. But we just want the name of a sailor. Or a vessel, maybe. We don't want to make trouble for anyone. We're not the law, just friends of these two wanting to make sure they're still OK. You know they're missing – run off together. It's been all over the news. You know the police have been here and found nothing. But they won't have been trying too hard. And they won't have been offering inducements like my friend and me.'

Another hundred-dollar bill joined the first.

'But, talking of inducements,' purred Richard hypnotically, 'you should know that they are limited. A few more dollars and no more time. We have reservations at Sora in an hour and we don't want to be late. So it's speak now' – two more hundred-dollar bills joined the first pair – 'or forever hold your peace . . .'

Silence. But a sweaty silence, wrestling with temptation. Four-hundred dollars was more than thirty-two thousand yen. A day's pay for a top-flight doctor or dentist. More than a month's wages for men like these.

Richard straightened. Pocketed the photographs and the cash. Turned and headed for the door. Nic fell in beside him. They stepped out on to the pavement and started walking along to where their taxi was waiting. By apparent coincidence a Mazda RX8 in police colours slid round the corner at the far end of the road.

'Now that,' said a quiet voice behind them, 'would make a first-rate drifter.'

Richard turned to find himself apparently facing down the male cast of the musical *Grease*. It was wall-to-wall sixties rebooted. There was slicked black hair. There were cool shades. Drainpipe jeans and what looked suspiciously like crepe-soled shoes. Almost as much black leather as covered the seats in his Continental.

'This is a surprise,' he said amiably. 'I was expecting sailors, not drifters.'

The young man who had spoken reached into the inside pocket of his leather jacket. Richard felt Nic stirring at his shoulder.

But only a phone came out. 'This your dude?' asked the young man. The screen showed Tanaka talking to a heavy-set Japanese in a navy donkey jacket. A sailor, clearly. The telltale bottles of the bar were in the background.

'Yes,' said Richard. 'But I'm not sure that picture's worth a thousand words – let alone five hundred dollars.' He emphasized the word *five*.

'Fair enough,' said the young drifter coolly. 'But this one is.' The drifter's thumb moved on the cell phone's keypad. Another picture appeared. This one was moving. In it, a Toyota Corolla was skidding sideways very fast across a wet and gleaming dock. Behind the car, security lighting showed the black wall of a ship's side, down which was suspended a gangplank. As the car slid across the phone camera's view, two figures, obviously a man and woman – but not so clearly Tanaka and Akia Rei – were hurrying up the gangplank.

The Toyota's spectacular slide slowed – the driver was clearly running out of dockside. The camera stayed focused on the car. But its movement brought the top of the gangplank and the ship's name into clearview. The car stopped. The picture froze.

If the figures caught in the act of stepping aboard were still not all that clear, the name of the ship was. *Dagupan Maru*, it said in Western script.

Ghost

'Can you make out her name?' called Liberty, leaning forward against the wheel and straining her eyes at the ghostly vessel drifting a couple of miles ahead. It was just after dawn on the fourth day of fast sailing and the sun rising behind them had cast its first great beams ahead of them to reveal the outline of a ship. The vessel was surprisingly close and drifting closer still, pulled towards them by the current while they were being pushed down on it by the wind. It had approached so close without them suspecting its presence during the night because it was apparently running dark and silent. No lights. No radio. They saw it in the bright dawn just before it registered on their simple collision alarm radar.

'Can you make out her name?' Liberty called again.

'Not completely. Looks like something *Maru* to me,' called back Bella Chung-Wolf. 'Her forepeak's a mess covered in dirt and rust. There's something else written there but I can't make it out. We'd need to get *way* nearer, even with these.' She waved the binoculars in the air to show what she meant. The steady wind whipped her long black hair forward and moulded the cotton shirt to her back. She had all the sure-footed athleticism of her mixed heritage, half Cantonese half Cheyenne, thought Liberty. But even so, as skipper, she should have insisted on life jackets if people were going running up and down the length of the steadily heeling deck. Even given the excitement of this unexpected encounter.

'Still nothing on the radio?' Liberty glanced down at Maya in the snug where *Flint*'s communications equipment sat stubbornly silent.

'We can't even call her up unless we have some idea of her name,' Maya answered.

'Maybe we could try something like, "*Hey, ghost ship drifting three miles off my starboard bow, this is sailing vessel* Flint; *how's things with you?*"' Emma Toda called from her place at

Bella's side on the bow. 'Something like that?' She and Bella giggled at the thought. Liberty thought better of asking Emma to explain a little more about the meaning of the universal *Maru* which seemed to be added to all Japanese registered vessels. But Emma was so proud of her Japanese background they would probably have had to endure a half-hour lecture before they were any the wiser.

'What about the authorities?' said Liberty, frowning. 'We ought to report her and get on our way.'

'Not a whisper,' answered Maya. 'We might as well be in deep space.'

'And there's no sign of life on deck?' she called back up to Bella, who obligingly put the binoculars to her eyes again.

'Nothing I can see. She looks like a ghost ship to me. A modern-day *Marie Celeste*.'

'Well, if we can't raise her and we can't raise the authorities, we have two simple choices,' said Emma, skipping back towards the cockpit, as sure-footed as Bella in spite of her square, muscular physique. 'We stay clear, head on, and report her as a hazard to shipping to the first radio contact we raise. Get them to pass on a warning to the nearest coastguard. Or we go aboard.'

'That's what we ought to do,' said the punctilious Maya. 'There could be someone aboard in trouble. We ought to make sure, you know?'

Liberty knew very well what was going on here. After the horrors of their stormbound run south and their near-fatal encounter with the Disney cruise liner, there had followed four full days and nights of non-stop simple sailing. Coming up to one hundred hours with the wind on their shoulder, brisk, kindly and unvarying. The ocean like an aquamarine carpet undulating easily before them. A white wake spreading ever wider behind them. No other vessel heaving over the huge horizon. Not a bird, not a fish, nothing to disturb the easy passage, day after day. The closest they had been to human contact outside themselves and the very occasional burst of activity on the radio had been the high white lines of the contrails as planes passed hundreds of thousands of feet above. The girls were getting bored.

But Emma and Maya were right. In the absence of anyone else either nearby or within radio contact, then it was *Flint*'s duty

to offer the apparently helpless vessel aid. And if they couldn't
raise anyone on her radio or communicate by any other signal
then they would have to go aboard and take a look. Though what
in heaven's name they were going to do if they found a ship full
of sick and dying sailors God alone knew. Hope and pray that
something that size would have a more efficient communications
system than *Flint*'s. And that Maya, the acting radio officer, could
get it to work.

It was this thought which pushed Liberty to her final decision.
The vessel drifting down on them looked to be about two hundred
feet in length. Her tonnage was hard to judge because she was
sitting low in the water, but Liberty would have been surprised
if she was much less than two hundred tons deadweight. She was
clearly a commercial vessel. Too small to be a freighter. More
likely a fishing boat. But a substantial, ocean-going ship. Which
might well be equipped with communications gear far more
powerful than theirs, even though, by the look of things, it was
probably not anything like as modern. But on the other hand, the
name *Maru* meant that it was Japanese. And whatever else they
did, the Japanese built some top-of-the-range communications kit.

Certainly, as *Flint* bore down on her, the difference between
the hull below her central bridge house and the equipment perched
above it was striking. The drifting ship had a long, low hull with
a white band on her immediately below the scuppers, sitting
brightly above black-painted sides that fell to a swollen, barnacle
encrusted waterline. Or it should have been a white band beneath
the scuppers. In fact it was tiger-striped with broad smears of
red rust. Above the scuppers themselves, the deck rails seemed
thin and ill-maintained, with sections designed to fold down
almost to the waterline, pulled back and secured up in grilles
like hockey nets.

From what Liberty could see, the green-painted non-slip of
the deck was in little better shape than the pocked, blistered and
rusting sides. And the deck furniture was, if anything, worse.
But, under the relentless searchlight of the rising sun, the bridge
house itself rose square and pristine above the rotting mess below.
Two levels up, it stood almost glacially white, with wide windows
facing forwards. And immediately behind it stood a communications mast that positively gleamed. A big white banner bearing

an identity code in Western letters and numbers, aptly enough ending in thirteen; and above that the almost showroom-new radar, sonar, fish-finding and communications complex, its brand-new brilliance marred only by the filth of the lines and rigging all around it. And, now that she noticed it, the matching equipment which capped the stubby foremast looked in pretty good nick as well.

Behind the bridge and the communications mast, halfway to the poop, there was a rusted square gantry that seemed to mark the beginning of a work area even worse maintained than the foredeck. And on the square stern itself sat a tall crane no doubt used for controlling any nets that the ship might want to deploy. A battered Japanese fishing vessel almost certainly, concluded Liberty. With a promising-looking range of communications kit that nobody aboard was apparently willing or able to use.

The decision as to who was going to board her was easy to make, therefore. They needed someone who knew about Japanese stuff and someone who knew about radios. Emma and Maya. 'OK,' ordered Liberty brusquely. 'Bella, come and take over the communications. Emma and Maya get ready to go aboard.'

There wasn't a huge amount of preparation to be done. Emma and Maya dressed in their thickest cotton shirts, jeans and deck shoes. They shrugged on life jackets in case they fell into the water during transfer from one vessel to the other. They grabbed torches because there seemed to be no power aboard the ghost ship. They each took a two-way that would communicate with the radio Bella was in charge of, though Liberty was careful to order that they should stay together at all times. Beyond these simple things, there was nothing much else they could take at this stage. They had no guns – and Liberty would never have considered sending anyone aboard if she had the slightest notion that there might be violence. They had a carefully selected range of medical and emergency supplies aboard *Flint* but the boxes they were in were unwieldy and Liberty didn't want to risk them unless there was clear and urgent need of them. So the simple, basic equipment they gathered together within the first few minutes looked as though it would be all they would take. But then, as Liberty steered *Flint* along her shadowy length on the ocean's quicksilver surface towards her mounting shadow rising slowly up the sun-bright side of the ghost ship, Maya had another idea.

'We should *film* this,' she announced. 'I can take the camera and video what we find. It would be great footage for our next news update.'

'Good thinking,' Liberty agreed at once. 'And if you set the camera to *transmit* as well as *record*, then Bella and I can watch your progress on the laptop.'

Maya raced below and was back with the little camera in an instant, then she ran back to the bow and filmed the last few minutes of the approach while Bella tested the clarity of the picture she received on the laptop and Emma in turn tested the two-ways. The immediacy of that contact lifted a nagging weight of worry off Liberty's shoulders at once. Because she could not get over the sneaking feeling that the vessel was somehow more dangerous than it looked.

However, the explorers had more to do than test their equipment, record their adventure and prepare to go aboard during the final moments of *Flint*'s approach. They had to get the sails down so that the yacht could at last come upright and lose the way she had acquired under the steady pressure of that unvarying easterly wind. Liberty was willing to use the motors during the final approach, but her yacht-handling proved more than equal to the task. Maya merely had to reach up as *Flint* eased under the anchor and past the ropes dangling from the rusty forepeak and grasp the midship rail just above her head, securing the bowline carefully as *Flint* at last came easily to a halt beside the well of the foredeck in front of the square, white bridge. Emma, in the meantime, lowered the foam-rubber fenders that would protect *Flint*'s pristine polystyrene sides from the rusty metal of the vessel they could now, from this close, identify as *Un Maru*.

Emma looked up at the name and glanced back towards Liberty with a smile. '*Un*,' she called, straightening. 'Her name is *Un*. It means *Luck*. Also it is the name of one of the temple dogs that guard the entrance to a Japanese Shinto shrine.'

'*Luck*,' called back Liberty. 'But what *kind* of luck, Emma? Good or bad?

'Well,' called back Maya decisively, 'let's get aboard and see, shall we?'

Un

It felt strange to Liberty at once that *Flint*'s deck was level and the vessel was no longer rushing down the wind. As Maya and Emma pulled themselves up and aboard the *Un Maru*, an eerie moment descended. Other sensations threatened to overwhelm her in that intensely strange instant. The stuck-pig squeal of the fenders squashed between the vessels' sides. The banshee whine of the wind in the rigging and in the deck rails that Emma and Maya were clambering over. The thud of the following sea beneath *Flint*'s solid counter. The way the deck shivered. How the tortured fenders squealed again, even more loudly.

'My God!' said Emma over the two-way, her voice loud enough to make both Bella and Liberty jump. 'You should *smell* this!' and the strange second was gone.

The wind backed suddenly as Emma spoke and Liberty could indeed smell *Un Maru* for an intense but blessedly brief instant The Japanese vessel's peculiar odour was an adenoid-searing amalgam of rust, diesel, sweat, sickness and rotting fish. No sooner did Liberty feel her stomach heave in response to the deeply offensive stench than it was gone, and the fresh, clean easterly wind was back.

The laptop screen came alive. Liberty's concentration on the unsteady picture was so intense that she seemed to be aboard with Emma and Maya. The green lawn of the deck heaved before her, raised into sickening molehills of rust and mess. Then the picture swung upwards. Above and before her were lines of rigging, red, brown and yellow with rust, sagging off the horizontal, bowed and bellied away from the vertical. Except that, about eight feet up there were straight lines running fore and aft from bridge house to forepeak a yard or so in from the port and starboard safety rails. These were supported by a couple of light gantries like tall, slim goalmouths for a soccer match. Under the nearest, stood a white-painted, red-streaked box that looked as though it contained hatch controls. Immediately aft of it, in the middle of the deck, an open hatch gaped, square and black.

'Anybody aboard?' bellowed Maya, making Liberty and Bella jump.

'And answer came there none,' observed Emma. 'Where shall we start?'

'I guess we should start in the bridge house,' suggested Maya, talking to Emma, but broadcasting her thoughts over the two-way.

'Yeah,' agreed Emma. 'Get ready to hold your breath, girl.'

'And take care,' ordered Liberty.

The camera's picture swung towards the bridge house, showing that the green non-slip deck coating stopped well before the rusty white wall. Emma's square shoulder and short ponytail lurched into view as she took the lead. A moment later they were at the starboard side. A deck door, which opened slowly beneath Emma's most forceful shove, screaming so loudly it made more shouting unnecessary, allowing sunlight to stream some way at least into the corridor immediately behind it. The camera jiggled as Maya stepped over the raised section and then wavered further as she reset the brightness.

Even after the banshee scream of the door she bellowed again, 'Hello, the ship? Is there anyone aboard? Emma, can you shout in Japanese?'

'*Ohayou gozaimasu*,' shouted Emma, even more loudly than Maya had. '*Otetsudai shimashouka*? It means *good morning, can I help you?* Will that do? I'm from Sacramento, not Sapporo.'

'That's fine,' said Maya. 'And it was loud enough to wake the dead in any language. Let's get moving.'

Emma switched on her torch and led the way to a companionway that Liberty reckoned must lead upwards to the bridge and downwards to the accommodation, storage and engineering sections. 'Up,' said Maya.

'Away from the stench,' agreed Emma, going partway to explaining her companion's terse monosyllable.

The battered, blistered steps led up between scuffed and black-scraped walls with dangerously unsecure banisters, round one blank-walled turn and immediately into the command bridge.

'Uh-oh,' said Emma as she stepped first through the command

bridge door, 'looks like we're by no means the first people to come aboard lately.'

Under the blistering brightness of the early morning sun, it was obvious at once that Emma was right. All of the control and navigation equipment had either been pirated, ripped free and left strewn on the deck or smashed to pieces in situ.

'Looks like we won't find much comms equipment,' growled Maya as she followed Emma's shoulder into the looted hollow of the radio room. There was a chart room next door, where all the charts and pilots were scattered: lying ripped, broken-backed and torn to pieces on the battered table and the littered deck.

The camera showed the women's progress back through the wreckage and down the companionway to the A deck corridor. Then Emma's torch led them downwards. The foot of the companionway opened into a communal area whose benches were clearly designed to also serve as bunks, whose central table doubled as work table and refectory board and all of whose cupboards gaped, their contents burst and scattered everywhere with an abandon that might have embarrassed a Vandal.

'Now this,' said Maya grimly, 'is what I call the crew's *mess*!'

A short corridor led forward from the wrecked crew's quarters past the foot of the companionway to a pair of smaller rooms on either hand, and what looked in the torchlight like a galley straight ahead. One room on the starboard was completely untouched. Immediately inside the doorway sat two temple dogs. The strangeness tempted the women to step in silently.

'*A*,' whispered Emma as the picture showed a pug face with its mouth open. 'And *Un*,' as the camera showed its closed-mouth twin. Beyond these stood a wooden shrine gate leading inwards. Somehow it did not look strange or out of place here in a cabin aboard a drifting hulk.

'It is the *Torii*,' said Emma. 'The temple gateway. Step through it into the spirit world.' She did. Maya, with the camera, followed.

There was a bowl full of clean-looking water with ladles beside it. Freshly folded towels. Further in, there was a small bamboo-sided collection box miraculously untouched, a table against the inmost wall with a box of bamboo sticks, some luck charts and some wooden tablets.

'It is a Shinto shrine,' said Emma, her voice low and reverent.

She gestured at the tablets on the table. '*Ema*, with pictures of the divine steed. A *Shuzu*,' she said, touching a decorated stick topped with a little bell. 'If we ring it, the gods will know we wish to speak with them. And an *Omamori*,' she picked up a talisman like the tablets with their vivid horses. 'It will bring good luck.'

'We should take that,' said Maya forthrightly. 'You never know when we'll need a little luck.'

Then they turned and walked out of the place. Opposite it was the ship's head. The briefest glance in here sufficed to show that it too remained undisturbed – though for very different reasons.

Then there was a small galley, everything in it ravished and scattered like the store cupboards in the crew's mess. The deck awash with cooking oil, rice, flour, noodles, broken eggs and rotting fish scattered everywhere. Cupboards gaping, doors off hinges, the cupboards themselves half off the walls; the simple gas-fuelled range torn off its fittings, sitting at a crazy angle, the gas bottle beneath it reeling drunkenly, only held erect by the metal hose connecting it to the burner, like a pirate hanged in chains.

The left-hand wall of the wrecked galley contained a door that gaped half open. Placing their feet with extreme care amid the slippery mess on the floor, Emma and Maya crossed to this and stepped through into another short corridor leading forward. At the end of this there was a more substantial door and it didn't take much for Liberty to work out that this was the coffer dam immediately beneath the forward wall of the bridge house that separated the propulsion and living areas from the main cargo area.

Emma pulled the bulkhead door back and stepped over the raised section into the vessel's main hold. It was a sizeable area, lit not only by the horizontal beams of the torches but also by a vertical column of white light which seemed to explode in and down through the square hatch left open in the deck above. The hold was empty, its distant walls a rotting shell seemingly supported by rust-red metal ribs.

'You cannot . . .' choked Maya. 'You cannot imagine the stench in this place.'

'OK,' said Liberty. 'You'd better get out before you suffocate, I guess.'

'We don't need to see any more, do we?' asked Maya quietly, depressed by the destruction all around them as they picked their way back through the galley. 'There's no one here. Nothing more to see.'

'Better just check aft,' said Liberty. 'Take a quick look in the engine room.'

'OK,' agreed Maya grudgingly. 'But I don't see that we should film any more of it.' And the laptop screen went blank.

'Just walking through the mess of the mess again,' came Maya's voice over the two-way. 'The passage behind leads between a couple of doors. Opening into . . . cabins. Captain's and engineer's, I guess. Trashed, same as everything else. Bunks smashed. Bedding scattered. Mattresses gutted – if you can call these things mattresses. Back into the corridor . . . Leading back and down a short companionway to an internal bulkhead door. Opening inwards . . .'

Abruptly the laptop screen lit up again. Maya's camera followed a pair of torch beams in a slow pan round an engine room. The engine and all the ancillary equipment seemed to be almost floating in a great dark sea that came most of the way up its rusty, battered sides and stretched away into the cavernous shadows, apparently coming halfway up the engine room walls.

'Is the surface of the water really black?' asked Liberty. 'Or is that a trick of the light?'

'It's black,' gasped Maya.

'Because it's oil,' choked Emma.

'The *fumes* . . .' Maya coughed.

'You'd better get out,' ordered Liberty. An engine room flooded with fuel oil had to be a very dangerous place indeed. Even in a powerless, abandoned ghost ship. Stories she had heard from the Mariners and their children whirled in the half-remembered recesses of her memory. Of supertanker holds exploding during cleaning because the static generated by too-powerful hoses set off the lethally explosive gases. Fumes ignited by the spark from the fibre of a nylon shirt.

Were Maya and Emma wearing or carrying anything that might set the volatile atmosphere ablaze? Did they have anything on or near them that might cause static? Anything powerful enough to generate a spark? The torches? The camera? The two-way radios?

At the very least, she remembered, her flesh going cold at the thought, the gas given off by fuel oil could be dangerously poisonous. 'Hurry,' she urged. 'Switch off the camera and get out fast. And close the door behind you.'

'Emma,' said Maya's voice distantly on the two-way. 'Emma . . .'

The picture on the laptop screen swung wildly through one-hundred-and-eighty degrees to show the corridor reaching back. Then the square receding lines of the perspective seemed to spin and tumble as the camera fell to the deck.

Humpback

R obin sprang awake. She looked around, blinking, all her senses on the alert. Something had just happened. Something bad. She looked at her watch. Just after six a.m. It would soon be dawn. She had been asleep for two hours.

It was Day A on the watch rotation. At the end of Day B, at four a.m. this morning, she had crept sleepily down into her bunk having relinquished the wheel to Flo Weary. Everything had been plain sailing then. They had enjoyed four days of a steady westerly trade wind that had driven them forward at the better part of thirty-five knots tacking across it in the traditional sawtooth pattern along their north-easterly course from Tuvalu past cursed Howland Island, heading for the vastness north of Hawaii and their rendezvous with Tanaka's bottle.

It was the kind of a run that *Katapult* seemed to love best of all. But, as with each of those last four days, there had been little to do except to perform the occasional tack. There had been nothing to see, no one to talk to except for their crew mates and the occasional wider contacts. And nothing registering on the radar or sonar except for the occasional reef.

But now there was something wrong.

'*Robin!*' Flo Weary's voice echoed down from the green-grey glimmer of the communications area, and Robin registered that Flo had called her an instant earlier, just as she was jarred awake. 'Robin! Did you feel that?'

'What?' asked Robin, rolling out on to the deck of *Katapult*'s main crew cabin and pulling herself as close to upright as she dared. The deck leaned a little – a little more than she expected, in fact. She paused, one hand against the solid column of the leaning mast, feeling the power of the wind on the sails pushing the mast over against the buoyancy of the starboard outrigger. But the deck was unexpectedly steep. The outrigger wasn't sitting right.

Thank God she had crawled slovenly into bed fully dressed.

'We hit something,' called Flo loudly enough to make Robin's watch-mate Rohini stir but not wake. It usually took something really major to wake the Indian round-the-world yachtswoman.

'I can't see how we did,' said Akelita from her place by the laptop, comms and safety equipment. 'There was nothing on the radar or the sonar. Well . . .'

'*Well* what?' demanded Flo. 'Was there something or not? Because we sure as hell hit something. Or the starboard outrigger did.'

Robin was up beside them now, stepping past Akelita to stand with Flo at the helm. The great mainsail strained above her the boom just touching her tumbled golden curls, the whole hull vibrated with the speed they were running at, crossing the steady airstream from one long tack to another, for maximum speed, running as close to the wind as they could. The air was steady, fresh and bracing. It blew the cobwebs of sleep away. The new day was just beginning to expand as the sun rose on the eastern rim of the world, almost dead ahead. The sky was light, speckled with the palest ghostly stars and the lightest of blues. The hissing, chuckling sea was beginning to gain substance, colour, shadowy green beneath the quicksilver blue of the sky's reflection. The morning was simply vast.

A point of intense green appeared on the far horizon almost dead ahead, as though a flare was exploding behind a sheet of bottle-green emerald. It was the sun, rising beyond the translucent, water-covered curve of the earth. And out of the nearby sea,

silhouetted against it a humpback whale suddenly soared into
the lower air, as though in answer to Flo's terse question.

Almost the whole of its twenty-metre length came out of the
water, seeming to tower threateningly ahead of them for an instant
as though it could stand on its tail indefinitely, crucified against
the dawn. The light in the Eastern sky caught the barnacle encrus-
tations on its long, sharp jaw and the leading edges of its wide,
wing-like fins, seeming to etch its black outline in rugged white.
It seemed to turn in the air, giving the entranced, horrified women
a glimpse of its pale, seamed jowls and belly. Then it exploded
back into the water like a depth charge.

'Shit,' said Flo roundly. 'Could we have hit *that*? At the better
part of forty knots? With the starboard outrigger? Christ!'

'Well, we hit something,' said Robin tersely. 'And the outrigger
looks wrong . . .'

'*Feels* wrong too,' added Flo. '*Katapult*'s not riding right.'

'I can't think of anything else that could have come and gone
so fast it didn't register on any of our equipment,' said Akelita.
'I hope the poor thing wasn't hurt.'

'OK,' said Robin. 'Let's hope not. And let's hope *Katapult*
didn't sustain too much damage either. Akelita, keep an eye out
for any more humpbacks. As far as I know they swim in pods
or family groups. Flo, ease off our speed while we think this
through – and we'll need to tack as soon as practical. We'll rely
on the port outrigger as much as we can for the moment. Once
we're steady, Flo or I can go out on the starboard wing and take
a closer look. We'll make an assessment as soon as we can, and
see whether we're going to need to call for help. We should be
fairly clear about our situation by the next routine contact at
noon. In the meantime, Akelita, where's the nearest land?'

They didn't have a spinnaker up – like *Flint* they were relying
on the simple sloop rig of mainsail and the foresail – so it was
easy enough to swing across the steady easterly wind and let the
canvas lean towards the port outrigger instead of the starboard.
The simple manoeuvre was enough to wake even Rohini, however,
and Flo handed over the helm to the Indian woman while Akelita
kept looking alike for whales and islands.

By the time *Katapult* had settled into her new position, Robin and Flo were dressed in life vests and safety harnesses. The vests themselves went over the black bibs of the harnesses which had shoulder straps and a gusset strap. The black webbing was guaranteed to withstand weights in excess of fifty kilos. In theory the girls could safely have bungee jumped in them. Flo led the pair of them up on to the foredeck to the right of the mainmast, and they paused to clip their carabineers in place like mountaineers before they walked forward to give the damage an initial look-see.

This time, Robin's attention was focused on immediate minutiae rather than on the vastness of the morning. Under Rohini's practised helmswomanship, the port outrigger behind the straining mainsail was porpoising just below the surface of the ocean, cutting through the water like a speeding dolphin, Robin knew. On the other hand, the starboard wing she was examining was raised slightly, its torpedo-shaped outrigger just above the waves, skimming like a flying fish the better part of twenty feet in length.

Robin's eyes narrowed thoughtfully. Between the main hull and the flying outrigger, was an articulated wing, hinged against the central hull, capable of being raised and lowered – like the sails – either by the yacht's central computer or by the crew on manual override. The top edge of the hinge was normally a rule-straight black line, for the major part of the articulation was designed to push the outrigger down into the water, the tension between the forces exercised against this and the sails generating the vessel's fearsome speed. It could be raised to the vertical, Robin knew, but only if secondary, articulated hinges were employed. A massively strong variant of the kind of system that allowed modern cupboard doors to swing wide. But both of the hinge systems seemed to have been knocked out of kilter by the outrigger's impact against the unfortunate whale. That straight-edged black line was wider towards the bow than it was towards the stern. And the delicate curve of the wing, designed to have the perfection of a Spitfire's aerofoil, stepped back slightly at the hinge-point of its leading edge.

'What do you reckon?' Robin asked, glancing up at Flo's frowning profile.

'We did good getting it up and taking the pressure off,' answered Flo, sweeping her fingers back through the wild pre-Raphaelite tumble of her red curls. 'We can't rely on its vertical movement unless the hinge sides are true and parallel. And it might even tear off, I guess, if the damage at the front gets any worse.'

'Is there anything we can do to help matters now?'

'Fix it, you mean? I don't know. I mean, I know the design of the hinge mechanism pretty well. My dad designed it, after all. It's really robust. I guess, if we can get the right angle on it we might be able to snap it back into place. Might be worth a shot.'

'Let's go for it, then,' decided Robin.

'It's not really designed to have people crawling around on it while *Katapult*'s under full sail, mind. There's not much in the way of handholds and so forth. We'd need to be really flaming careful.'

'Flo. We're in the middle of the Pacific Ocean, for Christ's sake. The nearest land is three miles straight down. Apart from the whale that did this, the nearest life forms are likely to be sharks. Of course I'm going to be careful.'

'Just so's you know.'

Flo stepped gingerly over the starboard deck rail and eased herself on to the outrigger wing. She stopped, seeming to will the soles of her deck shoes to take the firmest possible grip. Then she slowly sank to her right knee and took hold of the wing's leading edge just beside the step-back of the damaged hinge. Surf exploded up into her face. Her streaming Titian hair was suddenly slick and heavy with moisture. 'Come on out,' she called, and all at once Robin realized how much noise the wind and the water were making as *Katapult* thundered across the restless plane where they came together.

Shaking her safety line like a rat's tail behind her, she too stepped over the knee-high safety rail out on to the upward slope of the wing. She steadied herself as Flo had done, feeling the way the hull reacted to the movement of her weight across the critical balance of wave, wind and straining sails. The white composite surface she was standing on had been treated with non-slip paint, but even so, the pressure of the wind behind her and the weight of the water breaking back to slap into her face were dangerously disorientating. She swept her own suddenly sodden locks back, glad that they were nothing like as long and heavy as Flo's were. Then she took a careful step forward to stand beside her crewmate.

Flo looked up at her. 'See?' she said.

'What?' shouted Robin, sinking slowly to her right knee.

'This hinge-clip is sprung. Here. See? That seems to be all that's wrong,' Flo bellowed again.

'I see. What does it mean?' asked Robin, leaning closer, putting the knuckles of her right fist on the sandpaper roughness of the non-slip.

'It means we can fix it if we can get it to snap back into place,' Flo explained.

'How can we do that?' demanded Robin.

'It must have snapped out when the impact with the whale pushed the bow section of the outrigger back. Then the whole thing settled back a bit.' Flo didn't answer directly. But Robin nodded vigorously to show she was following her companion's reasoning.

'I see that,' she answered. Then she repeated, 'So what do we need to do?'

'I guess we'll have to get to the aft of the wing and try to push it forward,' decided Flo. 'And hope that does the trick.'

'Can we do that?' asked Robin sceptically.

'We can try,' said Flo. 'We'll give it a go from the aft section of the wing itself first, then maybe jury-rig something from the main hull later if we have to. Come on.'

Flo led the way back across the ten metre breadth of the wing's inner edge. At least it was a little easier to move, thought Robin grimly, with the wind in your face and the water slapping your backside instead of the other way round. Though in actual fact Flo's body was protecting her face while her backside was getting the worst of the bargain – and then some.

Still moving slowly and laboriously, Flo squatted back on her haunches, then sat gingerly on the wing. Lying back and stretching out, she tried to position herself so that her hands could hold the edge of the composite level with her hips while her feet could push against the side of the main hull as though she were the base of a triangle or the crosspiece in a capital letter A. As she heaved and strained, Robin gingerly copied her, lying outside her, for her legs were longer. She could feel the roughness beneath her back and shoulders; the smooth edge under her palms beside her hips. Her feet struck and slipped against the side of the hull beside the cockpit almost level with Rohini's shoulders.

One moment she was squirming backwards, trying to balance on an edge, with her hands slipping on the slick, streaming composite and the soles of her deck shoes slithering over the side of her vessel, the next she was under the water. She had an instant of disbelieving shock. Then she thought, *Oh, shit, this is going to hurt!*

Her safety line snapped taut and her harness jerked forward to pull her helplessly through the streaming surf at the better part of forty knots.

Johnston

R obin had never felt anything like it. Had she been able to catch her breath she would have screamed blue bloody murder even though she was not a woman easily reduced to *extremis*. Her life jacket inflated automatically as soon as she hit the water and was forced up beneath her chin by the relentless pressure. The unbreakable grip of the mountaineer's carabineer juddered down the safety rail making Robin feel as though a large number of soldiers in massive hobnail boots were giving her a good kicking. Until, with a jerk that almost tore her apart, it stopped. And things got worse. She found herself smashing through *Katapult*'s wake like an extremely well-endowed mermaid trying for the aquatic world speed record.

But the life jacket was nowhere near equal to the forces it was trying to overcome, so every second or so, Robin's head would be dragged under as though Poseidon himself was pulling at her legs. Her eyes were full of water: she could feel the lower lids sagging and ballooning like water-filled echoes of the canvas airbags pummelling her boobs. Her ears were filled with pressure that was simply agonizing. Her nose was running like Niagara and it felt as though the Congo, the Nile and the Amazon were all trying to flow down her throat at once.

Her safety line was now just the right length to allow *Katapult*'s rushing wake to hurl her against the yacht's hull with the regularity of a pendulum. Sometimes one of her shoulders hit; sometimes an elbow, sometimes her back or her front. She tried to put her hand out once, hoping for some control – and almost broke her wrist. Her legs waved behind her with all the strength and reliability of overcooked spaghetti and even though she was only wearing deck shoes, the force with which they banged together all but broke her ankles.

But all of this was as nothing compared with the exquisite agony of the gusset strap. The thin webbing that ran between her legs dug into the tenderest parts of her anatomy with a level of pure discomfort she had not experienced since childbirth. And, aptly enough, just as she had done in the midst of having the twins delivered, she knew exactly which bloody man had got her into this. And she suddenly remembered with almost shocking clarity every name she had called him in the hospital delivery room then. So of course she started calling him the same names all over again.

Which was why the first word that Florence Weary heard as she finally succeeded in securing the back of Robin's life jacket and pulling her head and shoulders up on to *Katapult*'s square afterdeck was enough to shock even a woman of enthusiastically Australian heritage who had spent her entire life in the company of sailors.

'Steady on there, girl,' she said. 'That's a bit harsh.'

'Not *you*!' choked Robin. 'Bloody *Richard*!'

'Oh,' said Flo, with sisterly understanding. '*Right!*'

She heaved again and Robin's legs flopped up on to the afterdeck like the tail of a dying halibut. The pair of them rested, side by side, fighting to regain their breath.

'Thanks,' said Robin after a moment's choking near silence.

'My pleasure. I got you in, so the least I could do was fish you out.'

'Not *the least*,' gasped Robin. 'You're going to have to do a certain amount of anointing and bandaging. I feel like I've been keelhauled.' She blinked the last of the seawater out of her streaming eyes and wondered whether she felt strong enough to wipe her nose. 'Did we fix it?'

''Fraid not, possum. We'll have to beach her and try again.'

'Beach her? Where, for God's sake? We're in the middle of the Pacific! Seven-hundred-and-fifty miles south-west of Hawaii, the last time I looked.'

'Right,' said Florence. 'And according to Akelita that puts us about five miles upwind of Johnston Atoll.'

Johnston Island was protected from the trade winds and the waves they brought with them by a semicircular reef. It would also have been protected from *Katapult*'s approach had not Rohini been forewarned of the fact by the British Admiralty Pilot, Sailing Directions Volume Sixty-two, which that bloody man Richard had insisted that they carry. Several of the earliest boats sailing these waters had ended up wedged on these reefs. So they came in carefully from the south-east, skirting round the lower end of the wall of surf that suddenly, almost inexplicably, appeared from the lazily heaving ocean surface like an avalanche going nowhere, and piled itself high enough along the crest of the coral to all but obscure the low, flat-topped landfall behind it.

'It looks like a big aircraft carrier more than an island,' observed Akelita as she strained up out of the snug to look through the clearview, checking what she could see against what her equipment was telling her.

'That's because it's mostly man-made,' said Rohini. 'The Americans have been adding and adding to it to make it long enough to hold a runway. You're right: it's really nothing more than a static aircraft carrier.'

'Time to take the sails down and motor in,' called Robin, climbing stiffly out of the cabin. 'Where's the harbour?'

'Over there,' answered Akelita, pointing. 'There's a jetty and everything.'

'We'll need a shelving beach or a slipway,' warned Flo, following Robin up, wiping antiseptic cream off her hands.

'Says here that there's some pretty reliable communications equipment available there, too,' said Rohini, who had the Admiralty Pilot open where she could see it. 'It used to be an American airbase till relatively recently . . . *the Military Radio station, a UHF/VHF air-ground radio, and a link to the Pacific Consolidated Telecommunications Network satellite.* It says here. Amateur radio operators occasionally transmit from the island, using KH3 as a call sign. Think we can get hold of any of that stuff and use it? Our equipment has been unreliable lately.'

'One thing at a time,' said Robin. 'Let's get there, let's get *Katapult* moored safely and then we can get a good look at that hinge system. What's the water depth here in the lagoon, Akelita?'

'Shallowest is three metres, deepest looks like about ten.'

Katapult motored gently towards the jetty under Rohini's experienced helmswomanship while Robin and Flo stiffly wound the sails away. Then Flo secured the bowline to the rickety little jetty and all four of them sat for a moment, catching their breath and simply looking around.

'Bloody big for an aircraft carrier, though,' said Flo after a while. 'Must be more than a mile long.'

'True enough,' agreed Akelita. 'But like Rohini said, there's not much more to it than the runway, the handling areas, the control tower and ancillary buildings. And there's been no one actually stationed here for the better part of a decade.'

'There must have been visitors, though,' said Robin, shading her eyes as she looked around. 'What was that you were saying about people transmitting from here using the KH3 call sign, Rohini?'

'It said they did it,' answered the Indian woman slowly. 'It doesn't say *when* they did it.'

'Let's go ashore and explore,' suggested Akelita.

'Of course we will,' said Robin easily, 'but our main priority is to get that wing fixed. And in any case, Rohini, there's something at the back of my mind about this place. What does the pilot say?'

'It was the base for the American Operation Dominic series of nuclear tests in the fifties and sixties,' answered Rohini. 'Rocket launches, nuclear explosions. There's some debate about how well the radioactive material was cleared up. It's mostly plutonium, and it's all buried somewhere out there, apparently; covered by something called Safeguard C. Doesn't sound all that safe to me.'

'Shit,' said Flo.

'Wait,' ordered Rohini, 'It gets better. The island was also used in the sixties and seventies as a dumping ground and disposal area for the full spectrum of biological and chemical weapons used by or confiscated by the US. Everything from Agent Orange to PCBs and PAHs . . .'

'PAHs come from oil,' said Robin. 'They are part of what makes fuel oil so poisonous if it begins to evaporate in a confined space. Effectively a potent poison gas . . .'

'And there's apparently a load of Sarin nerve gas buried out there too,' added Rohini.

'My God,' said Robin. 'Is there no end to it? One way or another it looks as though we're just sailing through one huge garbage patch after another. Talk about a dead sea! Professor Tanaka doesn't know the half of it!' She stood up and looked around at the low heave of the island as its grey-green scrub-covered flank mounted dully towards the flat blackness of the runways and the half-ruined buildings beyond. 'Let's fix our outrigger, take a quick look around, see if we can find some of this comms equipment Rohini mentioned then get on our way again.'

The beach of coarsely ground coral sloped down to the curve of the little anchorage just beside the jetty, so the women were able to pull *Katapult* into shallow enough water for Flo to get a close look and start working on repairs. The multihull sat high, with her forepeak up on the beach itself and the outriggers resting in the shallows on either side. The curve of the outrigger wings made two short tunnels, one either side of the hull, where they reached out and down to the surface. Allowing for the water of the bay beneath them, the tunnel roofs, with the hinges at their apex, stood a little less than six feet high. The tall Australian waded in and vanished beneath the starboard outrigger. Robin followed her, in spite of the unguents smeared over her. Unlike her last encounter with it, this section of the Pacific was warm, restful, almost soothing. She waded deeper.

The underside of the wing immediately above their heads was lined with panels designed to give access to the hinge mechanisms. 'I reckon all I have to do is open the forward panels and reset the clips,' Flo said, her voice echoing in the enclosed space. She reached up easily and felt the first of the panels with her fingers, like a proud owner stroking the soft nose of a winning horse. 'We have the kit. It looks like a one-woman job to me. Why don't you go ashore with the girls while I get things sorted here? We don't want to fall too far behind schedule.'

As things turned out, Rohini, having read the entry in the pilot, was put off the idea of exploring too far, so she took the kit down to Flo and stood beside her ready to help. Akelita was almost childishly excited, however; and was certainly well enough versed with communications equipment to make full use of anything live they found. So it was she and Robin who walked purposefully up the deserted slope towards the nearest buildings. There was a thin, dispirited-looking scrub which gave a vaguely herbal savour to the steady easterly wind. But over that there was an odour of decay, thought Robin sadly. Given that this was a coral island in the middle of a remote atoll at the heart of the Pacific Ocean, it was depressingly reminiscent of a run-down city tenement. The ground beneath their deck shoes levelled out and the coarse-ground coral gave way to pocked and mouldering paving. The runway stretched away on either hand like a wide blacktop crossing some Arizona desert, beginning to twist and waver as the sun heated up the air. Had it not been for the restless roaring of the surf on the reef and the presence of the functional box-like military buildings ahead, they might have been walking across the highway in Death Valley. The skin on Robin's legs prickled as the gathering heat dried them off after her brief paddle.

'This,' said Akelita, looking around with a shiver, 'is not a good advert for humanity.'

'Even if we didn't know what's buried here somewhere it's still a bit of a shock,' agreed Robin, thoughtlessly scratching her thigh. 'What it looks like to someone raised on an island paradise such as Tuvalu I simply cannot begin to imagine.'

'Well,' said Akelita bracingly, 'I don't suppose you'd want to test nuclear bombs and bury poisonous nerve gases on somewhere beautiful.'

The conversation was enough to take them across the runway into the nearest semi-derelict building. It looked like it had been the control tower, three stories high ending in a windowed observatory that reminded Robin a little of a command bridge. 'If there's communications equipment anywhere,' she said, 'it'll probably be in here.'

The door swung wide with a push. 'It's been broken open,' observed Robin, looking at the splintered jamb. She led the way, walking into the shady corridor ahead. 'Maybe ransacked.' She pushed the nearest door wide to show a room that had once been some kind of book room, the volumes scattered across the floor now, torn and mouldering. There were telephones on a table but their old-fashioned plastic bodies had been smashed.

'Let's go up to the observation room. See what's there,' suggested Akelita. 'We should get a good view of the island, if nothing else.'

A functional set of stairs led up through two floors to the control room. As Akelita said, the circle of sloping glass windows gave a good view all around. *Katapult* rested on the sand of the little anchorage beach surprisingly close at hand. The runway reached straight and flat along the squared length of the enhanced island, and two smaller islands sat ahead of it, like tugs waiting to position this massive aircraft carrier. On their left the shallow lagoon reached palely out to the reef where the white foam rose and fell as the great ocean rollers broke across it and the steady easterly trade wind took diamond-bright droplets of their spray and blew them in rainbows towards the land.

Robin and Akelita stood for a moment looking out, because there was nothing within the room to see. The banks of equipment beneath the panoramic windows had all been rifled or removed. Wires and cables hung out of conduits along the walls like colourful creepers going nowhere, connected to nothing. Cupboards and cabinets stood gap-toothed and gaping, anything of use or value long gone.

Robin walked thoughtlessly towards the window, looking down on *Katapult*, suddenly overwhelmed with the desire to be gone from this place. Her feet and legs were tickling and prickling even more intensely as they continued to dry after her paddle beside Flo Weary to examine the underside of the damaged wing. The feeling was distracting enough to break into her reverie. She shifted her feet uncomfortably and looked down. Gasped. Stunned. Looked across at Akelita. Almost choked in simple horror.

'Akelita,' she cried, feeling an unreasoning wave of hysteria sweeping relentlessly over her. 'Akelita, *look*!'

From knee to ankle both of them were covered in swarms of big bright yellow ants.

Dagupan

I t didn't take very long for Professor Reona Tanaka to suspect that he had made a terrible mistake. Perhaps a fatal one. But by the time his suspicions grew towards certainty it was far too late to do anything about them.

First Officer Sakai met Reona and Aika Rei secretly behind Rage, as agreed, on the evening after they had talked to him in the bar, an hour or so before the ship was due to sail. Using the noise and bustle of an illegal drift meeting where a range of souped-up motor cars went screaming sideways across the rain-slick dock, they stole up the gangplank and crept aboard, certain that they were unobserved. Reona and Aika were carrying suitcases – which the sailor did not offer to help with. Reona also had his laptop case slung over his shoulder. He was still too excited, too infatuated, to see how totally he was breaking with his past now. And everything he had ever worked for. The instant he stepped aboard, his eyes riveted firmly on Aika's shapely derrière, his old life closed behind him, but he really only understood that later.

Reona followed the slim woman and the bulky officer across the ship's deck to the tall bridge house, surprised to find himself aboard a modern bulk carrier, with its bridge at the stern and four fat, squat cranes standing midships between five-square hatch covers stretching away in brutal perspective through the drizzling darkness towards a stubby mast on the distant bow. He had somehow tricked himself into thinking of the romantic freighters of the early 1900s with their three-castle design and their associations with black and white Hollywood films.

The functional brightness of the A-deck corridor with its white walls and green decking came as a second shock. It made him think of hospitals and laboratories, though it was nowhere near as clean and well maintained as his own. And it throbbed gently. Every surface around him seemed to be vibrating as the various power sources aboard growled and grumbled, supplying light and heat, electrical current, water pressure and, eventually, engine power. There was a purposeful bustle about the place that the throbbing seemed to add to. Crewmen in boiler suits hurried past. They seemed to be drawn from every ethnic group around the West Pacific rim. The only thing they had in common was the brutal expression on their variously shaded faces. None of them seemed to pay Reona any attention, though he felt Aika was the subject of some searching second glances.

Sakai led them along the corridor to a lift. The three of them crowded in. The first officer crushed against Reona, his donkey jacket smelling of cigarettes and fuel oil, the rest of him smelling sharply of sweat. The men did not look at each other. Reona stole a glance at Aika but she too was looking away, trapped against the first officer's other side. But he thought she looked excited, and was a little disappointed that he was not more excited himself. 'The port officials have been aboard and OK'd us for departure. Customs, immigration and so forth,' growled Sakai. 'We're just waiting for the pilot and the tide. You'll have to stay low till we're well clear, though. You do realize that? There are sometimes spot checks.' Reona's heart lurched with nervousness, but both he and Aika both nodded silently. The lift hissed on upwards through three decks with the atmosphere relentlessly thickening before it opened on to the vessel's command bridge.

Captain Yamamoto welcomed them coolly and accepted both their story and their passage money with a blank stare and a shallow smile. He was a middle-aged man with long white hair and a silvery goatee who seemed out of place among the taciturn officers and crew aboard his relentlessly workaday command. He was preoccupied with preparations for departure, however, and clearly wanted rid of them before the pilot came aboard.

Sakai immediately showed the disorientated young couple to the owner's suite, one deck below, and gruffly advised them to settle in. He looked around the room, narrow-eyed, then went and pulled thin curtains across the widows. As he did this, he informed them that he would send something up from the galley when the crew had their dinner. Other than that, they would not be disturbed until the ship was well under way. They stood a little forlornly in the middle of the day room as he worked and nodded that they understood his orders. He looked at them thoughtfully, then left them to their own devices.

Reona found the suite a pleasant surprise, for the *Dagupan Maru* herself had by no means impressed him so far. The door from the corridor opened directly into a decent-sized day room with a square window that had looked aft across the poop deck before Sakai closed the curtains. The walls and ceiling were painted in cream, and the whole suite seemed to be mahogany-panelled to waist height. There were framed prints of famous harbours around the South China Sea. The throbbing deck was carpeted. There was a desk convenient for his laptop, a small square table and a couple of chairs. While he put his precious computer in place, Aika dropped her case beside the table, shrugged off her damp coat, draped it over a chair and went through the next door. 'There's a little corridor with a shower room off it,' she called, sounding as excited as if she really was on her honeymoon. 'And a bedroom at the end. Oh, Reona, it has a lovely bed. Wardrobes. A nice mirror for my make-up. And windows that look to the side as well as to the rear, though you have to peep round the curtains . . . I can see the dock and those silly boys in their racing cars. And it's so big! Bigger than your room at the university and my room put together! How fine!' There was a rhythmic squeaking and Reona hurried through to find her bouncing on the double bed like a child, arms and legs wide. She caught him looking up her skirt like a naughty schoolboy and laughed at his blushes.

They were still unpacking when a sudden peak in noise and activity coupled with a slight lurch warned them that the voyage was beginning. They both ran over to the port-side window and peeped round the curtain, watching in wonder as the dock appeared to slide slowly past, vanishing surprisingly quickly into the drizzling darkness. 'What an adventure!' she whispered, turning to him with her eyes wide.

Suddenly breathless, Reona found himself undressing her, slowly at first, but then with dangerous urgency at her imperious dictates. 'Be careful,' he gasped at last, holding her hands still for an instant. 'We don't want to tear our clothes! We haven't all that many spares!'

'Oh, come on!' she laughed, opening the wings of her warm silk blouse to reveal a basque of black lace and red silk that plunged provocatively past the waistband of her conservative-looking skirt. He had already caught a tantalizing glimpse of black lace stocking tops and matching red silk knickers. 'Live a little. See! I bought you a special present at the sexy underwear shop! Isn't this just what the naughty girls in the dockside Soaplands houses wear?'

He laughed with sudden excitement, thinking although it was a present for him, it was she who was wearing it. For a moment longer, at least.

Reona was never quite able to put his finger on the precise moment when it stopped being an adventure. Perhaps there was no moment – just a series of tiny incidents and growing feelings that only seemed to make any kind of a pattern when he looked back on them later. He had not expected this to be a pleasure cruise such as he had seen advertised on television travel programmes. With expensive shops, swimming pools and saunas; fawning stewards and dinner at the Captain's Table. This was a working vessel. The officers and crew had jobs to do and pandering to passengers was not one of them. But it seemed to him, even on the first morning after they had dropped the pilot and were safely under way in international waters, that Aika and he were being viewed as more than simple unexpected passengers – something between customers and cargo.

At first, when the short hairs on the back of his neck began to prickle, Reona supposed it was simply his sensitivity to the way the all-male crew were watching the only woman aboard – and the man who was all too obviously doing what almost all of them would like to do with her. Even her more modest outer garments could not disguise the truth of that. And then there was the fact that the only man aboard they knew – and who they needed to rely on to show them the ship and explain the routines, was suddenly too preoccupied by his duties to deal with them. And there were little things that they really did need to get clear.

One of the first was the laptop. Reona tried it in the cabin soon after he and Aika had satisfied several appetites by following their love-making with the food a surly crewman brought up to their cabin. He noticed two things at once. First, the reception was not strong enough to allow him vital Internet access, so he could not follow the progress of his priceless bottle nor of the two vessels racing towards it. Secondly, he was surprised to see that the battery had very little power. His first reaction to the second problem was to look around the cabin for a plug that would take his charger, but the sockets, although they were two-pin, seemed to be of a slightly different design to the charger he had brought, and it suddenly occurred to him that the ship would be running on its own power, as generated by one of the machines that made everything around him throb. It was in all probability on a different setting to the one hundred volt, fifty hertz he was used to in Tokyo. The last thing he needed was to damage the vital laptop now. Reluctantly, he switched off the power and closed the top. Then, a great deal less reluctantly, he went through to join Aika in bed.

Reona was up and about early next morning, roused by the bustle of a working ship at sea. Aika responded to his advances by grunting, rolling over and beginning to snore, so he got dressed and went out to explore, taking his laptop with him. He was hungry, but the feeling was more than overcome by a desire to check up on the position of those three vital dots, if he possibly could. And it occurred to him that if the metal walls of the bridge house were thick enough to break his laptop's communication with the Internet, then taking the machine outside – and ideally, up to somewhere high, might solve the problem.

His first ginger sortie out into the corridor the first officer had brought them along last night revealed that it ended in a door leading out on to a balcony which reminded him a little of a fire escape on a city tenement. He opened the door and stepped out into a fresh and bracing blue morning. He paused to look around, distracted by the vastness of the view across the quiet ocean. During the night, Japan had dropped below the horizon and there was nothing to see but the sea. Closer at hand, however, he soon discovered that steps led up and down from the balcony, climbing the outside of the bridge house. Slowly at first, and then with growing confidence, he climbed up these towards the top of the bridge itself. Two levels up, he stepped through a kind of a gate on to a flat green area that seemed to him almost as big as a football field.

There was a repainted funnel to the rear, which seemed to be giving out very little in the way of smoke or fumes. The front stretched sideways as the top of the two bridge wings which extended the bridge itself to right and left. In the middle, at the front, there was a tall, white-painted mast that looked surprisingly substantial. Placed between the funnel and the radio mast there were other white-painted housings that he was not certain about. Logic dictated that at least one of the big white boxes would contain the lift mechanism, but what the others might be he had no idea.

Still looking about in wonder at the top of the bridge and the vast morning that his new position revealed, he wandered forward until he was standing near the mast, at the front of the green deck, looking down the length of the main deck at the four squat cranes and the five square hatch tops they stood above. Unlike last night's brief glimpse in the drizzling darkness, this morning's long look revealed clear lines, a purposeful precision. The distant bow cut through the huge green ocean with a solid certainty. The wake churned along the sides of the powerful vessel, then split into a wide V across the ocean behind it. Here, thought Reona, a little overcome, was a vessel with a purpose. A ship who knew where she was going.

Then it hit him. He, Reona Tanaka, needed to know where she was going. Needed to know where she needed to go. Needed to dictate that course. He ran across to the nearest white housing that looked about as tall as a table. He put his laptop case on it and opened the side. He pulled out the laptop and opened it. Switched it on and put up a swift prayer to Un, god of Luck. The screen cleared. The lights above the keyboard all lit up. Including the one promising Internet access. With his heart in his mouth, he guided the cursor up to the icon for his search engine. Clicked on it. Continued to pray. But it too worked perfectly. He was safely over the first hurdle. Now all he needed to do was to access the cloud programmes that stored the vital information on *Cheerio*, *Flint* and *Katapult*'s locator beacons. 'Come on,' he whispered to himself, as the computer consulted the vital storage facility. '*ComeoncomeoncomeON* . . .'

'*Hey!* What are you doing here?'

The challenge was so sudden, so unexpected and so close at hand that he whirled round in a panic and nearly knocked the laptop flying.

There was a low-browed young man in overalls glaring at him like a fighter just about to throw a punch.

'I was trying to get on the Internet. I can't access it in my cabin so I thought—'

'Why didn't you connect it to the ship's system?' demanded the young man suspiciously.

'System? What? I didn't know.'

'*Dagupan Maru* may not be much to look at but she's up with the twenty-first century!' sneered the sailor.

Reona blushed. 'I didn't know. I've never been aboard a ship like this one. And she seems a very fine ship to me!'

The stranger seemed to relax a little. 'Senzo Tago.' He introduced himself. 'Junior engineering officer.'

'Tanaka Reona,' bowed Reona formally. 'Greenbaum Professor of . . .' his voice trailed off as he realized that in fact he wasn't Greenbaum Professor of anything any more.

But, 'I know who you are,' said the engineer. 'You're famous! I've seen you on the TV and on the Net. And you and your girlfriend are the talk of the ship in any case. Now, what's the matter with your laptop?'

'Nothing. Except it needs charging. I . . .'

'Hey, is that the new Sony? I've heard about these but I've never seen one. Awesome . . .'

An hour later, Junior Engineering Officer Senzo Tago had overseen the incorporation of Reona's laptop into the ship's systems, and Reona was happily tracking the signals given out by the three locators he was most worried about.

He was so preoccupied – and had been so during the whole process – that he had entirely failed to notice several things. He remained ignorant of the fact that Tago had kept looking through the half-open doorway at the bedroom where the sleeping Aika had rolled on top of the covers and now lay absolutely naked and clearly visible. Had he noticed either this fact or the expression on the sailor's face, he would have been deeply disturbed.

He did not know either – could not be expected to know – that engineer Tago had actually been sent on to the bridge on purpose by the first officer. Had been given orders to do with the laptop exactly what he had done. And to be sure he did *not* explain to the all-too trusting ex-professor that now his laptop was part of the system, everything he could see on his screen could be monitored on the bridge.

And, that it could, in fact, be transmitted to the private office high in the Luzon Logging Building in Quezon City, Manila, where another professor – one who still held his post, his position and his power – was able to see it all quite clearly too. Almost as clearly, in fact, as he was able to observe the video footage from the cabin that the naked Aika Rei was sleeping in.

Flags

Richard Mariner and Nic Greenbaum made it back from the docks to the Mandarin Oriental in time for the dinner which Nic had won and Richard was to pay for. They made it by the skin of their teeth, with hardly time to freshen up before they were rushed to the thirty-eighth floor. Service at Sora began at eight thirty local time or not at all, for it was a performance as much as a meal.

'This is even worse than going to the theatre,' said Richard mock mournfully as they hurried past the truncated gymnasium, the end of which had been adapted to house the sushi restaurant whose name meant 'Sky' in Japanese. 'I turned up five minutes late in Stratford once and was locked out of the first act of *Hamlet*. I never did work out what on earth was going on! Spent *four hours* trying . . .'

For just about two seconds, Nic believed him. Then, '*Yeah*,' drawled the American. 'I had the same problem at a cricket match. Place called Lord's.'

'Really?' asked Richard innocently. 'How much did you miss?'

'None of it. I just couldn't work out what the hell was going on. Spent *five days* trying . . .'

The restaurant was exclusive as well as time-specific. There were eight seats grouped around an L-shaped wooden bar which looked priceless, ancient and lovingly maintained. What was it about the Japanese and their wood? thought Richard. Six of the guests looked out over the night-time vista of Tokyo lights through floor-to-ceiling, wall-to-wall windows. From this height, Richard really could see why they called it 'Sky'. Richard and Nic sat in the pair with their backs to the window, lucky to be here at all. The whole room was tiled and flagged in dark grey, onyx on the wall, marble on the floor and the theme was taken up by the grey, black and white of the mats, cutlery and chopstick rests in front of them. The lighting was overhead and, to put it mildly, theatrical. Even the bonsai tree got its own spotlight.

'What's the next move now that we've found out where Professor Romeo and his Juliet went?' asked Nic more seriously, as he opened the exquisitely tied white box in front of him to find that it contained a perfectly folded napkin.

'Find out about this ship, *Dagupan Maru*,' answered Richard at once. 'What flag it's flying; where it's registered and who owns it; what it's carrying and where it's bound for.' Then, more sensitive to atmosphere, perhaps, than Nic, he added in a lower voice, 'But we'll leave that till tomorrow. This show's about to hit the road. Remember *Hamlet*. Remember Lord's.'

They fell silent and faced forward.

The beautifully suited and tailored Japanese men and women in the six seats beside them stopped frowning and tutting. The two young men in brown chefs' outfits and flat hats bowed – and the meal began. Began, in fact, with a drink. A young woman in a jade-green kimono asked each one what they would prefer. She approved of Nic's choice of sakes and frowned over Richard's choice of waters and teas, but he had worked in Hong Kong and Shanghai: he knew what it was to be viewed as a round-eyed barbarian. Then the young men behind the counter began to introduce, discuss and prepare the fish. One spoke Japanese, the other English. They were both, although youthful in appearance, masters of their art, though they shared as much with Richard Burton as they did with Raymond Blanc.

For the next three hours, the two sushi masters delivered bite-sized course after bite-sized course, each designed to build upon

the last in an ever-growing mountain of taste, each produced
with a flourish, like an elegant magic trick. Almost every member
of the fish and crustacean families available in the waters on
and off Japan was served in one form or another – raw or mari-
nated, in shell or out, with wasabi or with ginger – most of them
laid on a bed of rice and wrapped in seaweed. Richard drank
thimble-fuls of water while Nic sipped his sake icy from a glass
and thimblefuls of tea while Nic sipped it steaming from a
porcelain cup. Apart from that, he matched his companion course
for course. If not from soup to nuts, at least from *amuse* to *miso*.
Which was in many ways, Richard thought with sleepy content-
ment as he drained the *miso* bowl at last, almost the exact
opposite.

It was midnight when they left the restaurant, and although
Nic had slept well the night before, he had sipped his way through
a fair amount of sake tonight. Richard, though sober, was tired.
They both went straight to bed.

Richard's final thought before sleep claimed him was, unusually, not of Robin.

It was of a mysterious bulker called *Dagupan Maru*.

Richard woke with the name of the runaway lovers' ship still in
his head and as he showered and shaved, he tried to work out
where he should start to look for her. In the old days he would
have started with Lloyd's of London, for most of the working
ships in the world had been registered there at one time or another.
But that venerable institution nowadays really only kept records
of vessels that the members' agents had checked and insured.
And increasing numbers of owners in the current financial climate
insured their own bottoms – and prayed they'd never have to
replace them.

There was the British Department of Transport List but that
only contained details of British registered vessels that fell under
the aegis of the UK Authorities. But even here there was a certain
amount of uncertainty about vessels – and businesses – registered
in the Channel Islands and the Isle of Man. Each of the major
maritime nations had the equivalent, also with its individual
anomalies. But there was no central database, even of the major
players and their vessels, let alone of the anomalies and theirs.

And in any case, just because a vessel sailed from a certain country's ports and was crewed with a certain nation's seamen it no longer guaranteed that either one was the vessel's home country. That it *flew their flag,* as the saying went. A literal saying, however, for by maritime law all ships had to have the name of their home port written on their hull and the flag of their country of registration flying at their masthead.

But names and flags told you little, for flags of convenience were the modern norm as canny owners tried to overcome union rules and national laws about working conditions and safety procedures. There was certainly no central list of vessels under the nearly forty flags of convenience currently in use – from Panama, where the American ship owners had gone in the early days to break the powerful US shipping unions – to Liberia, the more modern favourite. Countries (sometimes little more than island states) whose 'flags' had broadened into offshore havens for all sorts of things – businesses, real and fake, working or shell, that didn't want their records checked by taxmen or financial authorities any more than they wanted their vessels and their crew conditions checked.

Richard gave a wry, lopsided grin, as he began to run the familiar list through his head, starting, aptly enough, with the legendary old pirate ports of the Spanish Main: Antigua, Aruba, Barbuda, Bahamas, Barbados, Belize, Bermuda, Cayman . . . If Captain Jack Sparrow were alive today, he thought grimly, he knew where *The Black Pearl* would be registered; what flag she would sail under, besides the skull and crossbones.

He would just have to hope that the Japanese Transport, Port and Pilotage Authorities had the details he wanted – and that they would be willing to share what information they actually had with him. The word *Maru,* whether it meant 'circle', 'completeness' or 'castle' also meant that the ship was Japanese. He would have to start with that and see where it got him. But where was she registered? Whose flag fluttered at her forepeak or her jackstaff? By the time he had slapped Roger and Gallet aftershave on his lean cheeks, he had decided that the best place to start was at the twenty-four-hour secretariat at Crewfinders. He glanced at his Rolex. Seven thirty a.m. in Tokyo meant eleven thirty p.m. in London. Audrey would be on duty.

Richard flipped up the top of his laptop and hit the email button. Crewfinders was in his electronic address book. He sat, still steaming with a towel wrapped round his waist, double-checked that Skype was down, and started typing:

Dear Audrey: This hasn't happened, but please imagine it has and act accordingly. Bulk Carrier *Dagupan Maru* several days out of Tokyo (destination unknown but current position presumably somewhere in the North Pacific) wants a replacement captain/first officer. I need to know everything about this vessel. Cargo, command (if possible), flag and owners as soon as you can. If you run into any difficulties, get Jim Bourne's Intelligence Section at London Centre involved. Reply to this address or call my Japanese cell on the number you already have. I will be starting with the Tokyo Harbour and Shipping Authorities and seeing what they will put on public record. Richard.

He flagged it *urgent* and pressed SEND.

Then he had a thought. He logged into *MarineTraffic.com* and put in *Dagupan Maru*. After a moment, the vessel's basic details came up beside a blurred photograph, snapped from some distance by the look of things. He scanned swiftly through the details. Ship type, year built, length and breadth, tonnage and so forth. His eyes leaped down the screen looking for more up-to-date information. Something to get him started. Flag: *Barbuda*. Last position: *Vancouver*. Current position: blank. Last known port: *Vancouver*. Information received: *thirty days twelve hours sixteen minutes ago. Not currently in range.* Voyage-related info: *departed Vancouver*. Destination: blank. Recent calls: *none*.

He scrolled down to the next page, eyes narrow and busy. Vessel's Wiki: Type – bulk carrier. Owner, Manager, Builder, hull number, class, service status, all blank. He hissed with frustration. Tonnage and dimensions: *no new information*. Communications, capacity, cargo, engines, officers, crew: all blank.

'She's a ghost ship, near as, dammit, sailing under a flag of convenience,' he said to Nic half an hour later as they craned over the laptop sitting amid the wreckage of their breakfast.

'Well, let's hope the Tokyo Port Authorities have a bit more info,' said Nic, round the last of his waffles, bacon and maple syrup.

'And that they're willing to share it with us,' nodded Richard, pushing aside a half-eaten croissant.

Richard and Nic had met in K'shiki on the thirty-eighth floor where they settled for the Western-style breakfast. Over coffee, after closing the disappointing laptop, they planned their working day, which was going to begin – and probably end – down on the docks. And they planned their evening by booking a table in Signature on the floor below.

'Tapas is supposed to be brilliant, too,' said Richard, pushing the laptop away as though he blamed it for the lack of information. 'A bit like Sora but different food. The sweet at the end for pudding looks exactly like bacon and eggs. There's all sorts of fun stuff. Quite an experience, I'm told.'

'Yeah,' answered Nic, who was footing the bill this evening. 'But after last night I'd like something a little less theatrical. And in any case, Tapas is booked solid.'

The Tokyo Port Authority Building might as well have been booked solid too. They were dropped off in front of the imposing building, which was surprisingly old and sturdy-looking amid the high-rise and neon-lit extravagance of much of Tokyo. They had to push their way in through the door and repeat their names and appointment time to several stony-faced receptionists before they got through to the interior. And even here they simply joined another series of queues. Not even shipping magnates like Richard and Nic could walk in off the street and expect to be seen at once – even though both men had arranged for their head offices to phone ahead. They ended up hanging around a little listlessly, watching sheets of grey rain falling over Tokyo Bay on a dull and darkening morning that even Disney was having trouble brightening up. 'Maybe we should grab a bite of lunch then split up,' suggested Richard at last. 'I could try the pilot office while you work your way up the queue here . . .'

But the idea wasn't put to the test. They were called through even as Nic said, 'Hey that's a good . . .'

The young woman port authority official was called Nanaka Oda, according to the ID badge on her lapel and the label on her desk. She rose to greet them and then sat when they filled the comfortable seats opposite her.

'You require information about a vessel departing Tokyo port some days ago?' she enquired formally, glancing from each of them across to her computer screen.

'The *Dagupan Maru*,' confirmed Richard. 'All the information you can give us, please.'

'Why you require this?' she asked frostily.

'We are interested in the vessel and her whereabouts,' answered Richard.

'You have authority for this enquiry?' she probed.

'No. Do we need any?' asked Richard innocently.

'For some information, obviously so!' she snapped.

'What can you tell us without authority?' persisted Richard.

She gave him a lingering look then turned to her computer. Her fingers flashed across the keyboard, and she began reading in a monotone. '*Dagupan Maru*. Vessel's details as follows. Ship Type: bulk carrier. Year Built: 1992. Length and Breadth: one-hundred-and-ninety-four metres by twenty-three metres. Gross Tonnage: eleven thousand tons. Dead Weight: twenty-nine thousand tons. Last registered flag: Barbuda. Call sign . . .

She had hardly even started before Richard realized she was simply reciting the information from *MarineTraffic.com* he had consulted already. But he sat and let her read it right through to the end, hoping that the port authority would have updated some of the information – or that she would be able, and willing, to add to it.

But no. When the chilly Nanaka reached the end of the Marine Traffic information, she stopped.

'Is that it?' asked Richard unbelievingly. 'Is that all you can tell us?'

'Yes,' she said decidedly. 'Unless you come back with authority, I can tell you no more!'

As they rose to leave, Richard pulled a business card out of his pocket. 'Miss Oda,' he said, as forcefully as he could. 'If anything else comes up, please give me a call. I've written the number of my Japanese cell on there. Any time.'

She nodded and took the card with a tiny bow, avoiding the burning blue intensity of his gaze.

And it suddenly struck him that this was more than simple civil service jobsworth obstructionism. Nanaka Oda was actually frightened to tell him about the *Dagupan Maru*.

Convenience

'Look,' said Nic as they hit the street again. 'I've got an idea. Why don't you see what you can get out of the pilotage people? I'll try another tack. Gettit? Tack! Like yachts . . . Oh, never mind. Liberty would have laughed.'

'What's your plan?' asked Richard.

'You have your contacts. I have mine. I'll run up to the TV centre and see whether there's any *news* about *Dagupan Maru*. You'd be surprised what gets on the services these days. And besides,' he laughed, 'I know where there's a really good burger bar up there.'

'Hey, that's a good idea!' Suddenly Richard wanted to be on his own with a little time to think things through. 'We'll keep in contact by cell and meet up at the Mandarin – even at the restaurant if push comes to shove. OK?'

They parted then and there, and Richard turned down towards the pilot's office, leaving Nic on the roadside waving hopefully at passing cabs.

Richard walked thoughtfully down towards the grey water of Tokyo Bay, sinking back into his darkening thoughts. It would require quite a lot of influence to make the Tokyo Port Authority so obstructive. And he could think of nobody in Tokyo – or Japan for that matter – who would want to take the trouble. Nobody legitimate, at any rate. Still deep in thought, he decided to grab a quick plate of sushi at the Ty Harbour Brewery on his way. He sat, alone and still thoughtful, surveying the old market, and ate a light lunch in many ways the equal of his dinner yesterday evening. Then, pulling himself almost physically out of his preoccupation, he went on down to the Harbour Pilot's Building.

Here his luck changed. The pilot who had guided the *Dagupan Maru* out into the Tokyo Roads was there, available, willing and able to speak to him.

His name was Sato, and he turned out to be a garrulous, middle-aged man with sleepy-looking brown eyes and a round, childlike face. 'Yes,' he said affably, over a cup of tea in the pilot officers' lounge. '*Dagupan Maru*. Sailed with the evening tide more than a week ago now. Ten days ago. Ten days tonight, in fact. Captain Yamamoto was in command as usual, though he must be nearing retirement age by now. I think First Officer Sakai really runs the ship . . .'

'Any idea of her cargo?' asked Richard, trying not to stare, mentally ticking off the things he most wanted to know; the things most likely to help him discover her background, track her course and find her current position.

'She was laden with timber, I understand – that's what her paperwork said, what I saw of it. Macassar Ebony.'

Richard had never heard of that particular wood, so he asked the next question on his list. 'Where was she bound?'

'She was bound back to Vancouver,' Sato answered easily.

'Passengers? Did you see anyone you weren't expecting to see?' Richard probed gently.

'No,' answered Sato slowly, drawing out the negative thoughtfully. 'There was no one aboard apart from the crew, as far as I'm aware. I saw no evidence of anyone.' Sato sat forward, meeting Richard's gaze earnestly. 'As I say, I saw the lading documents and the port authority clearances. Customs, immigration and so forth. But nothing more than my duty required, really. There were no passengers mentioned. Everything is written down in the port authority pilotage and ship movement logbooks – though they're all on line these days of course.'

'Is there public access to those records?' asked Richard hopefully.

'Only with the proper clearances, I'm afraid,' answered Sato, putting down his teacup with a decided *chink!*

And that was all the pilot could tell him. His personal pager sounded then and he excused himself courteously. 'Ah. Duty calls, I'm afraid. My cutter awaits. Another vessel requires safe guidance out into the roads. The sister ship of *Dagupan Maru*, by great coincidence . . .' He rose, bowed and he left.

In the cab on the way back to the Mandarin, Richard took a call from Nic almost as soon as he had told the cabbie where to go – and long before he had any chance to collect his thoughts and assess what he had learned. 'It's the cargo that was in the news,' said the American. 'I'll go into more detail over dinner, but here's the headlines. *Dagupan Maru* apparently sailed with a full load of Macassar Ebony.'

'I can confirm that,' said Richard frowning. 'The pilot Mr Sato told me . . .'

'OK. Well, Macassar Ebony's apparently incredibly rare. It's sure as hell not supposed to be trafficked in bulk. Nowadays the trees only grow in Sulawesi, Maluku and Borneo in Indonesia. And there are hardly any of them left. That's one of the reasons the wood's worth so much. More than gold, ton for ton, the guys here say. Certainly nobody legit would get the chance to get enough to fill a ship out of the rainforest. Not even those guys you had a set-to with in Indonesia, the guys clearing the jungles illegally logging out all the precious hardwoods and slaughtering the wildlife . . .'

'Luzon Logging, yes . . .'

'But apparently there was a whole palace or something built of the stuff. Up in Tohoku Region near Sendai. Not a really ancient national heritage job. Turn of the 1900s. But a big place, you know? A palace and all of it made of Macassar Ebony. But then the palace was destroyed in the great earthquake of 2011, the one that brought the tsunami, screwed up the power stations. That one. Well, the palace was pretty badly damaged and before the local authorities could repair it these guys came in and took the wood. Thousands of tons. Priceless in today's market. Pretty shady. There's been a court case – but what can I say? The whole lot's gone and it looks like it's aboard the *Dagupan Maru*. Definitely is, if what you say the pilot saw is right.'

'Excellent work, Nic. That's the cargo and that's why they might want to be a little secretive about it. Any news about the hull? Who owns her?'

'According to the news morgue here, she's registered to an outfit called Aruba Holdings in Barbuda. That's about all. But wait! This just in as they say . . . The timber is apparently owned by some guys calling themselves Cook and Company, registered in Cayman. They're the ones advertising it for sale in the States at any rate. But of course when you say "the States" . . .'

'You mean, "Anyone who can get themselves or their representative to the States" . . .'

'Like you say, old buddy. Flags of convenience fly both

ways – and anyone can fly into the good old US of A from almost anywhere in the world and do business . . .'

Over dinner they discussed what they had discovered so far and what they planned to do next. 'So,' started Richard, as he tucked into his Parma-wrapped langoustine tails, 'they had more than one reason to keep *Dagupan Maru*'s comings and goings quiet. Illegal passengers and borderline contraband cargo.'

'I wonder who these guys are,' mused Nic, doing much the same as Richard in terms of ham and shellfish. 'Aruba Holdings and Cook and Company.'

'More flags of convenience, as likely as not,' said Richard. 'I wonder whether it'd be worth hiring a private detective, or at least some kind of enquiry firm, to look into them . . .'

'Don't you have that top-flight commercial intelligence section you call London Centre back at Heritage Mariner?' mused Nic. 'I thought they were among the best in the business.'

'Already on the case,' said Richard.

'Then I vote we wait and see what they say. No sense in training a bloodhound then hiring a spaniel to do the same job.'

'I suppose so,' said Richard. 'But it's just that the waiting is—'

'A bitch. Yeah.'

They fell silent as the empty plates were whisked away and the next course arrived. Richard had gone for the rosemary roasted Dover sole. Nick for the grilled rack of lamb. 'But still,' said Richard, dropping his voice, 'the more I think of it, the more I worry. I was thinking this all through from start to finish on my way down to the pilot office this afternoon. It seems to pan out like this: Reona and Aika Rei aren't on a pleasure cruise and if they were they certainly chose the wrong ship. What they *did* choose was a vessel that didn't mind taking people aboard in secret and smuggling them out against the law. And, more importantly, perhaps, we now know that it's one that was going close to the course of that damn bottle. That has to be what they're after. The good ship *Cheerio*. *Dagupan Maru* must be passing near it on the way across to Vancouver. And our young lovers seem to be after it in secret. Secrecy is so important that they're willing to risk their lives for it. And there's only one thing I can think of that's worth that kind of risk.'

'The lottery ticket,' Nic said with a forkful of lamb, gnocchi and endive halfway to his mouth. 'The lottery . . .' he repeated.

'I don't know,' nodded Richard. 'What are the odds that the professor's won the lottery with the ticket he put in the *Cheerio*?'

'Or his gorgeous girlfriend has. And this is all about getting it back?'

'One-hundred-and-ten-million dollars, if they can get it out and back in time.'

'The odds of winning in the first place are so long that the rest probably wouldn't matter. Like if you get hit by lightning on a golf course – what are the odds that you were holding a five iron or a putter when it happened?'

'I didn't know you played golf,' said Richard.

And his cell phone started ringing.

He put down a fork laden with creamy Dover sole and pulled it out of his pocket. 'They'll frown at long phone calls in here,' he said. 'I'll take this outside.'

Outside the door of the restaurant was a waiting area with a bar on one side and a wall-mounted television on the other side. As dinner had just started, the little bar was empty apart from the barman. Richard paused here and put the phone to his ear. 'Yes?'

'News channel twenty-four,' said a cool voice that reminded him forcefully of Nanaka Oda at the port office. Then the line went dead.

'I say,' called Richard to the barman at once. 'Could you put that on news channel twenty-four?'

The screen switched from a garish make-up advert to the grey of the security-lit docks. Richard thought he recognized the rotund shape of Police Officer Ozawa among a group of policemen in the background. A reporter in close-up was speaking rapid Japanese and an English translation was scrolling across the bottom of the screen:

'. . . was a long-serving and respected member of the pilot office. He leaves a widow and two married daughters. Foul play is not suspected. The police are certain that this was nothing more than a tragic accident. Pilot Sato was just reboarding his cutter when he appeared to slip and fall into the water. Despite efforts to save him . . .'

'What is it?' asked Nic as soon as he saw Richard's face. 'Is it Robin? The kids?'

'No. Not quite that bad.' Richard sat back down and pushed

aside the best Dover sole he had ever tasted, his appetite gone. 'But it's bad enough. You'd better get on to the chap you talked to at Tokyo TV this afternoon and tell him to watch his back . . .'

The pair of them went through every implication they could imagine. Starting with the last fact Sato had let slip – the ship he died beside was *Dagupan Maru*'s sister. Was his death actually an accident? Or, as Nanaka Oda's call seemed to suggest, was it something more? And, if more, was the motive for the tragedy because Sato had talked to Richard? Or that he had seen something ten days ago aboard *Dagupan Maru* herself? And, whatever might be the answer to these conundrums, what impact, if any, might that have on the knotty problem they had been wrestling with before Richard's phone rang?

'Whatever,' decided Richard, as the coffee cups were cleared away, 'we're stuck at the moment, until we get updates from *Flint* or *Katapult*. Or from Crewfinders. We really need to know where the girls are and what's happening . . .'

'And, perhaps more importantly still,' said Nic, 'we need to know who these people Aruba Holdings and Cook and Company really are.'

The answer came through at four next morning and it came to Richard's cell phone. He was in such a deep sleep that he almost didn't answer it in time, but he caught it on the last ring. 'Mariner?' he croaked, pushing the bright chill of the thing to his ear.

'Evening, boss – or morning where you are. Sorry to come through at this ungodly hour but I thought you'd want to know as soon as we did.'

It was Jim Bourne. That fact alone sent adrenaline through Richard's bloodstream like Turkish coffee spiked with Red Bull. 'Jim,' he said, sitting up and swinging his legs over the side of the bed. 'Fire away.'

'Crewfinders hit wall after wall,' said Jim. 'So they called London Centre in and we've had to do a fair amount of bulldozing I can tell you. Where shall I start? The flag?'

'OK. I take it she's no longer under Barbuda's flag?'

'Right. She and her sister were moved a year ago. All very hush-hush. New flag would have been a dead end too, except for the fact that you left some favours outstanding there. They've moved the flag to Tuvalu.' He paused as Richard gasped, swore and switched on the bedside light.

'Tuvalu,' repeated Richard.

'Tuvalu and Vanuatu are now offering flags of convenience apparently,' confirmed Jim briskly. 'Tuvalu has been since the early 2000s. That's where *Dagupan* is registered now. Owners still registered as Aruba Holdings – but Aruba is just another Flag of Convenience state. So we're calling in some of the favours you left outstanding in Tuvalu. Guy called Willy's on the case.'

'OK, Jim, that's good to know. What else?'

'*Dagupan Maru* herself. We've done a super search that *MarineTraffic.com* would kill for. I've emailed you the full details but the headlines are as follows: the ship is registered as heading from Tokyo to Vancouver. That's 4,088 nautical miles. She should be on a heading of four four point three degrees north-east, getting ready to swing south-east on the Great Circle. Her speed is ten knots. She's been sailing for ten days. That's two-hundred-and-forty hours. She should have proceeded . . .'

'Twenty-four hundred nautical miles,' said Richard. 'I do mental arithmetic, Jim, even at four a.m.'

'And that distance at that heading should put her at five one point six degrees north, one seven two degrees west,' continued Jim, unabashed. 'BUT she's actually at four five point two degrees north, one six nine point five degrees west. Well off the Great Circle route and far farther south than she ought to be.'

'How do we know that?' snapped Richard. 'She's switched off her locator.'

'She has,' answered Jim. 'But the professor's switched on his laptop and the university can track that.'

'Where's the bottle?' asked Richard after a moment.

'Three four north, one six three west. But that's not necessarily the right question.'

Richard sat up straight, running his fingers through his hair. Until suddenly and shockingly, a mental picture of Sato the dead pilot appeared in his mind. Sato, killed coming back from *Dagupan*'s sister ship. 'Where are the girls?' he croaked.

'Robin's last position was Johnston Island, one six point seven degrees north, one six nine point five degrees west.'

'That's due south of *Dagupan*. Liberty?'

'Four five point two degrees north, one four four degrees west.'

'That's due west of her. And they're all heading in for the bottle in the middle. So the cargo's not all that important after all,' he added thoughtfully.

'The Macassar Ebony?' said Jim. 'I wouldn't say that, but if the owners know anything about timber then they'll know the price of the cargo is only going to go up and up. They can afford a little side trip if they feel the urge.'

'Or if they have a good enough reason.' Richard was thinking, *A hundred-and-ten-million good reasons*. 'And are they the kind of people who know anything about timber? These Cook and Company people?'

'Ah. Right. Yes. Cook and Company are a shell company. As far as we can ascertain they are owned by Aruba Holdings whoever they are. Hull and cargo. Same owners. Risky of course, but potentially profitable if the gamble comes off. And they do seem like gamblers, these people. It's all in the email.'

'But you can't tell me who those owners are? The people who re-registered the flag at Tuvalu?'

'No . . . But I think I know a man who can. Hang on . . .'

The line hissed for a moment, then Jim was back. And his voice had lost all of that know-it-all bounciness from earlier. 'That was Willy on the other line reporting in from Tuvalu. It took some doing, but he's seen the records and there isn't any doubt. Aruba Holdings is a shell company entirely owned, lock, stock and barrel, by Luzon Logging of Quezon City, Manila. It's a bit of a nightmare, Richard. *Luzon Logging* . . .'

Professor

Aika Rei was growing more and more certain that she was being watched. The feeling grew stronger as time passed. Reona told her she was overreacting. That it was natural that she should be the centre of attention. She would have attracted the crew's admiring gaze even had she been fat and middle-aged.

But she sensed that her professor was withdrawing from her and she began to feel more and more unprotected.

It was not that Reona was tiring of her – he was as attentive as ever, especially when it came to matters of the pillow. Indeed, he was becoming ever more experimental and graduating into being an extremely satisfactory lover. At night she would tease him that he was passing through his doctorate in the bed and becoming a professor of passion too. But during the long, increasingly tedious days, he was beginning to be seduced by his original mistress back into his research.

To a great extent Aika Rei blamed the electrical engineer, Senzo Tago for this. The way in which he set up the laptop as part of the ship's powerful communications system and then kept returning to check up on it, to refine it and perfect it, allowed Reona access to all the information and research that he kept in his university cloud files as well as permitting constant monitoring of the Cheerio bottle and the two yachts racing towards it. Helpfully, Tago also put a little red dot that tracked *Dagupan*'s position and progress across the screen as well as one for her objective's position and one for her competitors'. Then he found a way of adding the ship's observations about patterns of weather, sea and current to the whole. Reona became so entranced by this ever-changing situation that he completely failed to notice the way the engineer leered at her behind his back.

And Senzo Tago was by no means alone. During the early days of the voyage, Aika was happy to explore the ship and all the common parts that the crew could frequent. She was excited to do so, in fact, her head full of well-financed plans, schemes and dreams as well as the elevated feeling that an intense and burgeoning love affair can bring. She was not at first put off by their surly suspicion of the lovely young woman and the unworldly professor in their midst. Of her habit of suddenly appearing, with him or without him, as entranced observer of some workaday ship's routine, in skirts that seemed either tight or short – or both. Of her arrival at the doorway of some section of the engine room, storage facility or work area, in the tightest jeans and a cut-off T-shirt that moulded to her bust. She explored the off-duty areas and discovered there was little indeed for the off-watch crews to do except to sleep and eat, but did not at first begin to assess the effect of the boredom on the men. She was a spectator at their on-deck football and baseball matches without noticing the way they were all watching her.

At first she did not even notice the way in which they started playing with her, treating her as their toy. She appeared without suspicion at her place for lifeboat drill with First Officer Sakai's crew in the middle of the night wearing the skimpiest of see-through dressing gowns. She supposed it was simple safety procedure when the same thing happened two nights later. And three nights after that. Without a second thought, she visited the canteen and joined the self-service queue for food at meal times, assuming that the way she was jostled – especially when alone – was just the result of the crew's eagerness to eat.

She thought only of changing into her most sensible footwear when invited to inspect the engine room maintenance levels with their mesh-grille flooring, and did not wonder at the sudden interest among the engineers in anything that might be happening one level below her, or immediately beneath the flare of her skirt and everything underneath it that might be revealed to someone looking upwards through a transparent deck.

She thought nothing of the sudden failure of their private en suite facilities and spent several days relieving herself, washing and showering in a specially isolated section of the crew's facility before it hit her that none of this was quite as isolated as it seemed.

The incident that really changed things, that woke her up to some of the risks she and her professor were really running here, was nothing to do with her place as ship's sex toy at all. It was to do with the cargo.

It was the tenth day since they had come aboard and *Dagupan Maru* was ploughing her lonely way through a wide, calm ocean. The sky and the sea were as predictably boring as the routine aboard. There were no clouds, no winds, no waves of any note; no ships. There hadn't even been any seabirds to watch during the hours since dawn, and it was well past noon now.

Aika Rei had gown bored with watching Reona crouching over his laptop and the arrival of Senzo Tago with yet another piece of programming had been motive enough to drive her down to the crew's canteen for an early lunch. Because she ate early, before the change of watch, the place was all but deserted and she settled in a corner with a bowl of *soba* noodles and *dashi* soup, content to be alone, so she could slurp them noisily like the good Tokyo girl she was. The only other people there was a work gang of four unfamiliar men, hurriedly finishing their thick *udon* noodles and *kamaboko* fishcakes liberally sprinkled with *shichimi* seven-pepper seasoning. Perhaps it was the fact that they were not paying any attention to her at all that piqued her interest. When they rose and scuttled out, she left her half-eaten food and followed them.

They were heading for a section of the ship she had not yet explored. Her interest quickened further as she followed them down one of the port-side interior companionways into the decks below the front of the bridge house, away from the more familiar engineering sections behind it. She did not know it, but they were hard up against the cofferdam that separated the living and working areas from the cargo holds. And, by the time they slowed, they were four decks down and hard up against the skin of the port-side hull. The lighting was poor down here; there were more than enough shadows for Aika Rei to hide in as the men, still preoccupied with the business that had brought them down here, gathered together around a big bulkhead door.

It was only when the little group of crewmen began to loosen the two big handles holding this closed that they began to look around nervously – and Aika realized that she might be caught up in something problematic here. But she stayed, because, after ten days, the fear was preferable to the boredom. And she saw herself as a decisive and adventurous woman. It took a lot to frighten her off, as her presence aboard in the first place attested.

And that was why, when they eased the big door open and stepped in one after the other, leaving the door slightly ajar, that Aika Rei decided to follow them. She found herself in a narrow passage on the floor of what looked like a huge warehouse. There were light fittings on the walls and on the deckhead far, far above, giving some kind of illumination to the place, but their dimness and simple distance simply emphasized the enormity of the hold. As far as she was concerned, she was in the largest space she had ever come across in her life. And yet she felt constricted, almost claustrophobic. Because it was packed. Instead of air, almost every cubic centimetre of the place was packed with wood so dark that it looked black to her. There was a smell of smoke and it seemed to her at first that the black wood must be charred and burned. But no – when she reached out a hesitant hand to touch a plank of the stuff, it was as cool and smooth, as polished and soapy as jade. And the sawdust smell beneath the burning was rich and sweet, almost like perfume in her nostrils. She glanced back and was relieved to see that there were handles on the inside of the door as well as on the outside. Then she began to creep forward, only to freeze.

'. . . *millions* . . .' came a whisper, apparently from between the ebony planks themselves. '*It's worth millions* . . .'

'. . . *says it's worth more than jade, ounce for ounce* . . .'

'. . . *more than gold* . . .'

'But it's in beams and planks!' came a voice closer at hand. Louder, more sceptical, less awed.

The more practical one, thought Aika Rei: *there's always one* . . . She edged further into the massive, wood-filled space, straining to hear them more clearly.

'Look at it!' the sceptical voice continued. 'Scumbag Tago looked it up on that stupid professor's computer while he was out at dinner with the slut he's shagging. It used to be a fucking *palace,* for fuck's sake. Of course it's in planks and timbers, trunks and logs. There's nothing here for you to steal, Izumi. Even if it is worth as much as jade. Or gold. Feel it – it's as *heavy* as gold too. To get something out of here, smuggle it past that bastard Sakai and off the ship in Vancouver, you'd need something as small as your *dick*! And everything in here is almost as big as mine . . .'

'Yours only gets that big, Nagase,' sneered one of the others, 'when you're getting an eyeful of the hot slut!'

'At least it gets that big, Ido, old friend. Especially when I peep through the spyhole in her shower . . .'

Realization hit Aika Rei with almost physical force. *She* was the person they were referring to in such shocking terms! She stopped breathing, as though punched in the stomach. It was her shower they were spying on. *Her* shower! She was so shocked and angry that she was actually about to give them a piece of

her mind, as though they had been dirty-minded students in one
of her lectures, but just at that moment the bulkhead door behind
her slammed wide.

'Come out!' bellowed a massive voice. 'Izumi, Nagase, the
rest of you! We know you're in there!'

'Shit!' hissed Izumi. 'It's fucking *Sakai*. He's going to fucking
kill us.'

'Better take it like a man, then, Izumi,' answered Nagase.
'Unless you want to bend over and take it like a woman! Here
I am, First Officer Sakai. General purpose seaman Nagase coming
out as ordered!'

There was the narrowest of spaces for Aika Rei to squeeze
into. It was deep and blessedly dark. She made herself invisible.
Willed herself silent. Imagined herself undiscoverable. The largest
of the four men swaggered past. His footsteps echoed confidently
enough until they were stopped abruptly by the ringing, almost
bell-like sound of a metal bar being slammed across his skull.
There was a softer crumpling sound as he slumped unconscious
to the deck. 'One down, three to go,' bellowed First Officer Sakai.
'Don't make me come in and get you!'

The next two tried to run out as a pair but they didn't get any
further than Nagase. They too went down with that telltale crumpling sound as the cracked-bell tones were still ringing in the
air. 'Come on, Izumi! Don't keep us waiting!'

'Fuck you, Sakai! I'm not going to let you crack my skull
open so easily!'

'You can't stop it, Izumi. You know that. You've broken the
rules. You suffer the consequences. You're only drawing it out,
making it worse for yourself.'

'I didn't! I didn't break any rules. I wasn't going to steal
anything!'

'That's only because there's nothing in here small enough to
steal and you know it! What did you think? A palace was going
to be made out of neat little nickable sections just right for you
to try and smuggle ashore? You'd better thank your lucky gods
that it's not. Have you any idea what would have happened to
you if this had gone any further? You know nobody crosses the
company. Nobody pisses off the professor. Our professor – not
that sad little git with his sorry slut in the owner's suite. And let

me tell you this, Seaman Izumi, while you still have ears to hear with, *our* professor's *coming aboard*! Did you know that? The man himself! And you do not want to be in anybody's bad books when the professor comes aboard. That's why Nagase here did the wise thing. His dick's not as big as a roof beam but at least he'll still have one when this is all over. Which is more than you'll have if the professor hears anything about this, and you know it!'

Still the coward Izumi hesitated, and Sakai added those last, few, fatal words: 'Come on, for fuck's sake, Izumi. You know the professor only wants to play with the two in the owner's suite after he gets the lottery ticket. Well, with the slut, at any rate. Don't make him waste his time on you . . .'

Izumi capitulated. The cracked bell sound was preceded by a whimper and followed by the soft crumpling sound. The door slammed shut. Aika Rei threw up her *soba* noodles and *dashi* broth all over the deck at her feet.

During the time it took her to stumble to the bulkhead door and release the inner handles, she began to see her whole existence in an entirely new light. But, try as she might, she could not begin to see any kind of a way out of this suddenly terrifying situation either for herself or for her poor Reona.

Her professor was not in their suite when she finally made it back. A couple of hours earlier she would have assumed he had gone to lunch without her. Now she was at once terrified they might have murdered him already. She went into their bathroom and used a dry towel to rub the sickness off her shoes. The main door opened and she ran out, almost weeping with relief to find Tago there. Her revulsion was so great that she spat, 'You know they all call you *Scumbag Tago*?'

He looked at her like a surly child. Then he sneered. 'You should hear some of the things they call *you*!'

'I *have*, you little shit! Now get out! And tell whichever sick fuck turned the water off in here so you could spy on me showering downstairs to turn it back on again. I'd *rot* before I washed down there again. I'd go to the toilet out of the *window*, you sick scum!'

He went, apparently more than a little shaken by the venom and profanity of her outburst. Alone – really terribly alone, now

– she collapsed on the chair she put her coat on the first time she had walked in here as innocently as a child, and really began to wonder what was actually going to become of herself and her beloved professor Reona Tanaka.

But if Reona was *her* professor, she thought, then who was this other professor? The professor that even the fearsome First Officer Sakai seemed to be terrified of. Why was he threatening to come aboard the *Dagupan Maru*? And what on earth did this other professor want with *her*?

Aika Rei was still stuck at this point when Reona reappeared the better part of an hour later. He didn't notice her expression, for he was bursting with news.

'Good news,' he said as he came in. 'I bumped into First Officer Sakai and he says the bathroom's been fixed. We're back to our own private en suite!'

'Reona,' she began, a little weakly.

'Oh, and we're to have a visitor!' he interrupted her, too full of boyish enthusiasm to be stopped. 'Apparently the CEO of the company wants to come aboard himself; be there in person when we catch up with the *Cheerio*.'

'Darling,' she tried again.

But he overrode her again. 'And he's not just the chairman of the shipping section; he's the guy who runs the whole thing. Luzon Logging – the lot. He sounds really important, incredibly powerful – maybe even more powerful that Mr Greenbaum and Captain Mariner. Professor Satang S. Sittart's his name and Sakai says he can hardly wait to meet us!'

Wreck

Liberty was in action without a second thought. The minute the picture from Maya's camera settled at that strange angle she was up out of the cockpit and running across *Flint*'s warm, polystyrene and composite deck towards the side of the derelict vessel so ironically called *Luck*. 'Maya!' she called into the two-way. '*Maya!* Can you hear me?'

There was the hissing of an empty channel. Liberty's whole long body went cold, even though she was in frantic motion.

'Hey!' called Bella, looking up from the laptop, shocked by the suddenness of the disaster and by Liberty's explosive reaction to it. 'You take care!'

'I will,' called back Liberty. But she didn't really believe her own words. 'Maya?' she called again. 'Emma?'

There was only quiet hissing in reply.

The deck of the ghost ship was a quick scramble up and its look and layout were already familiar from the pictures Maya and Emma had sent back. The only thing the pictures had not revealed was the fact that, like *Flint*, the derelict vessel was stirring rhythmically as the big ocean rollers passed beneath her keel. That explained the unexpected movement she had been so swift to dismiss, she thought. And the heaving seemed to be intensifying. She glanced up at the hard blue sky as she stepped over the rotting safety rail, suddenly aware that the weather might be on the change.

But Liberty had much more immediate concerns. She ran across the green non-slip and the grey section behind it. She did not pause until she reached the starboard bridge-house door, then she swung it wide until it slammed against the wall behind it and clipped wide open, shaking in its retaining clip as the echo of the bang it made faded into the moaning of the wind. She gulped a deep breath of relatively clear air and stepped over the raised section into the bridge house itself.

Sunlight streamed in behind her, lighting the lateral corridor to the top of the companionway, but the warmth of the outside vanished immediately into a clammy chill. The pictures had not prepared her for the stink, any more than they had for the restless movement, and even that quick eye-watering breath she had caught when the wind backed hardly prepared her for the stench. She hadn't thought to bring a torch – hadn't really thought at all – so she slowed a little as she plunged into the shadowy stairwell like a reluctant bather entering an icy pool.

No sooner had the shadows closed around her than the composition of the dark air changed. The sickening aroma of rotting fish was all but lost beneath the eye-watering smell of diesel gas. As though she was swimming in petrol, Liberty plunged on, taking the shallowest breath she could, praying that she could hold out against the deadly fumes, forewarned and forearmed.

The turn of the stairwell was the darkest part of the journey, for as she went on down into the wreckage of the crew's mess, the light cast by two torches illuminated where she was walking. They did so, she noted grimly, because they were shining along the deck from the sides of the two fallen women at the far end of the engine room corridor. Even so, the low, lateral beams made it easy enough for her to pick her way through the rotting filth on the deck.

Emma had made it almost to the door of the crew's mess. She lay on her face with the torch out ahead of her, as though she was pointing the bright beam at some danger hidden in the dark ahead of her. Maya lay immediately outside the half-closed engine room door with the camera and the second torch. Liberty stepped past both women and pushed the cold metal door closed then slammed the handles into place. Only then did she turn.

Liberty had already calculated that she would have to take Emma first because she would never get Maya past the American-Japanese woman's stocky body. Not in a passageway as narrow as this one. Wearily, feeling the weight of her own arms and legs beginning to drag her down, she took Emma by the back of her life vest and lifted her as though she were some kind of suitcase. The torch rolled free of Emma's slack grip and continued to point urgently through the mess into the wreckage of the galley with its tank of cooking gas. The rolling of the beam gave the whole thing a weird, unsettling movement, adding to the motion of the hull, seeming to set it swinging more forcefully still.

Emma's arms and legs dragged along the floor of the passageway as Liberty pulled her out. Her wrists and knees slithered through the filth on the mess floor and bashed against every stair on the long upward haul. Little by little, one step at a time, Liberty's mind closed down until only her iron will was keeping her going. Her long legs only just functioned. Her back and shoulders seemed to be on fire. Her hands, and especially her fingertips, were points of almost incapacitating agony. She didn't dare breathe too deeply so she couldn't call for help. Her head sang and her heart thundered so powerfully that it felt as though her chest was going to explode. But somehow Liberty managed to pull Emma up into the dazzling brightness of the lateral corridor and out on to the windy weather deck.

'Bella,' she croaked into the two-way, the moment she dared fill her lungs with the wonderful air that had almost made her puke ten minutes ago. 'Double-check the way *Flint*'s secured and come aboard. I'll never be able to do that again. Not alone.' She rolled Emma over on to her back, sank to her knees beside her and tried to check for signs of life. Her adrenaline-filled hands were shaking so much she could hardly hold her friend's warm throat, let alone find a pulse. Besides, the strain on her fingers of treating the rubberized canvas of a life jacket as though it were the handle of a suitcase had left her nails torn and her fingertips utterly numb. She put her ear to Emma's lips. Could not hear breathing. Could not feel anything other than the steady wind on her cheek.

'That's really fucking risky, Liberty,' warned Bella. 'And the weather's on the turn . . .'

'It's really fucking *vital*, Bella! *Get here now!*' Liberty pulled herself back up and turned towards the clipped bulkhead door. 'You really don't want to finish this trip three-handed,' she emphasized. 'Maybe two-handed – *with a couple of corpses for company*! Get here or it'll be too late.'

She paused, leaning against the doorway, willing herself to hurry up, feeling as though she was wearing a suit of lead. Then, with startling suddenness, Bella was there beside her and, shoulder to shoulder, they went in. 'Goodness!' whispered Bella. 'It's cold in here! And that *smell*!'

'Don't breathe,' grated Liberty. 'Take one deep breath and hold it. It gets worse.' She did what she advised, then took the lead down the dark companionway, feeling Bella close behind her. She had to put her hand on the wall to steady herself several times before she stepped down on to the lower deck once more. They went side by side through the crew's mess, with the torch beams lighting up their feet among the rubbish, then Liberty took the lead again stepping into the narrow corridor. She slowed carefully so she could stoop and retrieve Emma's torch without Bella bumping into her, then she gestured to her dark-haired companion to pick up Maya's torch as well. They paused for an instant as Liberty tried to work out the best way for two women to carry a third along a corridor only just wide enough for one. Then she stooped and took hold of Maya's life jacket just as she had taken hold of Emma's. Bella stood back and Liberty heaved the inert mass of Maya's head and shoulders past her knees. Then, blessedly, Bella stooped and grabbed the waist section of the sturdy vest, taking half the terrible weight.

Liberty swung the torch beam dead ahead and began to stagger forward. As she did so, she realized with simple horror that the gas tank in the kitchen did not just seem to be swinging. It was actually swinging. Quite wildly, in fact. And even as the two would-be rescuers pulled Maya into the filthy mess, the tank finally tore free of its fixing and crashed to the floor. But one more horrified glance was enough to tell Liberty the worst. It was the pipe that had broken – not the connection. And that realization was confirmed at once by the fact that the roaring in her ears became real – the roaring of escaping gas. Cooking gas was pumping out of the bottle and through the broken pipe to mix with the already lethal fume-filled atmosphere. The smallest spark would set the whole lot off now.

Simple horror seemed to lend Liberty even more strength. She heaved Maya on to the steps of the companionway so fiercely that for a moment she was pulling Bella as well. Then Bella caught something of her terror and the pair of them bundled Maya up the companionway, round the bend and up again into the brightness of the corridor. Side by side with Maya dragging between them, they raced down the wider A deck passageway and out on to the deck.

Liberty tensed to let go of Maya and grab Emma, but the Sino-American woman was already on her hands and knees, puking weakly on to the deck. The wind had picked up even further. There were clouds threatening in the distance, and the colour of the ocean had changed to a deeper green. The swells were big enough to be moving both *Flint* and *Un Maru* more wildly. The fenders between the hulls were screaming like souls in torment. 'Quickly!' gasped Liberty. 'Let's get aboard *Flint* and away. Emma! Can you walk?'

Answering with actions rather than words, Emma pulled herself to her feet and staggered alongside Liberty and Bella to the side of the derelict wreck. Liberty went over first and turned at once, reaching back and up for Maya's dead weight. Then Emma half fell aboard before Bella stepped more delicately – but no less urgently – over the safety rail and down. Then she too turned and began to untie the rope securing the two working hulls together.

Liberty staggered down into the cockpit and the moment Bella shouted, 'Free!' she engaged the motor and eased the two vessels apart. With Maya still face down on the deck and Emma on all fours beside her, Liberty brought the motors up to full ahead, looking back fearfully over her shoulder, trusting that the darkening ocean ahead was clear. It was only when Bella joined her in the cockpit, settled into her accustomed place beside the equipment and whispered, with profanity that she had never been heard to use before today, '*What the fuck . . .*', that Liberty thought to look down. And saw the laptop screen.

In their rush to get clear they had forgotten the camera. It was still where Maya had dropped it and it was still switched on. The little light gave just enough illumination for them to still make out the corridor at its crazy angle and the openings leading into increasingly shadowed rooms beyond it. The crew's mess and the galley, almost invisible in the darkness. *Un Maru* was moving sufficiently forcefully to make the camera itself rock from side to side, and the combined movement gave the impression that the derelict vessel was in the grip of a terrible storm. The corridor heaved and lurched. The angles of the doorways seemed to reel crazily. For a truly mind-bending moment it seemed that the door into the mess and that into the galley were moving out of synch, at different speeds and attitudes.

And everything in the distant galley seemed to be alive. Cupboard doors flapped, dark veneer exteriors invisible, white laminate interiors catching the light. The last of their contents slid around, from side to side and back and forth, little more than dark shapes coming and going into and out of the darkness as the doors swung to and fro, outlined against the white of the interiors. Until, at last, the cupboard hanging crazily above the dismounted gas stove top fell off completely.

They never knew how or why, but something in that final fall sparked off the gas. The galley exploded into flame. A cloud of yellow brilliance filled the mess, which instantly added to the brightness and the flames. A great ball of fire billowed into the engine room corridor and came rolling along the deckhead above the camera, which recorded its own destruction with shocking faithfulness. A black-streaked yellow cloud rolling forward, contained by the geometric precision of the walls and deckhead above them and seeming to drip flaming streamers into the fume-rich atmosphere immediately outside the diesel-flooded engine room. And then the screen went blank.

House

L iberty jammed the motor controls hard forward and looked fearfully back over her shoulder at the all too slowly receding shape of the drifting hulk. A muffled *BOOM!* echoed down the wind. A gout of thick black smoke burst out of the open bridge house and came towards them. Red fire followed. It came flooding out of the bulkhead doors the women had left open. It exploded through the glass and came licking out of the windows. Then with a deafening report, the oil in the flooded engine room went up, the fumes heated to detonation point by the warmth coming through the bulkhead. Liberty hadn't even registered that *Un Maru* possessed a funnel until she saw it rise like a rocket and cartwheel into the water, trailing smoke. And the whole deck of the vessel seemed to tear itself open.

Liberty could almost see the wall of force spreading across the water towards them, like a squall. *Flint* slammed forward as it hit her, digging her bow into the back of a wave and heaving wildly. For a moment, the air was very hot, very noisy, and full of the stenches that had marked the *Un Maru* when she was still alive. But there was no debris. No hard rain of nuts and bolts. No withering shrapnel of glass shards. The blazing hulk refused to sink. It sat there, low in the water, its funnel and bridge house gone and its decks open to the elements, burning, guttering, floating.

'Now whoever built *that*,' said Liberty wonderingly after a while, 'should have done some work on the *Titanic*.'

The chuckle Maya gave was the first sign that she was still alive.

One by one they pulled themselves together and began to look to their boat. They stowed the fenders and set the sails. They reported to a distant, whispering radio contact that *Flint* was OK, and her crew were fine. They did not detail their most recent near disaster. Instead, they reported the current state of wind, weather and water. They calculated that they were currently at four five point two degrees north, one four four degrees west, and heading west along their course as agreed towards their rendezvous with *Cheerio* at a mean ten knots under full sail. That there would be no more video footage because their camera had sustained fatal damage. And finally that there was a burning vessel drifting as a serious hazard to shipping, a second or two of longitude east of the position they had just given.

The wind strengthened, *Flint*'s mainsail swung out to starboard and their speed picked up a little. The clouds in the east behind them started scudding in low and dark as a squall came chasing them westwards. It was this as much as anything that pulled them out of the lethargy that followed the adrenaline high which had got them through the adventure. They needed to sort out their storm rig, and were lucky that the weather gave them sufficient warning to change their gear before they did so.

They even had time for a hot meal at eight bells, though the traditional marker of noon aboard did not signify the traditional change of watch. Not under their current rotation. It might have given Liberty a chance for a noon sight, had she been minded to double-check the GPS with more old-fashioned methods. But the clouds had closed down and the exercise would have been pointless. So they sat, rigged and ready for foul weather with their speed falling off in the following wind, eating a mess of reconstituted scrambled eggs and baked beans which, by some magic, Bella rendered not only palatable but delicious.

But in the end, the squall never caught up with them. Its southern skirts scattered them with rain and pulled the wind round a point or two, then span away northwards. The wind eased and shifted southwards in the early afternoon and they began to think of running across it, gybing into a course that took them first north of their westerly course and then south again to meet it. It would be hard work, but it would keep their speed up.

The wind's new quarter seemed to bring the weather some further second thoughts with it. Conditions began to moderate towards a clear calm and the swells, never really amounting to all that much, began to settle into their accustomed deep-water set. The girls began to relax once more, and fell to more active yacht-handling. This was a race, after all. And they were still more than four days away from the spot their target was calculated to be at when they met it. About the same distance as *Katapult* by the look of things.

The clouds thinned and the afternoon sun came out, westering on their port bow as they continued their northerly reach. Their wet weather gear came off, replaced by jeans and blouses. The wind stayed steady enough to keep vision clear through the rest of the afternoon, and it seemed to *Flint*'s crew that things could only get better from here. Liberty let her ease off a point or two so the hull didn't vibrate so badly.

Then, just after the watch changed at seventeen hundred hours local time, '*What's that?*' demanded Bella, who was using the last of her off-watch time to do a little lookout-keeping. The tall Chinese-American was back up on the forepeak with the binoculars once again. 'Liberty, there's something dead ahead.'

Maya called, 'Just a minute,' and checked on her instruments, while Liberty looked down from the helm to see what the radar and sonar could make of whatever Bella could see.

'Well,' announced Maya decidedly. 'It looks like there's something there. Radar's picking it up but I have no clear picture of what on earth it is. If the kit's to be believed, it goes on forever. If there was anything on the sonar I might be convinced it was an island.'

'An island?' demanded Liberty. 'Out here? There's nothing on the chart.'

'Nothing for miles,' confirmed Maya. 'And I mean hundreds and hundreds of miles. We're due to hit *Cheerio* long before we hit anything like land.'

'Then what on earth is it?' mused Liberty.

'If we stay on this course then we'll find out because we're heading straight for it,' called Bella.

'Well, I hadn't planned to be until we change watches at nineteen hundred hours, then we can run back south all night,' said Liberty, more to herself than to anyone. 'Maybe get a smooth run. Manage a little sleep.'

'Well, that's OK,' answered Maya. 'We'll be close enough for a look-see by nineteen hundred.'

'But after this morning we'll be pretty bloody careful as we close up with it,' said Liberty feelingly.

The wind continued to let them run north of west along this reach as the sun settled westward. Bella continued to look ahead, but the low brightness began to interfere with her vision and so she came back to the cockpit, then went below to do some more cooking. The watch was due to change at nineteen hundred hours, so they ate curry and rice at eighteen hundred. Maya kept an electronic eye on what they were approaching as she shovelled spoonfuls of the fragrant food into her mouth, but it was not until the last few moments before darkness at eighteen forty-eight that Bella got another opportunity to check with the binoculars.

And the moment she did so, things changed yet again. 'Liberty!' she called urgently. 'Come here and look at this! You won't believe it! All of you, come and take a look.'

'One at a time,' warned Liberty. 'Emma, take the helm for a moment, please.'

A minute later she was at Bella's shoulder with the mixed-race Chinese-Cheyenne's hair blowing in black strands across her face. She spread her feet a little and leaned her lower belly into the curve of the safety rail on the forecastle head of *Flint*'s slim hull. Her hip fitted snugly against Bella's, and the tight line of the forestay with the full-bellied sail behind it separated their feet then rose solidly up behind them, holding the pair of them safely. Spray kicked up to the level of their knees, chuckling beneath the counter like a naughty child and the wind whispered past them.

'What?' Liberty asked, straining to see ahead. The northern horizon was dark, but oddly not with clouds. The sky was glassily clear and light. It was the sea that was dark. She shaded her eyes and squinted across the glare coming in from the port quarter. The horizon looked strangely uneven, rising in unnaturally square-looking sections. For a moment she wondered whether it could be a fleet of ships beating down on them, with the setting sun gleaming across their tall sides and square bridge houses. Frowning, she took the binoculars from Bella and pushed them to her eyes.

It was all Liberty could do to stop herself from shouting with shock. For what was approaching them was not a fleet. It was a town. Had the sonar given it any undersea foundations, she would have sworn it must be an island with a considerable settlement sitting on top of it. But no. There was no land there. Maya's sonar readings had confirmed that clearly enough. It was all afloat. Something stirred in her memory, something she had read or seen while planning this trip. Something dismissed as being too ridiculous. Too unlikely to be relevant.

'Bella,' she said. 'Go back and take the wheel. I want Emma to see this. I really wouldn't have believed it possible . . .'

And yet she could see a house, clear as day. An honest-to-goodness house, with another behind it, a third in the distance. Tall, two-storied, solidly roofed family dwellings. Square windows catching the last of the light. And cars. Half-a-dozen family saloons: Hondas, Nissans, Toyotas, apparently parked haphazardly outside the dwellings. A mass of wood, some of it rising up like fences on a suburban street. It stretched from side to side across the horizon. Liberty tried for a moment or two to calculate the simple size of what she was seeing. Trying to understand it seemed so far beyond anything she was capable of.

'Mother of God,' she breathed. 'What the hell is this?'

'Tohoku,' said Emma, easing into Bella's vacant position at her shoulder. 'It is the wreckage that the tsunami washed out to sea from Japan after the Tohoku earthquake in 2011. I have heard tell of an island of it floating slowly across the Pacific, but I never thought I'd actually see it. Some day it will reach British Columbia, they say. Maybe Alaska and Washington State in the US. For the moment, it seems, it is here.'

'Shit,' said Liberty. She looked at the floating island with its cars, fences and houses for another unbelieving moment.

Then she was in action. 'Stand by to gybe,' she ordered briskly. 'We're on the southward reach as of now!'

Spray

The first thing Flo Weary thought when Robin and Akelita came running full-tilt down the grainy grey-gold beach and splashed side by side into the water of the Johnston Island anchorage was '*Where in God's name did those two get yellow tights from?*' When her two companions raced silently past her, Flo was just wading up on to the beach with a satisfied smile on her face, certain that she had fixed the wing so that it would function just as well as it had before the whale hit it. The outrigger itself was still in the water, though not fully submerged. Its torpedo shape was well over a metre in depth even before it rose into the up-arching wing and a metre or so was under the water, leaving a little less than a metre between its sleek, aqua-dynamic bottom and the coarse seabed beneath it.

As the astonished Australian watched wide-eyed, Robin and Akelita dived beneath the surface, wedged their bodies into this space and remained there for minute after minute, their legs wriggling like massive shrimp-tails. After about thirty seconds, the wavelets on either side of the outrigger started to get a yellowish-looking scum on the top of them. Fascinated, and still utterly unsuspecting, Flo turned round and started wading back out, frowning with concentration as she looked at the weird phenomenon. By the grace of God, as she later observed, her eyes were pretty sharp, and a childhood experience with a swarm of green ants in Cairns made her realize what was going on pretty quickly. And so she turned in a flash and was back aboard, yelling, 'Rohini? Where's the insect repellent?'

Perhaps it was the Cairns experience or perhaps it was simply her native caution, but Flo had made sure *Katapult* was well stocked with Rentokill. She waded back in with a pressurized can of the stuff in each hand. She came as close to the bright yellow creatures as she dared, and then sprayed the struggling swarms with two streams of the deadly mist. No sooner had they stopped twitching and begun to float away out to sea than Robin burst out of the water, panting like a walrus, taking great gulps of air and tearing at her clothes. 'Up on the beach double quick,' ordered Flo. 'Strip off and I'll give you a speedy spray. Better safe than sorry, girl.'

Akelita followed, also streaming and gasping, and was given the same brusque orders. The lovely Polynesian baulked, her ecological sensitivities outraged, and might have refused altogether had she not seen her skipper dancing from foot to foot, stepping out of her panties to stand naked on the shore. Even so, she crinkled her nose. 'What are you going to spray me with?' she demanded, beginning to pull her own clothes off as she waded up on to the grainy coral.

'Near as I can figure it, nothing more than essence of chrysanthemum,' answered Flo shortly. 'The alternative is *ants in your pants*. Literally. And ants in your pants just to begin with.' She looked speakingly at the Polynesian Islander's luxuriant pubis. 'You do not want an ants' nest there, girl! Especially if they start biting. They haven't started biting, have they?'

Both women shook their heads.

'There you go! You got something to be thankful for. It's only by the grace of God that I realized what was going on. Grace of God and personal experience. Now,' said Flo, shaking the cans. 'Chrysanthemums. Plants. Where's the harm?'

'Even so,' said Akelita. 'Plants can be dangerous. Look at stinging nettles. Look at poison ivy. I don't want *poison ivy* up my . . .'

'Stop negotiating with Akelita,' ordered Robin. 'Come over here and spray me head to foot. And don't spare my blushes. You won't believe the places I can still feel them crawling in . . .'

'Sparing your blushes didn't even occur to me,' Flo assured her. 'Hold your breath and close your eyes. I'll start at the top and work my way down . . .'

Half an hour later, Robin and Akelita were dressed in fresh clothes and their wet togs, also drenched in Rentokill spray, were out on the poop behind the cockpit. They were drying off there because the crew on watch could also watch them – in case anything small and yellow attempted to escape and stow away aboard.

But to be fair, no one had much leisure to look at drying underwear. *Katapult* was still in the calm, shallow mid-section of the Johnston Atoll, behind the surf-wall of the reef, but Robin and her crew were completing a series of complicated exercises designed to test the outriggers and bring maximum pressure to bear on the joint that Flo had just fixed.

They had all the computer systems switched on so that the central control programmes could monitor and assess the way things were working. Robin was at the helm, therefore, and looking ahead, checking the set of the sails and the stress on the outrigger wings. Flo was crouched over the laptop, assessing the figures scrolling past. Rohini was on the radio, trying to get a strong enough signal to allow a report. And Akelita was keeping as close an eye on the sonar and the depth gauge as possible while the vessel skimmed through the reef-fanged waters.

Robin was beginning to feel, with some relief, that *Katapult* seemed to be functioning as well as when they left Tuvalu. Indeed, Robin allowed, she seemed to be functioning as well as she had been the last time *Katapult* won the gruelling Fastnet race. Back on form with a vengeance, she thought almost fiercely. And it suddenly occurred to her that she really wanted to win this race too.

Flo's voice cheerfully called up the figures confirming that everything was at optimum. Rohini's quieter tones repeated *Katapult*'s call sign over and over as she tried to report their position, contact *Flint* and catch up with *Cheerio*'s current whereabouts. Suddenly she was speaking rapidly, trying to get through her report before she lost contact once again. Robin frowned briefly. The scratchy signal came and went, but the Indian yachtswoman, used to single-handing and the need to pass the maximum information in the minimum time, was able to get sufficient reliable information to update their contact. Then connection faded again before she could get much new information in return.

Akelita said quietly, 'Shelving down from three metres to ten dead ahead.'

'Everything seems to be back up to spec,' Flo reported to Robin, almost the instant that Rohini stopped speaking. 'Looks like we're good to go.'

'There's a good channel straight ahead,' confirmed Akelita. 'We don't even have to alter course to get back on track.'

'OK,' said Robin at once. 'Time to leave this tropical paradise. Close down the computers, Flo. Get ready for some sail-handling, girls. Rohini, now you're off the radio you're in charge of the sails with Flo. Akelita, can you navigate us back out past the head of the reef then we may need to lay in a bit of a course correction to get us bang on target for the next way point we're aiming for. Five hundred nautical miles north-east along our proposed course. If memory serves, that'll be two four degrees north, one six six point five degrees west, somewhere between Hawaii and Midway.'

Even as she stopped speaking she was automatically calculating how much time it would take them to achieve the next leg, based on the mean speeds they had managed before they hit the whale. And what she hoped to get out of her lively command and her increasingly weary crew once they were back out on the ocean and in the grip of the easterly trade winds.

They had come in through the reef from the south-west. Now Akelita took them out between the islands on a north-easterly heading, keeping the reef to port. Rohini and Flo set the sails by hand as Robin directed and then came back into the cockpit. Akelita called out the names of the islands as *Katapult* skimmed past them, beginning to gather speed as the wind took her once again. As soon as the sleek multihull was beyond the end of the runway on Johnston Island itself and out of the malign influence of the humans and the yellow scourge they seemed to have brought with them, Akelita handed the depth gauge, sonar and radar displays over to Rohini and skipped up to the forepeak, calling excitedly over her friend's sailing directions, shouting out the species of increasingly abundant wildlife they could see.

They whispered past Sand Island first, the little grey-gold hump on their starboard given further prominence by the columns of seabirds hovering above it like smoke. 'Petrels and shearwaters,' Akelita informed them as she lowered the binoculars.

Akau, on their port side next, was larger, and in any case it was framed against the surf on the reef. There were monk seals sunning themselves on its coral beaches, Akelita observed, and tropicbirds and terns, nesting above and around the sleepy monk seal males and their sleek harems. There were more seals and one or two turtles on the last island, Hikina, and by the time they passed it they were back to racing speed. Nesting on the beaches among the seals and the turtles there were millions of boobies, and the island's upper reaches were home to majestic red-throated frigate birds that followed them, etched against the hard blue sky like dragons as they passed the end of the reef and swung back on to their course for the next five-hundred-mile leg of their voyage.

'We plan on one more waypoint at French Frigate Shoals then forty-eight hours hard sailing,' said Robin some hours later, as they sat around the cockpit eating their evening meal. 'But you know we'll hit light winds after we pass the next point. We were lucky to get through the doldrums as well as we did, but it's the horse latitudes next and the winds will fall just as light.'

'Aw, come on, skipper,' interrupted Flo abrasively. 'Don't go getting all "*cup half empty*" on us.'

'Independently of whatever we find there,' added Akelita, almost angrily, 'we'll still have to try and get to the bottle, even if there's other rubbish there.'

'Looking at it in a "*cup half full*" way,' said Flo bracingly, 'the more rubbish we hit the better. Except that I want to win this frigging race as much as Akelita does. I want to take that bottle home. Aussies do not like coming second, girls. So, I'm sorry. You'll just have to suck it up and get ready for victory.'

'Unless we hit light winds as well as a Sargasso of rubbish,' warned Robin.

'But if we do, then so will *Flint*,' countered Rohini, taking sides with Flo and Akelita. 'She's about the same distance out but coming in on the opposite course. Whatever we hit from the south-west, she'll hit from the north-east – and right about the same time, all things being equal.' She looked around the cockpit, wide-eyed with growing excitement. 'Looks like we're set up for a real tight finish.'

'And the bottle's going to be there?' asked Robin. 'Everyone's still one-hundred-per-cent certain about that?'

'By the look of these projection figures, it'll be right on the button. And still well afloat. Though God alone knows what else will have washed down around it.'

'A few days hard sailing with a following wind and a bit of luck,' said Robin. 'Then we'll just cruise home to Vancouver. With the winning bottle. We have the supplies. We have the time. We'll average five knots instead of fifteen on the long runs and hope for a bit of a holiday.'

'Oh,' said Akelita. 'Oh, yes, I'd like that.'

'I'd like that too,' said Flo. 'But I'd like that *and a man* one hell of a lot more.'

'Oh, yes,' agreed Akelita. 'I'd like one of those too.'

'*At least* one,' emphasized Rohini with a chuckle. A chuckle that spread round the cockpit and turned into proper, full-throated laughter.

And as Robin contentedly joined in the hilarity, suddenly found herself wondering what *her* man was up to . . .

Measures

'Luzon Logging,' said Nic, frowning. 'That means Satang Sittart's involved. That's bad.'

'He may not be involved directly or personally,' countered Richard.

'That a risk you want to take?' demanded Nic. 'I mean, I was there on Pulau Baya Island when he went down from the topmost step of the three-storey staircase right to the bottom of the river in two seconds flat, weighted down with what looked genuinely like a ton of bricks. I was there when they pulled him out and got the first good look at his ears. Or what little was left of them. You know he blames you and Robin for the damage that was done then and all the agony and humiliation he has been forced to suffer since.'

'I know,' Richard admitted. 'But we can't do anything about that now. And in any case, we don't know that Sittart is even aware of the situation with the bottle and the yachts, let alone involved in it.'

Nic gave a brutal laugh. 'One of his ships is well off course, heading for the graveyard of the Pacific chasing a bottle that might just be worth one-hundred-and-ten-million US dollars. Of course he's aware of it, Richard. And I'll bet it's only a question of time before he gets involved. *Personally!*'

'OK, but the point I'm making is this: the information Jim Bourne sent me from London Centre about the *Dagupan Maru* is worrying enough even before we add the professor into the picture.'

'It must have been pretty damn worrying for you to get me up at this ungodly hour . . .' said Nic with a wry laugh, looking at the black, white-figured face of the Breitling watch that protected the inner side of his left wrist, as though the steady beat of his pulse could help the fabulously expensive mechanism keep time. 'It's still not five a.m.!'

He strode across Richard's reception room lowering his left hand and raising his right – which held a cup of coffee. There was a half-empty cafètiere of Blue Mountain High Roast on the table beside Richard, lately placed there near his laptop by a young man from room service. Both Richard and Nic were dressed in casual trousers, and open-necked shirts, as befitted the time and the place, if not the serious nature of the meeting. 'What has Jim sent over?' the American asked, stopping his pacing and returning to ease his long body on to the sofa beside Richard so that he could see the laptop screen more clearly.

Richard had scrolled down past the information on the vessel's hull and engines and the screen was full of information about the captain and his senior officers now. 'Captain Yamamoto for a start,' he observed grimly, gesturing at the lines of neat black text and the damning information that they held.

'Oh,' said Nic grimly as he scanned the bold headlines. '*That* Yamamoto.'

He lapsed into thoughtful silence and reread the news articles Jim had digested for them. The digest came from several news articles from Manila, Tokyo, Seattle, Hong Kong and London, detailing the notorious incident that so nearly had the captain stripped of his command – and sent to prison. Because it had involved so many deaths. 'I still can't figure how he walked away from it . . .' said Nic after a while. 'How many kids were on the yacht he ran down? Eight?'

'Ten,' answered Richard grimly. 'She was a Transpac fifty-two out of Seattle, heading round the world. Planning to stop off in Manila for more supplies.'

'That's a big vessel to run over – even in the middle of the night, and even if your command is the better part of four hundred metres long and your bridge is a solid thousand feet back from the bows. Did any of the kids survive?'

'One,' confirmed Richard. 'That's how the authorities identified the vessel and were able to bring the case against him in the end. He didn't stop and search for survivors. He just sailed straight on.'

Nic shook his head. 'And he didn't report anything. Didn't lower a boat and try and help. Didn't even notice he had run down something the size of a Transpac fifty-two . . .'

'His first officer took the rap,' said Richard, scanning Jim's information. 'Though he got away with eighteen months' hard time and kept his papers. Sloppy bridge watch in the middle of the night. Radio equipment faulty. Collision Alarm radar playing up. And apparently no one aboard even noticed the impact. It was a complete mess.'

'So what you're saying is that the first officer was really only another aspect of the way this guy Yamamoto was running his command . . .'

'Looks that way. But the worrying thing is—' Richard stopped. Thought for a moment. Started over again. '*One of the worrying things* is that the yacht he ran down was twice the size of either *Flint* or *Katapult*. And even though *Dagupan Maru* isn't as big as his last command, she's more than big enough to repeat the exercise if he feels so inclined.'

'And why would he?' demanded Nic. 'Why would he feel so inclined?'

'Independently of the fact that he also seems to be going for the bottle, you mean?' demanded Richard cynically.

'Yeah,' spat Nic. 'Independently of that.'

'The gossip around the trial was that the Transpac simply got in Yamamoto's way while he was trying to meet a tight schedule. Demanding owners, not willing to cut anyone any slack – and Yamamoto keen to be their number one commander, so they say.'

'You mean he did it on purpose? It wasn't just sloppy seamanship?'

'Yes. He's a *"get there no matter who gets hurts"* kind of a chap, according to Jim's note here. He just ran them over when they got in his way. Not criminal negligence. Malice aforethought. Murder.'

'How on earth did he walk away from that?' Nic shook his head in simple bewilderment.

'No one could prove it,' shrugged Richard. 'The Transpac was pushing its luck sailing across the main shipping routes into Manila harbour anyway. And Yamamoto met his employers' schedule to the minute, so the grateful company arranged for his defence when it came up before the Maritime Court in Quezon City.'

Light dawned on Nic's face. 'And those employers were . . .'

'Luzon Logging.' Richard nodded. 'But wait.' He rode over Nic's bark of cynical laughter. 'It gets better . . .' Richard scrolled down further. 'The name of the first officer who took the rap and did the eighteen months hard time in Manila City Jail was . . .'

'Sakai Inazo,' breathed Nic. 'And he's aboard the *Dagupan Maru* with his old commander.'

'Not only that,' added Richard, 'but someone paid his hundred-dollar regular squeeze for what they call a "condominium" in the prison – a relatively private area with a real bed and some access to regular sanitation and proper food. Though even so, the man must have been pretty tough in the first place to survive, let alone be healthy enough to go straight back aboard so soon after he came out again.'

'Do tell . . .' Nic paused for a heartbeat. 'What do you think's going on here, Richard?'

'Look at the cargo, Nic. Most of a palace made of priceless wood that's only just out of legal review by the skin of its teeth; one step ahead of a judicial restraining order, a couple of sea miles in front of the customs people by the look of it.' He looked across at his friend and business partner.

'Hard men on a desperate voyage,' murmured Nic. 'Little short of pirates.'

'And would you look at the rest of the crew,' emphasized Richard. 'They all have some kind of criminal record. This guy Senzo Tago, their electrical engineer, has done time for peddling child pornography on the Net . . .'

'Heaven knows what that involved if he was doing it from the child sex capital of the world,' growled Nic. 'What do they reckon? One-hundred-thousand child prostitutes in and around the Ermita district of Manila alone . . .'

'That was his address.' Richard read it off the screen. 'Four forty, Santa Lucia, Ermita, Manila. Down by the docks, aptly enough. According to this, his defence was that he was just running an online dating agency on the side from his ship's duties. Online dating *for seven- to ten-year-old girls* according to the charges, Jim says' – he sat up, stretched, reached for his coffee and added – 'it's probably apropos of nothing, but you know there's also a flourishing trade in girls of all ages from Manila to Japan. All of it one-way. Most of it by sea . . .'

'Did Luzon Logging defend him as well?' grunted Nic.

'They did,' Richard confirmed. 'And they defended this man Nagase against a charge of pimping – with grievous bodily harm. This chap Izumi for murder. He's only just been released. And as for this fellow Ido . . .'

'Enough already,' said Nic. 'What's your point?'

'*Dagupan Maru* must be one of Luzon Logging's special *go anywhere do anything* ships. The kind that were smuggling protected hardwoods out of the supposedly protected forests of Indonesia during the end of the last century and the beginning of this. Destroying irreplaceable habitats and slaughtering endangered wildlife. Now they're moving priceless timber out of the reach of Japanese courts. And using men who are expert in dealing with Phillipine prostitution rackets at one end – and no doubt the Japanese Yakuza at the other end – to do it. What sort of cargo do you think Captain Yamamoto and his merry crew are used to dealing with?'

'OK. If I accept that they smuggle anything, including child prostitutes, what then?'

'Then I'd say they are clearly the last men on God's green earth that you want to be racing for Reona Tanaka's bottle – against your *daughter* . . .'

'Or against your *wife* . . .' countered Nic grimly.

'Not to mention six other women they are likely to catch up with in the middle of the least-visited corner of the emptiest ocean in the world . . .'

Nic was silent for a moment, eyes narrow, mind clearly racing as he sipped his coffee – apparently without tasting a drop. 'So, how do we warn them?' Nic asked at last.

'Radio, email, whatever will get through,' said Richard. 'But they are passing out of an area of weak signal into an area of almost no signal at all. And besides, speaking for Robin at least, if her blood's up she'll go for that bottle no matter who might be standing in her way.'

'Yeah. Liberty's the same,' admitted Nic. 'Once she gets the bit between her teeth, there's no stopping her.' He took another sip of coffee. 'So how do *we* get out there to watch their backs and keep them safe?'

'That's the trouble,' said Richard. 'There's nothing *there* to get out *to*.'

'Nothing?' echoed Nic. 'What do you mean, nothing?'

'Look at it like this,' said Richard. He downsized Jim Bourne's email to the toolbar and clicked up his Google Earth account. 'If *Dagupan Maru* had followed the normal course between Tokyo and Vancouver, it would have taken her up on a great circle route into the Bering Sea through this strait here between the Aleutian Islands off Alaska, see?' The screen went blue. The Aleutian Islands appeared, like a string of pearls between Alaska and the eastern end of Russia. The point of Richard's cursor automatically gave the LatLong reading wherever it pointed. He held it over the island he was indicating. Five two point seven; one seven four, it read.

'Yeah . . .' said Nic uncertainly.

'That airbase there on Shemya Island?' Richard insisted.

'Eareckson. I see it . . .' Nic nodded.

'You know what the next inhabited town south of there on latitude one seven four is?' asked Richard.

'No idea,' admitted Nic.

'Auckland.'

'*Auckland, New Zealand?*'

'Yup.' Richard nodded forcefully. 'Then Wellington. Then Antarctica. In fact, Antarctica is the *only* major land mass south of Eareckson. Because North Island is only that – an island. The only land south of Anchorage, Alaska is Hawaii. Hawaii is the only heavily populated area in the North Pacific Ocean.

Otherwise it's islands and atolls – Wake, Midway, Johnston, Howland.

'I've heard of Wake and Midway . . .' Nic frowned.

'Only because they're inhabited – mostly by United States forces personnel. You haven't heard of the others because nobody lives on them. Robin's heading for French Frigate Shoals as her next way station; it's the only land left on her route before she hits Vancouver – but there's no one actually living there. It's a deserted runway for emergency landings for flights between Honolulu and Midway.' Richard paused and looked over at his frowning friend. 'French Frigate Shoals will be the nearest land to where the bottle is due to end up,' he said forcefully. 'And French Frigate Shoals are the better part of a thousand miles south-west of where the bottle's due to be when they all reach it. You see the problem? There is literally nothing there.'

'OK,' countered Nic. 'So how do we put something there?'

'That's a good question,' admitted Richard. 'But it's only the first question of several if we're going down this road.'

'Fine,' snapped Nic, pulling himself erect once more and beginning to prowl round the room once more. 'So the first question is: how do we put something there? What's the next question?'

'The next question is,' answered Richard thoughtfully, 'how do we get ourselves out to whatever we do manage to put there?'

Out

Professor Satang S. Sittart left the Luzon Logging building in Quezon City, Manila, in a chauffeured Bentley Arnage at eight on the dot and took the ten a.m. PAL Airbus a380 from Ninoy Aquino International Airport to Narita International, Tokyo, two mornings later. Like his enemies, Richard Mariner and Nicholas Greenbaum, he had access to private jets but, like them, he took commercial flights when they were convenient.

One of the many benefits of Sittart's position and influence was that he hardly needed to bother with customs and immigration when he did go commercial. Two-hour check-in times and so forth were not for the likes of him. He stepped straight out of the tan leather luxury of the Arnage into the almost equal graciousness of the first-class departure lounge, therefore. And here, suited by Manila's leading tailor in black silk, shod by its leading custom cobbler in black Oxford shoes and carrying only the black kid-skin travelling case containing his laptop, he fitted right in and took his ease until an obsequious attendant informed him in a whisper that his flight was called.

One of the few benefits derived from the damage to his ears was that the professor no longer experienced any discomfort from changes in pressure, so he was happy to relax in his first-class accommodation as soon as his flight was airborne and allow the lissom air hostesses to fill his sparkling glass and his much darker fantasies equally efficiently and fully. Particularly as she had been unwise enough to grimace very slightly when she first saw the box-like hearing aids he wore clamped astride the polished ivory dome of his skull, though she had taken his laptop and put it in an overhead compartment with a modest smile.

But he soon shrugged off his darker musings, for he had more immediate matters to occupy his mind. And, oddly enough, they were almost identical to the preoccupations filling the minds of Richard Mariner and Nic Greenbaum. Except that the North Pacific Ocean, graveyard or not, was Professor Sittart's ocean. He had assets in place. And he knew exactly how and when he could reach them. Though he was still prone to lapsing into the deepest of brown studies as he finalized the details of exactly what he planned to do when he reached his final destination. The final destination, indeed, of several other people too. Or so he planned.

After a while he called the stewardess and asked her to reach down his laptop from the overhead compartment. The sight of her cafe au lait skin glimpsed as her blouse buttons strained apart was the last distraction he allowed himself before he placed the laptop on the table in front of him and began to scroll through its capacious memory.

A car was waiting for him as he exited Narita International Airport at four fifteen local time. He reset the all but priceless Patek Philippe on his wrist to one hour ahead of Manila time and then he sat silently in the back during the eighty-minute drive into the heart of the city. The laptop went on to a fold-down table, and the car, unlike the a380, allowed Internet access. He accessed his office files and read his most recent emails as he purred along the Kanto Highway like a tiger beginning its hunt. He did not look up from his work until the highway swung into the heart of the city and began a southward curve round Tokyo Bay.

Sittart favoured the Grand Hotel in Shinagawa and had taken a suite on its top floor facing east from which he could look over the bustling docks. The doorway from the corridor opened into a reception room with coffee table and soft chairs, a flat-screen TV that doubled as a mirror and a writing desk with Wi-Fi access. The silent air smelt faintly of lotus blossom and a vase of flowers stood on an occasional table by the window. A bathroom opened off one side and a bedroom off the other. A third door led through to an intimate little dining room whose corner windows allowed diners to overlook both the docks to the east and the lights of Takanawa District with the Sengaku-ji Temple beyond them to the north. The east-facing windows stood along one wall of the central reception room and then continued along the bedroom wall on the far side of the huge bed. Sittart walked straight to the reception room window and stood there, framed against the stormy sky, like a Rajah considering his domain.

The sun was setting away behind him and its rays pierced the ragged overcast strongly enough to send the hotel's long shadow creeping relentlessly out over the water and the myriad vessels working or waiting upon it. Sittart felt that was a pleasing symbol of his own spreading power and influence. He came as close as he ever came to smiling. He continued to stand, lost in thought, as the bellboy unpacked his case and put its contents in wardrobes, drawers and cupboards.

When the boy was finished, he looked across at the back of the hotel's latest guest, framed against the darkening sky with the strange boxes on either side of his head giving him an almost alien look. The bell boy decided against trying for his usual ten dollars. Certainly, the elegance of the luggage and the perfection of the tailoring – let alone the glimpse of the top-of-the-range Patek Philippe – would normally have promised ten dollars and maybe more. But there was something about the strange, silent guest that seemed to forbid even the fleeting intimacy of a tip.

Oddly for such a powerful man, Sittart added nothing to the pristine perfection of the accommodation. No character or personality. Once his personal effects were packed away, the room seemed almost to be empty again except for the slim laptop sitting in its kid-skin case on the coffee table. And, when the black-suited Sittart stepped into a shadow behind a massive silk curtain and apparently disappeared into the darkness there, the room seemed for an instant to be completely untenanted. Except that, the moment the door whispered closed behind the departing bellboy, his cell phone began to ring.

Sittart stepped back out into the middle of the room as he pulled the phone out of his pocket. He glanced at the screen before he pressed 'connect' and held the instrument close to his face, watching the display. The phone was cutting edge and top of the range, but Sittart used few of its more advanced functions. He had chosen it because it had a powerful internal speaker which was always set to maximum volume. The voice he heard matched the identification portrait he was watching. Both belonged to Nanaka Oda, one of the Tokyo port officials he kept on a secret retainer from one of Luzon Logging's many slush funds.

'Yes?' His Japanese was harsh – his natural tone in any language held something of a snarl.

'There are several matters which we need to discuss.' Her voice was steady. Unusually so. Most people talking to the professor tended to sound a little nervous.

'Go on.'

'Not on the phone. We need to meet.'

'You know where I am. Come here.'

She did not hesitate, which was, again, unusual, especially in a woman, the professor noted. 'My shift has just finished. Shall I come now?'

'At once.'

'Ten minutes.'

He broke connection and continued to stare at the woman's

ID photograph for a moment longer. Then he looked around the room with something of a start, as though he was seeing it for the first time. Which, in a way, he was. His mind, which had been distant since he had glanced at the coffee-coloured curve of the air hostess's breast, seemed to become aware of immediate sensations once again. And he realized that he was hungry.

Automatically, he glanced at the courtesy folder beside his laptop. Then he looked across to the old-fashioned telephone handset. He crossed to it and looked down, frowning. It was not the hands-free speaker phone he had ordered. He hated using old-fashioned handsets because he had to press the receiver to his boxlike hearing aid. He scrutinized the phone more closely, trying to work out how a hands-free function might be engaged. This consideration brought the subject of his almost dreamlike concentration back to mind again, but he dismissed all further thoughts of Robin and Richard Mariner for the time being. Nanaka Oda would be here soon. He would make her order food. Perhaps even allow her to share it with him while they talked. The idea appealed to him. She seemed to have some interesting potential. He picked up the red leather folder and opened it at the room service menu. After a moment of more silent consideration, he put it down again and crossed to the bathroom.

By the time the phone he hated so much began to ring, he had washed his hands and moved his laptop to the Wi-Fi-enabled desk. As the phone rang, so a red button flashed. He pressed it and so discovered that the phone did have a speaker facility not unlike his cell and he pressed it without raising the handset after all. 'Yes?'

'It is reception, Professor. There is a lady here. She says you are expecting her.' The voice was distant and tinny. He could only just make out the words. The phone was not really efficient enough for his requirements.

'I am!' he shouted, overcompensating. 'Tell her to come up at once.'

Sittart, angered by the business with the phone and piqued by her unflappable behaviour so far, chose to test Nanaka Oda a little further by opening the door wide on her first firm knock.

He stepped forward almost threateningly as he did so, filling the door frame so that she was confronted with him suddenly and at unexpectedly close quarters. They had never met. As far as he knew she had seen no pictures of him. Yet she did not flinch at the sudden confrontation.

Their eyes met, almost on a level. And hers did not flicker at the sight of his lean face, his high cheekbones, his hawkbeak nose, his shark-thin mouth, his long dark eyes or the square black boxes clamped over his ruined ears, as the air hostess's had done. She was exactly like her ID picture on his cell phone. Round-faced but with a determined set to her mouth and chin. Dark hair, dyed to keep any grey at bay. Incongruous button nose. Dark eyes with a steady, almost calculating gaze. She smelt of perspiration but her breath smelt of mints as his smelt of the Parma Violet lozenges he liked to suck. A square woman one size too big for her clothes, but who wore them tightly zipped and buttoned anyway. Very different to the sort of woman he usually dealt with. Or the sort of pretty, vulnerable creature that filled his darker fantasies.

'Nanaka Oda,' she introduced herself, and tensed her body to bow but then she stopped, realizing that she would head-butt him if she did so.

He stepped back. 'Come in,' he ordered.

Again, she did not hesitate. She marched straight past him and crossed to the coffee table, then turned to face him as he closed the door and leaned back against it for a moment, eyes and mind busy.

He considered her for a moment longer in silence. Although they had never met, he knew all about her. He did not employ – even clandestinely – anyone with whose secrets he was not intimately familiar. Such knowledge was just another aspect of the power he liked to exercise over others. He knew she was single. That she lived out in Fuchu and commuted in and out on the Keio Line – of which Luzon Logging was a shareholder. But not under that name.

A couple of years ago, aged forty, she had withdrawn from the lonely hearts circle through which she had hoped to find a husband. The competition from slim and pretty young executive rivals had become too fierce. She consoled herself nowadays with Western films of a romantic nature and chocolate, which was why her clothes didn't fit well any longer. And, in spite of the reasonable wage she earned, she couldn't afford new ones in the larger sizes she really needed.

She had fallen into Luzon Logging's clutches in her late thirties five years ago when a last desperate attempt at matrimony with a much younger man had merely led to an unwanted pregnancy and an expensive abortion which the child's father was too busy getting out of the affair to pay for. The failure of the relationship had turned out to be lucky for her. The fleeing lover had been involved in a hit-and-run car accident and would be in a wheelchair for the rest of his days. A particularly bitter irony because he – and, briefly, she – had been involved in the illegal drifting craze down on the Tokyo docks. According to the professor's sources, she had been a promising drifter – while he had been a rising star. There was a potent question on her secret Luzon Logging file as to whether she had been at the wheel of the car that had hit him and then run into anonymity.

Such matters would be broached later, Sittart decided; and he could be certain of the fact. One of his many accomplishments was that he had the ability to control conversations with uncanny precision. 'We have much to discuss,' he stated, speaking too loudly and with a snarl in his tone as usual. 'But I am hungry. You will order food first and we will talk while we eat.' It did not occur to him to ask if she was hungry or whether this arrangement suited her.

'As you wish,' she answered equably.

He picked up the room service folder and gestured at the telephone handset.

Another man might have said, 'The tempura vegetables are particularly good here . . .' as a way of explaining his choices; of negotiating an expression of her thoughts. Sittart never even thought of such irrelevancies. He glanced up to ensure she was holding the handset ready and he barked a series of staccato phrases at her, which she repeated to room service. Twenty minutes later they were in the private dining room with a selection of meat and fish karaage, tempura vegatables, tonkatsu pork, gyoza potsticker dumplings and fried yaki udon steaming on the table between them. The professor picked up the short, sharp Japanese chopsticks, moved his choice of the food on to his plate, Western style, and began to eat. She sat with her hands in her lap and watched him until he glanced at her and ordered, 'Eat!'

Then, while they consumed the food, they began to talk.

Two hours later, Nanaka Oda was sitting in a black Toyota Corolla AE86 without number plates, tapping the throttle gently. In her mind she was five years back in time, in a top-flight drifting car, hopped up to the max on adrenaline and ready for action. The Toyota was sitting invisibly with its lights off on the rain-slick roadway just along from the pierside bar called Rage. Had she turned off the motor, wound down the window and listened carefully, she would have heard the distant snarl of her erstwhile lover's friends, drifting down on the docks.

But Nanaka Oda had better things to do.

Beside her, on the front passenger seat lay the untraceable mobile the professor had given her, with which she had contacted the same number she had called from her office three days earlier to warn Richard Mariner about the mysterious death of the too-talkative pilot. Something she had done on the professor's orders. An act calculated to win a little trust from the foreign giant. Just enough to make him take a risk and agree to meet her in the hope of getting a little more information.

Unknown to the too-trusting Englishman, the professor had also supplied the taxi to bring him here – the Keio Line was by no means the only transport system in which Luzon Logging had a stake. As agreed, the taxi stopped a little way back from the bar, under the flare of a street light. Two unmistakable figures climbed out of the back, paid, and began to hurry forward.

Nanaka Oda was in action at once. Her black Toyota, lights out, as invisible in the night-time downpour as Professor Sittart had been in the shadows behind the curtain in his room, reared forward. The hunting roar of its motor masked by the relentless drumming of the rain. The ruthless woman, reliving the ecstatic moment of revenge against her faithless lover, span the wheel as the car leaped onward, sending the black wall of its side drifting up on to the pavement, leaping high over the unexpectedly substantial kerb, where the two tall figures were suddenly diving sideways and away.

Too late, she thought, contentedly, far too late, my dear.

And the rear of the car connected with a most satisfying double thud.

Debris

S oon after the debris from the Japanese earthquake sank below the northern horizon the wind swung round towards the west and gathered force. Liberty was forced to tack *Flint* across a choppy and increasingly restless ocean that began to run against them up through force six of the Beaufort scale towards full gale force seven with a sea state to match. It was very different sailing to what they had experienced at first where they had just given up and run before the wind down past Portland towards San Francisco.

This time the weather was clear, the sky a hard, dark cobalt all day, as though it was made of polished blue steel. The sea gathered itself in long corrugations, pushed relentlessly towards them by the hot, strong wind. White-topped, steep-sided walls of green water that would have been acceptable – at a stretch – if they could have met them head-on. But the only way of making the progress they so keenly desired was to cross the increasingly powerful near-gale in huge sawtooth tacks, which meant they mostly met the onrushing waves on the port or starboard quarter. The white tops exploded against them, over them, making the whole hull shudder as they spewed across *Flint*'s foredeck and hissed up to the cabin like serpents. Every now and then, while she butted grimly on, green water swamped in from the poop and only the straining wall of washboards kept the insides anything like dry. But with the increasingly weary women running up and down to change tack a couple of times each watch, it was never really anything like dry in actual fact.

Therefore, as *Flint* shouldered through the water, so she performed almost all of the movements that naval architects call the six degrees of freedom. She *surged* forward and occasionally backward; she *swayed* from side to side, she *heaved* up and down while she *heeled* this way and that under the wind. She *pitched* and she *yawed* with an enthusiasm that made standing difficult, sitting uncomfortable, sleep next to impossible, and staying in a bunk or hammock nothing more than a dream. It was lucky no one felt like eating because cooking was out of the question, and any food or drink choked down came straight back up again.

But the wind eased back to force five in the night. The sea calmed and by the end of the next day's sailing, they were pushing through force-three weather, smacking over wavelets that hardly stirred *Flint*'s hull out of the gentle forward motion Liberty's expert sail-handling was forcing out of an eight-knot westerly breeze. The sun beat down all afternoon and by the change of watch at seventeen hundred hours all their clothes and gear were dry enough to gather off the decks and stow away.

It was a Day B rotation so Liberty and Maya were on watch while Emma and Bella cleared away and broke open the food locker. As the sun settled westerly on the starboard quarter, Liberty held the con while Maya sat on the cabin roof with their binoculars round her neck and the four of them feasted on canned beef stew, canned mixed vegetables and pasta, followed by canned peaches and condensed milk, followed by coffee and more condensed milk.

At eighteen hundred, Maya tried to raise a signal on their communications equipment but nothing was coming through. The red dots on the computer screen were moving according to programming and predictions now – they hadn't been updated live for some time. After a while, she gave up with a shrug. Later, in the quiet of the darkness, cutting across that warm, steady westerly under a low, full moon and a jewel box full of massive tropical stars, she tried to raise a signal once again. This time she was more successful. She made her regular report and asked for news in return. *Katapult* had reported in recently as well; she was past French Frigate Shoals – by the skin of her teeth, apparently – and running steadily up to meet them. Even as the report came through, the red dots on the laptop screen reset themselves, jumping forward to show that both the yachts and the bottle they were racing towards had made better than predicted progress. Unaccountably, another dot appeared, flickering on and off almost like a warning light, seemingly coming down from the north. No one Maya talked to had any idea what that was. A marker of some kind that Captain Mariner had added to the display while he and Mr Greenbaum were in Tokyo.

'Ask them about Dad,' demanded Liberty. 'He's been out of contact for longer than usual. It's not like him.'

But there was seemingly nothing new to report in that quarter. And the signal dwindled away after a few more minutes in any case. 'That's strange,' said the sharp-eared Maya unthinkingly. 'They sounded almost shifty there. D'you think there's something they're not telling us?'

'Probably just fallout from the fact that the professor's gone off somewhere,' said Liberty. 'Like they told us, what, nearly a week ago now. That has to have put some kind of spanner in the works.'

'Yes,' said Maya uncertainly. 'That's what it'll be, I guess.'

They fell silent then and talked little more, both of them prey to suspicions of their own. The moon was still up when they changed the watch at four a.m., moved on to a southward tack as they did so, and the whole thing was completed almost as easily as it would have been by daylight.

The good thing about holding the watch through to this hour was that the berths were still warm, thought Liberty drowsily as she settled down twenty minutes later into the berth she shared turnabout with Emma. Her head was on a pillow which could double as a life preserver that still smelt faintly of Emma's favourite perfume. Her right ear was near the inner curve of the starboard quarter only a couple of inches away from the North Pacific, separated from the enormity of water by the moulded, strengthened polystyrene skin of the hull. And, where there had been a restless reeling thunder of surf only forty-eight hours earlier, now there was a restful hissing chuckle.

And, suddenly, distantly, hauntingly, the lost and lonely keening of whalesong echoing up out of untold depths below.

But as she fell into an exhausted sleep, she still found herself wondering about her father.

*   *   *

When she woke in the morning, she found she had far more immediate things to worry about.

It was the tapping that woke her. It inserted itself into a disturbingly vivid dream of some wild half-remembered New England heathland like the ghost of Cathy in *Wuthering Heights* rapping insistently on the window. She sprang awake, sea-wise enough to remember not to sit up. *Tap*, *tap*, *tap*, went the sound straight out of her dream, immediately beside her head on the outer wall of the hull. She looked at her watch, an Omega Seamaster her dad had bought her years ago. Eight forty-five a.m. Four hours' sleep was enough to be going on with, she thought, and rolled out. Still a little groggy, she walked along the deck of the dark cabin towards the brightness coming down from the open cockpit. Then, still half asleep, she climbed the steps up into the morning.

It was the smell she noticed first. A strange, half foreign, half familiar odour. Oily and yet not oil. Rancid, and yet too chemical to be rotting. A stink she associated somehow with coasts, with bays and harbours; yet lacking the metallic tang which told of rusty hulls and anchor chain. Still, something she associated with anchorages, not oceans. It was a smell she had never come across this far out; yet there was an immediacy about it. And even as she fought to get a mental handle on it, she thrust her head out into the daylight.

Emma was standing, grimly, at the wheel while Bella was sitting on the cabin roof. 'What is it?' asked Liberty as she clambered up and out. 'Something's not right.'

'Take a look for yourself,' advised Emma shortly.

Liberty pulled herself right up out of the cockpit to stand beside her crewmate at the con. The next thing she noticed after the tapping and the smell was the fact that the wind had fallen light. Maybe force two on the Beaufort Scale. *Flint* was only making way because Emma was as accomplished a yachtswoman as Liberty herself, and was still able to catch the light airs in *Flint*'s tall sails with almost magical efficiency.

Liberty's gaze fell from the full belly of the main sail to the immediate prospect of the waters through which her command was making her steady way. And her face closed into a frown of horrified disbelief. For *Flint* was sailing through a sea of increasingly solid garbage. The surface of the ocean was all but hidden by a layer of plastic. There were bottles of every size, shape and colour – though the colours were faded to a disturbingly garish range of pastels. Most of them were clear but clouding and encrusted with marine life forms of every sort from weeds to barnacles. It was these, she reckoned, that had been tapping on the counter just beside her head as *Flint* surged steadily through them like an icebreaker through ice floes. There were commercial fishing floats and buoys the size of big balloons, most of them originally Day-Glo orange but yellowing and whitening now. Plastic bins and barrels of every size, most of them round, but a few she could see that were square-sided too. Between the larger pieces of plastic debris there was scattered a mass of smashed and broken, rotting and disintegrating matter, all of it still the unnaturally bright hues that marked it as man-made rather than natural. It was only when she looked over the side and gazed straight down that she saw any actual water. And when she stood up beside Bella and looked into the distance straight ahead along their course, the whole of the ocean seemed to be one impenetrable Sargasso Sea of decomposing plastic rubbish.

'I thought it wasn't like this,' she said at last, stunned. 'I mean I know the Garbage Patch exists in some form. But I thought like Dad and Richard said that it was in nurdles and particles suspended in the current. There isn't supposed to be a Sargasso of the stuff! Christ, it looks as though it gets almost thick enough to stop us dead ahead.'

'Let's hope that's just an optical illusion,' said Bella practically. 'It couldn't really get that solid, surely!'

'Hasn't slowed us any so far,' added Maya. 'And we've been sailing through it since before dawn.'

'Jesus!' gasped Liberty. 'How big is it?'

'Let's hope it's not the size of Texas like they say,' answered Bella. 'Or we'll never find the professor's bottle.'

'The professor!' shouted Liberty. 'That must be it! His theory must be even more accurate than he thought. Perhaps the currents have speeded up enough to get all the debris spewing out of China, Japan and Western America here in double-quick time. My God! We have to tell somebody about this!'

'Chance'd be a fine thing,' said Emma grimly. 'Radio's offline again. The rest of the safety stuff's not much use either with all of this crap packed around us.'

'Not that we know how to contact the professor at the moment anyhow,' added Bella brightly.

'I wasn't thinking of him,' said Liberty. 'I was thinking of Dad or Richard. Someone who can do something about this . . .'

'Isn't that what we're doing?' demanded Emma trenchantly. 'Isn't that why we're all out here at the stinking shithouse end of nowhere?'

'I guess,' allowed Liberty. 'But I didn't really think that all *this* would be here too!' And as if to emphasize her words, *Flint*'s starboard quarter rammed into a big orange buoy like an American football quarterback hitting his opposite number.

'Think it does get much thicker than this?' demanded Bella suddenly sounding nervous.

'*Hey!*' came Maya's irate bellow from below. 'What the f— Did we just collide with? Isn't anyone on *watch*, for Christ's sake?'

'Oh, great!' whispered Emma. 'Now we've woken the Wicked Witch of the West.'

'And her Witchiness is *pissed*!' added Bella. 'I hope you have your ruby slippers, Dorothy, or it's flying monkey time for you!'

Maya staggered up and pushed Liberty aside. 'What in hell's name?' she started. Then she stopped dead, staring around, goggle-eyed. 'Jesus Christ!' she said. 'What's that *smell*?'

And the answer hit both Emma and Liberty at the same time. It was the same smell that had nearly gassed the girls in the engine room of the ghost ship *Un Maru*.

Shoals

I t was not until *Katapult* reached French Frigate Shoals that Robin and her crew understood just how much damage the collision with the humpback whale had actually caused.

It was one of the multihull's most advanced features that the sensors for her sonar alarm system were located in the bows of the outriggers and the receiver in the central hull. This allowed 3D mapping of the submarine terrain over which they sailed. But its accuracy depended on the precise emission of the sonar pulses in the first place. The further out of phase they went, the more inaccurate the system would become.

Flo's focus on repairing the hinge – not to mention Robin and Akelita's adventure of the yellow crazy ants on Johnston Island – simply overwhelmed anything she might have done to check any further internal damage which could have resulted from the impact. Not that she could have done much, to be fair, without getting *Katapult* right up out of the water in any case. To make matters worse, the sonar worked well enough on the exit from Johnston Atoll to put their minds at rest and then was not really required for the deep-water run up to the shoals. Consequently there was no need to test or question its accuracy until *Katapult*'s pre-planned route brought her racing across the wind to the next way station on her carefully deliberated course.

By the grace of God they arrived at French Frigate Shoals with the dawn and the sun rising out of a calm sea into a cloudless sky polished by the steady trade wind, and framing the tower of La Perouse dead ahead so spectacularly that they could not miss it. The basalt islet, remnant of the solid heart of the long-dead volcano whose coral-covered caldera curved behind it, appeared with the sun dead ahead, and Rohini who held the watch sitting on the cabin roof, called back to Robin at the wheel, 'I see it! Robin, you should take a look at this, it looks exactly like an old-fashioned frigate under full sail! You'd think we were running down on the Flying Dutchman himself!'

'If you can see La Perouse,' Robin called back to her, 'then the shoal is lying right across our course. You should be able to see East Island behind La Perouse soon, then Bare Island just behind that.' She closed her eyes for a moment, remembering the image of the shoal she had seen on Google Earth as she was planning this leg of the voyage. It looked disturbingly like a foetus lying on its side in the ocean, with a large head under the bigger islelets to the north and a long spine curling south. But she could not bring herself to describe it in these terms. 'If I remember the pilot correctly,' she called instead, 'there's about fifteen nautical miles of reefs and shoals on a north-south curve between Shark Island in the north and Disappearing Island in the south. If you think of it as Robin Hood's bow, La Perouse is where the feather of his arrow would be. And where the arrow's pointed is right where we're headed. Arrow straight and arrow fast, with any luck.'

'That's very romantic,' said Akelita, popping her head up out of the cabin. 'But who the heck is Robin Hood?'

'I've spent enough time teaching you seamanship, girl,' teased Robin. 'Don't get me started on culture as well! Come here and check the sonar. The bloke who named this place – *le Compte de La Perouse* – nearly lost both his French frigates here, you know.'

'*You* taught *me* seamanship!' cried Akelita, theatrically outraged. 'There is nothing I don't know about the sea!'

Robin changed course as *Katapult* came up to the black tower of La Perouse. She swung on to a more northerly heading but she found that her route across the rolling ocean was limited by the trade wind streaming down towards them. It had swung to the north-west in the night and the further northward Robin pointed *Katapult*'s three bows, the more she found herself coming close to the eye of the wind, and even *Katapult* could not sail directly into a north-westerly trade wind. She stayed on the more easterly tack, therefore, aiming her command at the northern outreach of the reef that lay across their path. Planning to skim across the head of the gigantic foetus lying just beneath the surface in her imagination. Hopefully without damaging her command: without waking the sleeping blue baby. 'Keep an eye on that sonar,' she said to Akelita round a mouthful of their last breakfast bacon. 'I'm going to have to run through the northerly shoals south of Shark Island and come out between Trig Island and Tern Island where the airport is.'

'What!' laughed Akelita. 'Another airport in the middle of nowhere?'

'Like Johnston,' Robin answered. 'It's just an island with a landing strip taking up almost the whole of it. Unmanned. Emergencies only. But this one hasn't been a nuclear test site, missile launch pad or a dumping ground for chemical weapons and whatnot.'

'Even so, I don't want to go anywhere near it!' Akelita announced with a shudder. 'There might be *ants*!'

The wind picked up, pushing *Katapult* ever faster into the curving wall of shoals. The fact that Robin was holding her sleek vessel as close to the eye as she dared, set up even more tension between the wind pressure and the tall sails, driving the multihull ever more swiftly forward. Her starboard outrigger began to porpoise in and out of the surface. Cross-waves, born of the westerly edge of the trade, spread across the usually placid shallows ahead. The still-low sun glanced dazzlingly off the restless ridges, concealing the few white horses that were beginning to spring up as the weather crept relentlessly up the Beaufort scale.

The glittering combination of gleaming sun and dancing water hid from Rohini the upthrusting coral shoals Akelita's damaged sonar was reading as lying several metres deeper than they actually were.

It was Flo who saw the danger as she came up to wash the breakfast things. It had been their practice to put their consumable waste over the side. Everything else stayed aboard. But crusts, rind and bacon fat would only add to the welfare of the sea and the creatures within it by their reckoning, so over the side they went. And after she dumped them, Flo leaned down to push the unbreakable plastic plate into the surface of the water racing past *Katapult*'s central hull, aiming to give it a bit of a scrub. And as she did so, she saw a coral head race past, seemingly just beneath the surface. She paused, frowned, looked again, all too well aware of the tricks refraction can play with anyone looking into the water. But no. Another heave of reef sped by, covered in a fine scalp of green and yellow weed, alive with tiny jewel-bright fish. It wasn't an optical illusion: the top of the shoal was only inches beneath their speeding keel. If they had been in *Flint*, with the centreboard down they'd have been wrecked already.

'Akelita!' bellowed Flo. 'We're about to run aground. Where's the sonar?'

'I'm on it!' answered Akelita. 'It says we have three metres clearance all round!'

'Three centimetres maybe! Robin. Watch out! There's something badly wrong here!'

Robin and Flo had sailed together for a good long time. They trusted each other without question or hesitation. On the Australian's first call, therefore, Robin put *Katapult*'s helm hard over, loosened the main sheet and snatched the wind out of her sails. The boom swung dangerously this way and that but the crew had rehearsed the manoeuvre often enough to keep their heads low and hang on tight until the wild motion slowed. Stopped. The way came off her surprisingly swiftly and in a matter of moments she was idling, rocking a little lumpily in the chop, with her loose sails thundering angrily and her rigging whimpering in the wind. Robin tightened the main sheet enough to stop the boom swinging, but not enough to fill the sails again.

'All right,' she ordered crisply. 'Check it out!'

Rohini and Akelita joined Flo at the sides, looking anxiously down into the limpid water. And their eyes immediately told them the bitter truth. The sonar had been lying all along. It was something akin to a miracle that they were still afloat.

'What does the GPS say?' asked Robin. 'Maybe we can trust that!'

Akelita came back into the cockpit. 'Two three point eight five degrees north by one six six point two seven degrees west,' she answered.

'That's as near to the middle of nowhere as you can get I guess,' called Flo. 'We can't stay here, Robin.'

'Damn right. We'll motor out along the course I'd planned – or as near as we can.'

'How'll we manage that?' demanded Akelta.

'The old-fashioned way,' Robin answered brutally. 'Life jackets and lifelines on please, ladies, and get ready for a hard day's work!'

Akalita went astride the bow of the starboard outrigger and Rohini went astride the port one. They each carried a boathook the better part of two metres in length. Flo went on the fore-peak of the central hull with a weighted line knotted every boathook length, which was as close as they could come to fathoms. While the three of them were getting into position, Robin engaged the power and the computer so she could furl the restless sails. Then she engaged the motor and began to ease the restless vessel forward across the choppy water. Flo threw the weighted line forward and gathered it back in, testing the depth as the bright cord came vertical, while the two outriders sat ready to fend off any coral heads that came too close for comfort.

'By the *Mark*, *Twain*!' sang out Flo cheerfully.

'Thank you very much, Samuel Longhorn Clements,' called back Robin, relieved to find her crew still so chirpy. 'Do you actually mean that we have two fathoms clearance?'

Flo answered in the affirmative and threw the plumb again.

'Let's just hope reports of her demise *remain* a little premature,' added Rohini. 'Though if she has nearly four metres beneath her, I have to say I have a damn sight less than one beneath me. Coral head coming up! Hard a'starboard!'

And so, very much in the manner of *Broussole* and *Astrolabe*, the frigates commanded by Jean Francois de Galaup, Comte de la Perouse, who felt his way across these very waters while Robin's ancestors were celebrating Guy Fawkes day in 1786, *Katapult* proceeded through the shoals, guided by soundings that reminded the intrepid skipper of the *Hornblower* and *Aubrey* novels she had read with so much pleasure in her youth, shared so enthusiastically with her darling Richard and read to her children in turn.

By nightfall, Trig Island was a shadowy lump low on *Katapult*'s starboard and Tern Island's square end and higher runway stood above and behind the port, framed against the sunset as La Perouse had been against the dawn. They hadn't stopped for a midday break and they didn't plan to try reporting in until they were clear of the shoal. Because if they weren't out of here by dark, then they really were in serious trouble.

Dead ahead was an intermittent wall of breakers hushing smoothly over the coral-fanged curve of ancient drowned volcanic caldera rim. Robin glanced down at the GPS. The break in the disturbing wall of foam was dead ahead at two two point eight eight degrees north, one six six point two six degrees west. But, of course, what lay between the piles of surf standing like snow-drifts on her right hand and her left was an inrushing current of hard green water that seemed intent on either pushing her back or forcing her to one side or the other. And as she pushed the throttles smoothly forward, yelling, 'Watch out, Akelita! Keep

your eyes peeled and your boathook ready, Rohini!' She prayed
that the smooth green gap was wide enough to let her command
out into the deep water once again.

'You've got three fathoms under the keel,' yelled Flo. 'Keep
her steady and straight ahead.'

'You've three meters at the side here,' called Akelita.
'Though it's hard to be sure because of the foam. It feels like
it's piled up high above my head. And it's starting to come
down on me.'

'Here too,' bellowed Rohini, her voice beginning to get lost
beneath the roaring of the surf, the hissing of the current and the
throbbing of the motor pushing *Katapult* relentlessly forward.

Feeling as though *Katapult* must actually be sailing uphill
over the inrushing heave of clear green water, Robin gunned
the motor to the maximum and threw the intrepid little vessel
towards the open water. Looking straight ahead and holding the
wheel steady by an almost superhuman effort, she thrust
Katapult into the narrow gap. Both of the outriggers vanished
beneath the avalanches of foam tumbling inwards from the piles
of breakers riding up over the reef-topped rim. Even Flo at the
forepeak of the main hull seemed to vanish into spray. The
walls of white water came rushing up towards Robin with a
seemingly majestic inevitability, and yet she found she only
just had time to slam the cover over the cabin back hard against
the washboards before she too was seemingly caught beneath
a waterfall of foam, then *Katapult* was through. The roaring
was coming from behind her. Her boat was rushing downhill.
There was sun on the back of her streaming head. She blinked
the salt foam out of her eyes and looked for her three friends.
And they were all there, miraculously still in place. Clinging
on for dear life. But there. Safe.

'Rohini? Are you all right?' called Robin.

'Fine,' answered the Indian yachtswoman. 'But promise me
we're never going to do anything like that again.'

'I promise!' answered Robin feelingly. 'Come inboard as
quickly as you can.'

As Akelita and Rohini obeyed, both still miraculously possessed
of their boathooks, Flo paused for one last instant. Cast her lead
and let it run. And run and run and run between her fingers. 'No

bottom on this line,' she called at last. 'Looks like we're safely through.'

'We'll tidy up, dry off and report in – if we can raise a signal,' Robin decided. 'Then we'll have something really special for dinner. Akelita, what've we got?'

'We have the last of the frozen Chinese curry from the Vaiaku Lagi Hotel,' answered Akelita. 'That was really special. To me at least, because it reminds me of Tuvalu and home.'

And something about the answer made Robin think of Richard; probably the fact that it was in the upstairs room in the Vaiaku Lagi Hotel where she had last slept with him.

But thinking of Richard suddenly seemed to cloud the otherwise sunny relief at having brought her command and her crew safely through the shoals and back out into the deep ocean once again. And being under way again, with sails up and sheets taut, skimming across a steady trade wind as the sun set behind the rim of the watery world astern. And, as it turned out, nothing about the contact she made after dinner on a clear and steady radio signal served to put her worried mind at rest.

For neither Richard nor Nic Greenbaum was available.

Neither, in fact, had been in contact for a couple of days – apparently since Jim Bourne at London Centre had sent them a whole lot of information, to the Mandarin Oriental Hotel in Tokyo, about a ship called the *Dagupan Maru*.

Mess

'**B**ut what shall we do?' demanded Dr Aika Rei, and not for the first time. 'If we do not lead them to the bottle and give them the ticket they will hurt us – and I do mean *hurt* us – or kill us. Or both.'

'And if we *do*, then they will still kill us,' answered Reona Tanaka, terrified, glancing round their cabin, half convinced it must be wired for sound. Still unaware that the bedroom was also wired for video.

'They will kill *you*,' spat Aika Rei, making death sound

like the easy option. 'They have other plans for *me*!' She shuddered.

'But surely *he* will help us. He is an educated man, he must be . . .'

'Who?' Her face was blank. Uncomprehending. 'Who do you suppose will help us?'

'This professor they say is coming aboard. Professor Sittart.'

'As far as I know, he is their leader,' she hissed. 'He's more likely to hold the gun that kills you. Or to hold my clothes while his men . . .'

'But that's ridiculous! Things like that do not happen in real life!'

'But I overheard them talking about it!' she shouted.

'Well, all I can say is that you must have misunderstood what you heard. Or *over*heard.' His face was white. He looked desperately around the cabin.

Aika Rei's expression told him all too clearly what she thought of that suggestion. And of his fear.

So he tried another tack. 'The captain seems a civilized person,' he whispered forcefully. 'Perhaps we should try talking to him.'

But she shook her head again, frowning. 'He must be either as corrupt as his crew – or so stupid that he does not understand what's going on. In either case he will be of no help to us – and going to him may well just make things worse.'

'OK,' he temporized. 'What do you want to do?'

'We must wait,' she decided. 'Pretend we suspect nothing. Behave as normal. We are not the only ones heading for the bottle, remember. If we can somehow control the timing, then we could get there at the same moment as the other people trying to reach it. Perhaps they can help us.'

Reona thought, *But they are eight unarmed women on two little yachts. How can they possibly help us?*

While Aika Rei thought, *At the very least there will be eight more women to be shared among the crew and that has to make things easier for me.*

But the matter was decided and the plan agreed.

As *Dagupan Maru* ploughed south towards the red dot on Reona's map, therefore, the young professor and the lovely doctor behaved as though they were determined to maintain their fiction of being honeymooners, suspecting there was nothing in the world amiss. Though it was, perhaps, fortunate that Sittart was no longer taking any interest in the video footage from the bedroom, for it was here that the fiction of being insatiable lovers broke down.

The crew realized at once that something had changed. They picked up on his fear as accurately as a pack of hounds. But, like any group of people forced to rub along together in a confined space for a long time, they were adept at concealing suspicions. And besides, the first officer made it plain that the professor was coming aboard – and that he might well be interested in more than the bottle and the ticket it contained. Even those who knew the professor only by reputation knew the rules. You could look. But you'd better not touch.

So Reona and Aika Rei were able to proceed in blissful ignorance of the fact that they were fooling no one. And a kind of routine was maintained in which Engineer Senzo Tago came and consulted the laptop every morning, just as though he had no chance to see it on a slave monitor when he was working on the bridge. It was his job to keep the red dots bright, and Reona remained ignorant of the fact that First Officer Sakai was employed on the bridge at least twice a day in plotting the precise positions of the bottle and the ship on their ever-moving courses, calculating the constantly varying track for *Dagupan Maru* that would bring them most swiftly together. It was a routine that only three things could change, Sakai Inazo reasoned grimly as he worked. Landfall. Catching up with the bottle. The arrival of Professor Sittart. And the wise officer knew precisely in what order those events would occur.

Reona saw it first because now that *Dagupan Maru* was coming up to 3,400 nautical miles out of Tokyo docks, even the ship's powerful radio equipment was finding it hard to maintain the laptop signal, so he and Electrical Engineer Tago were back up on top of the bridge house where they had first met, in the massive calm of a mid-ocean morning. Tago was trying to find a way of boosting the signal in order to firm up the four red dots on Reona's laptop. 'What's that?' asked Reona. 'Up on the sky behind us.'

'Must be a bird,' answered the electrical engineer, glancing up from the radio antenna. 'We sometimes see albatrosses. I've tried to shoot them. I hear they make good eating. And it's *astern of us* not *behind us*.'

'But it glinted!' said Reona. 'It looks like its metal.'

'Metal! You must be seeing things!' jeered the engineer. But he straightened anyway. The two men stood shoulder to shoulder and looked up at a black dot which appeared to be approaching out of the wide blue sky. And it did indeed catch the sun and glint, suddenly, like a diamond against the royal blue of the heavens.

'Shit!' said Senzo, the instant it did so. 'You're right! It's a chopper. And that can only mean one thing! Fuck . . .' And he was gone.

Reona stood for a moment longer, looking up in simple disbelief. They were more than three thousand miles from land, he thought numbly. How on earth could a helicopter fly such a vast distance? Who on earth would want to make a helicopter fly so far or have any reason at all for doing so?

The answer hit him like a blow from a heavyweight boxer, and he too was gone down into the bridge house like a startled rabbit.

The whole atmosphere aboard had changed in the few moments he had been up on the deck. There were crewmen bustling about tasks and duties they had never bothered with up until now. He saw Captain Yamamoto heading purposefully for the bridge, and glanced at his watch in simple shock – the captain had never surfaced before midday during the whole trip so far. He arrived at their cabin to find Aika Rei being bustled out of the accommodation that they had shared. 'We're being moved,' she explained, her eyes wide with terror. 'They say they need the owner's suite at once. What is going on?'

'There's a helicopter approaching,' Reona answered, suddenly cold with the echo of her naked fear. 'It must be Professor Sittart.'

The helicopter settled on a landing area Reona hadn't even registered as existing on the poop deck. He and Aika Rei were part of the welcoming committee even though neither of them particularly wanted to be there. But the professor had radioed his orders ahead, First Officer Sakai informed them brusquely, as he picked them up and herded them aft.

Captain Yamamoto was there, together with several crew members the shy academic did not recognize as general purpose seamen Izumi, Nagase and Ido. Aika Rei knew them as soon as they started speaking, however, and pressed herself even more closely against Reona, simply shaking with fear.

They all bowed in the face of the downdraught and the threat of the rotors as the helicopter settled thunderously on to the deck, then there was a moment of stasis as the motor died and the rotors slowed.

After half-a-dozen heartbeats, a door in the side of the chopper slid back and an elegant foot shod in black Oxford shoes appeared, followed by a long leg clothed in black shot-silk trousers. A tall, skeletal man with a skull like a huge ivory ball stepped nimbly down as Captain Yamamoto rushed solicitously forward. Aika Rei, seeing the black boxes clamped so brutally over his ears, gasped with shock and horror.

But the stranger turned and reached back into the helicopter cabin as though unaware of the captain and his welcoming committee. He handed out a plump, square woman whose body was at least two sizes too big for the severe grey business suit she was wearing. She swept her short, black hair out of her eyes with a square, short-fingered hand as she arrived on the deck and looked coldly around.

Yamamoto bobbed before them until the tall man deigned to notice him. 'Ah, Captain,' he said with a snarl in his voice that carried easily across the deck. 'Allow me to introduce my associate, Miss Nanaka Oda. You will need to arrange accommodation for her. I trust my suite is prepared?'

'Of course, Professor. Everything is just as you ordered . . .'

As the three of them crossed the deck, Sakai sent his crew men to get the luggage and Reona was struck by the wide berth the three seamen gave the tall man and the square woman beside him. He looked around, wondering what he was expected to do next, intensely aware that Aika Rei was tugging insistently at his arm, hoping to escape before the professor noticed them. 'We have been in the air for two solid days,' the professor was saying

to Yamamoto. 'Hopping from one ship to another, with our helicopter like a dragonfly jumping across lily pads on a pond. It is
fortunate that Luzon Logging has so many vessels in the area.
But even so . . .' His voice trailed off, and suddenly Reona was
at the centre of his regard. 'Ah,' said Sittart, modifying his snarl
to a growl. 'This must be Professor Tanaka. A pleasure, Professor.'
His voice dismissed Reona, then lingered. 'And this must be his
lovely assistant . . .'

Aika Rei did not appreciate being addressed as though she
was some kind of an itinerant magician's stooge but, like Reona,
she bowed.

Sittart's focus shifted once again. 'So, Captain, after we have
settled in and freshened up we would appreciate a proper meal.
And I note that it is almost time for the midday mess in any
case. We would be very pleased if the professor and his assistant
could join us. *And*, of course, yourself and your off-watch officers,
if that is convenient.'

Reona and Aika Rei were bundled below. The cabin they had
been assigned was reassigned to the strange, square woman Sittart
had brought with him. Their luggage was simply thrown out into
the corridor once more and despite increasingly irate questions,
Reona could not discover where the pair of them were supposed
to be sleeping tonight. They were forced to use the washrooms
they had been assigned when their en suite had apparently failed.
And Reona was grateful that Aika Rei at least did not need to
shower. But by the time they were hurried back towards the mess
the question of their new sleeping arrangements had still not
been settled.

'Ask them!' hissed Aika Rei angrily. 'This simply isn't good
enough. We need to know where we will be sleeping tonight!
And if you won't make a fuss then I certainly will!'

Reona was not in the best of moods, therefore, when Aika Rei
and he were pushed into the dining area after a lengthy and
fruitless squabble with Sakai about their accommodation. The
Professor and Nanaka Oda were already there, attended by
Yamamoto and a range of officers that Reona had hardly met.
Sakai was notable by his absence, but Senzo Tago was there in
his place. The rest of the men – and one woman – were locked
in animated conversation as the food was brought in from the

galley. Reona only recognized the Indonesian cuisine because he had lectured more than once at the University of Manila. *Nasi goreng* fried rice was accompanied by skewers of pork and chicken *satay*, a side dish of *sayur lodeh* coconut sauce and by a fragrant *semur daging* beef stew which must have been ordered via the radio – for it took hours to prepare.

The professor did not seem to register their arrival as they were bundled into seats at the long captain's table. The food was in dishes down the centre and the two latecomers were hesitant about reaching forward to serve themselves. 'Don't be shy,' ordered Sittart suddenly, looking at Aika Rei. 'There's plenty for all. And the chef has outdone himself, I think. There is *gado gado* coming if you would prefer noodles.'

'No,' choked Aika Rei. 'I'm not hungry. This is fine . . .'

'Professor?' enquired Sittart civilly. 'Rice or noodles for you?'

'Actually, sir, I'm not hungry either . . .'

'As you wish,' answered Sittart accommodatingly, and a lively conversation sprang up, dominated by the professor himself. What did the officers think of the unfortunate rumours about the dangers of rubbish accumulating in the North Pacific? he enquired. They all decided that it was mere scaremongering.

What did they think about the possibility of plastic debris actually collecting there as though a Sargasso Sea might be created from mankind's detritus? he probed. Ridiculous, they all agreed.

At last the professor's long, cold eyes rested on Reona as though on an opponent in a duel. 'And you, Professor Tanaka, what do you believe?' whispered Sittart, with all the sick pleasure of a bully preparing his victim for a beating.

Reona pulled himself erect. 'I believe the danger is real and imminent, Professor,' he answered. 'That is why Captain Mariner, Mr Greenbaum and I embarked on the experiment with the bottle we are all currently pursuing. And, I have to say, sir, that the fact we are still pursuing it makes my proposition all the more likely!'

'Good,' growled Sittart gently. 'Very good. A man of conviction.' He looked around the suddenly silent table with his long, cold eyes. 'What we have here, gentlemen – ladies – is a man of conviction.'

'It is more than mere conviction,' snapped Reona, goaded. 'The experiment has proved it to be true. The currents are swirling the rubbish out here in solid pieces before it can break up. The bottle, Cheerio, is still just ahead of us. It is still broadcasting its locator signal. We know exactly where it is. Engineer Tago, is this not so? Its precise location is on the laptop for anyone to see! It is still out there in the water, still afloat, still broadcasting! My theory is correct. Our ship will come up with it within a day or so and then we will recover it. Then you will see!'

'Engineer Tago, is this true?' whispered Sittart. 'Is the location of the bottle on the laptop? Is it accurate? Reliable? Will we come up with it within a day or so? Do we need the professor here to guide us?'

'It is true, sir,' answered Tago. 'The signal is strong and true. It shows clearly and reliably on the laptop and has done so for a week. The professor has shown me how to access the information so we do not need him at all.'

'Good,' whispered Sittart, his voice like sand sliding over shot silk.

He produced a gun from beneath the table like a conjurer making a rabbit appear. And before anyone could react, he shot Reona through the middle of his forehead with it. Aika Rei screamed at the top of her lungs with shock but the noise was lost beneath the deafening clap of the gunshot in the enclosed space of the room. There was a surprising amount of smoke – enough to obscure the assassin for a moment, but not his victim. The unfortunate meteorologist jerked backwards as though someone had punched him very hard in the face. The metal wall on the far side of the dining room boomed like an untuned gong as the bullet hit it. A mark that looked unsettlingly like a large blackberry appeared in the middle of Reona's high forehead. A wisp of smoke seemed to issue from the middle of it. Taking his chair with him, he slid back for perhaps a metre as he sprayed brain matter out of the rear of his shattered skull. Then he slumped on to one side, fell off the chair on to the deck and lay still.

Sittart put the smoking gun on to the table as the echo of the outrageous noise began to fade away. No one at the table moved a muscle or said a word. 'That's settled, then,' observed the professor, as though discussing an argument of no real importance. 'And so is the matter of accommodation that was apparently worrying the professor so much. Heave his body over the side when we have finished here and put his woman's clothing back into the owner's suite with mine. She will be sleeping with me from now on.'

As so many things aboard *Dagupan Maru* seemed to, it fell to First Officer Sakai to clear up the professor's mess. After the meal was finished and everyone had left the dining room, he dragooned seaman Ido into mopping the floor and washing the walls while Nagase and Izumi wrapped the corpse in plastic sheeting and carried it up to the weather deck.

Here Sakai paused, looking out across the wide afternoon with something of a frown. There was a strange taint on the air. It smelt like diesel fuel, mixed with rust and rottenness. If there was an odour of dead water, he thought, this would be it. Then he shrugged, not being a particularly imaginative man, and gestured to his seamen to dump the late Professor Tanaka overboard.

Inevitably, as they did so, Sakai looked down to see the corpse fall. And he was surprised to observe that his ship seemed to be pushing through a floating island made of rubbish. And Tanaka fell on to this. There was a hollow *thud* rather than a final *splash*. He did not sink immediately. Instead, his body lay across two sizeable oil drums that had been lashed together with yards of indestructible plastic rope. The wind took the sheeting and blew it wide. Just for a moment, Sakai found himself staring into the eyes of the man he had brought aboard little more than a week ago. The barrels beneath Tanaka stirred, thumped together with a doleful *Boom!*

The dead man nodded as though he knew some secret deep beyond the living man's comprehension, and began to slide silently into the oily water.

Sakai went back to his cabin to wash – only to find it occupied by Sittart and his unnerving protégé. As he stooped to pick up the kit that was now piled in the corridor, in preparation for moving the second officer down the pecking order of accommodation, he overheard a snatch of conversation.

'This is a lovely cabin, Professor. It is larger than my rooms at home.'

'Don't give it a thought, my dear. Nothing is too good for the woman who has settled some old scores for me and rid me of two of my bitterest enemies.'

American Gambit

R ichard woke up.
He knew he was alive because of the pain. This came as a relief as well as a surprise. The last things he remembered with any clarity were being hit by the side of a skidding car and deciding, as he flew backwards through the rain-filled Tokyo air, that his luck had finally run out. But now, providentially, his head hurt. He opened his eyes and the brightness hurt. He moved his head and his neck hurt. He tensed to sit up and discovered that his whole body hurt. He relaxed back on starched, unfamiliar pillows and thought. *Where am I and what's going on?* At least thinking didn't hurt.

'Hey,' said Nic's familiar drawl, 'I think he's coming to, Jim.' And even that quiet observation hurt because Richard's ears hurt. And also because it necessitated a physical reaction and a reply.

Richard opened his eyes again. The painful brightness resolved itself into a white-painted room with two anxious faces standing at a bed foot looking down at him. 'Hey, Nic,' Richard croaked. 'You OK?'

'Yeah. And it's all thanks to you that I am. I owe you one. You pushed me out of the way and took most of the force. You're one big bruise. Head to foot.'

'Bruise?' asked Richard, flooding with relief. 'Nothing broken?'

'Doctors say not,' answered Jim Bourne. 'You'll be stiff and sore for a while and you've had pretty severe concussion, but no major breakages internal or skeletal. Apparently the kerb was enough to break the car's momentum and knock it offline. It's been found down by the docks. Burned-out. No clues. Could have been an accident as likely as anything else, given the amount of *drifting* that goes on down there.'

'Police?' asked Richard.

'Officer Izawa,' answered Nic. 'At some length. But as far as he's concerned, it was just a case of two reckless tourists bumbling about in a dangerous place and getting involved in the kind of accident that happens down there all the time. No deaths. No clues. No case.'

'Of course.' Richard nodded. Regretted it. 'How long have I been out?' he asked, easing his shoulders in preparation for more decisive movement. *Bruises,* he thought. *How bad can that be, after all?*

'In and out for two days and a night. It's eight a.m. now. Jim and I just got here. Jim flew in yesterday after you had that talk with Audrey at Crewfinders.'

Did I? thought Richard. *Then how come I don't remember . . .*

'But they say you slept well last night,' observed Jim cheerfully. 'You've had periods when you were compos mentis enough to be throwing out orders like Bligh of the *Bounty . . .*'

'And others when you were more like Rip Van Winkle,' added Nic.

'Two days!' Richard sat up without further thought. Discovered he could handle the pain. 'We've got to get moving!' Swung his legs out of bed and thought for a moment he must be wearing purple pyjamas. 'Get moving,' he repeated a little less decisively.

'Yeah,' said Nic. 'You made that clear when you were in Captain Bligh mode. But you're the only one holding us up now that Jim's here to hold the fort in Tokyo – and everything's in place like you ordered.'

Richard had only the vaguest memory of giving any orders at all but he wasn't about to admit this for fear of being held back to undergo further medical checks – especially now that he was getting the measure of just how badly bruised he was. He glanced automatically at his left wrist but there was a bandage round it instead of his trusty Rolex. His blood went cold with fear that the beloved timepiece might be broken.

'Eight a.m., local time,' confirmed Jim helpfully. He handed

over the watch from a bedside table and Richard checked it
– at least it seemed undamaged – and slipped it over the
bandage.

'What is this place?' he asked as he began to pull himself out
of bed, gathering the hospital robe more tightly as he moved.

'The Fuku Sunshan private hospital,' answered Nic. 'It's the
one my guys at Tokyo Greenbaum use. Part of the health plan.
You became an honorary employee when you saved the boss's
butt. As far as the health plan goes, anyway.'

'How close to the airport is it?' asked Richard as he tried to
push himself erect. And failed. Sat down again and gathered his
strength.

'Close enough,' answered Jim. 'And all your kit is here, packed
and ready.'

'Christian Hassang and the folks at the Mandarin said *Hi* and
Bye,' supplied Nic. 'They sent the flowers.' He gestured and
Richard looked through a doorway into a private room which
seemed to have become a greenhouse.

'I need a laptop and an update,' grated Richard. 'And some
clothes.' He tried again. And this time he made it to his feet.

'Clothes and laptop are next door somewhere under the
greenery,' answered Nic. 'Update's easy. All three vessels are
closing with the bottle. We're looking at maybe a day – probably
no more than that. Time's tight.'

'How are the girls?' demanded Richard, taking his first steps
like an over-adventurous toddler.

'They seem OK,' answered Nic shortly. 'Communications
come and go. We didn't tell them about our little contretemps.
Or about the lottery ticket. And I guess they're keeping stuff
from us too.'

'OK,' decided Richard. 'I'll have a look at the laptop while I
dress. Nic, what do I need to do to get checked out of here?'

'I'll go see . . .' Nic vanished.

'Jim. Is there a car?'

'A Merc in the private car park five floors down and a
Gulfstream in the corporate bay at Haneda Airport. Both fuelled
up and ready to go.'

Richard leaned against the wall as he stepped into his underwear then sat a little gingerly on a providentially firm sofa to

put on his socks. As he did this, he scanned the readout on the laptop screen over the top of his purple-splotched calves. *Cheerio* was flashing cheerfully at three two point five degrees north one six two degrees west. 'The middle of nowhere with a vengeance,' he mumbled to himself.

Reona Tanaka's laptop was switched on and accessing the Tokyo University cloud, which was registering it at 350 miles north of the bottle. *Katapult* was 200 miles east and *Flint* seemed to be about the same distance west of it. All four signals were as far away from dry land as it was possible to get. Three-and-a-half-thousand miles away from where Richard was sitting now, as the crow flew.

'Chuck over that shirt, would you, Jim?' he asked, his mind racing. 'And alert both the driver and the pilot that we're ready for the *off*.'

By the time Nic came back, Richard was dressed, washed, shaved and experimenting with the least painful way to carry his case.

'That's done,' said Nic cheerfully. 'They didn't like letting you go without another series of tests but I said you didn't have time. So they've given you this medication to take if the pain gets too severe or if you really start to stiffen up. Watch it, though. It'll make you drowsy.'

'If anything goes wrong I promise not to sue them,' said Richard.

'I told them that when I signed the waiver,' said Nic. 'You promise not to sue them. Or haunt them.'

'Very funny,' grated Richard. 'Let's hit the road.'

'Been there, done that,' chuckled Nic, taking his friend's suitcase and turning to lead the way out. '*Hitting the road* is what got us in this hospital in the first place.'

The car sitting in the private car park, gleaming beneath the watery sunshine of a promising-looking morning, was a brand-new Mercedes E Class Avantgarde. Among its other advantages, it was configured to allow full use of all the communications equipment they had with them, so Richard was able to double-check the readings he had scanned on the laptop as the taciturn driver pushed the saloon as close to its 150 mph top speed as law and circumstances allowed. Then he was able to contact the twenty-four-hour desk at Crewfinders in London and double-check the arrangements he and Audrey had put in place during a conversation he could not remember having more than twenty-four hours ago. While he did this, Nic contacted the airport again and alerted the pilot that they were on their way confirming that a flight plan had been filed and clearances put in place on the expectation that they would be lifting off as soon after ten local time as humanly and bureaucratically possible.

Then the three men went into closed conference while the car sped like a black rocket along a route which, Richard noted with a subconscious shiver, was all too close to the one that had taken them to Rage and the nearly fatal dock area. But soon enough they were turning on to Metropolitan Expressway 1, and not long after that, they had to close their equipment down as the Mercedes plunged into the tunnel designed to take them under the water and out on to the island which contained the airport itself. And nothing much more than the airport, in fact. A lot like a good number of islands, large and small, between here and Canada, thought Richard.

They eased past the Terminals One and Two, and sped directly down to the handling areas where they drew up beside the gleaming Gulfstream G650 in Greenbaum International livery that was parked on the apron. Richard made use of his initial stiffness and slowness getting out of the Merc to admire the jet that seemed to tower above him. It was as near as dammit, he knew, a hundred feet long from nose to tail and a hundred feet wide from wing tip to wing tip. The folding stairs were down and the three businessmen climbed aboard to find a range of officialdom awaiting them. Even allowing for three executives, half-a-dozen officials and four crew members, the passenger compartment seemed spacious and thinly populated. Richard stooped – painfully and uneasily – though he could just about have stood erect in the very middle of the cabin, and folded himself into a leather-covered sofa as soon as he was able.

A certain number of the necessary questions had already been answered by the pilots, flight engineer and the air hostess who were wearing the green uniform of the Greenbaum International flight crew. Nic was an old hand at this and what little he could not settle on behalf of Richard and himself was covered by Jim, as a senior executive with Heritage Mariner, who went with the men from Customs, Immigration and Security, when they all left the plane.

Twenty minutes later, the pilot reported that they had clearance and a place in the queue for lift-off. So it was, as planned, a little after ten a.m. local time, that the Gulfstream accelerated down the runway with its twin Rolls-Royce BR725 A1 – twelve engines powering up to maximum revs, and lifted into the watery sunshine of the lower air above Tokyo Bay.

At the earliest possible opportunity, the air hostess came over to the two occupants of the exclusive executive cabin and enquired, 'What can I get for you, gentlemen?'

And Richard answered, feelingly, '*Food!*'

By the time the Gulfstream was levelling out at 40,000 feet over Chiba and the east coast of Japan was falling away at a whisper less than the speed of sound behind her sleek belly, Richard was tucking into smoked salmon and scrambled eggs on pale but plentiful toast. The percolator was chugging cheerfully and the aroma of Blue Mountain high roast Arabica coffee was filling the atmosphere.

At last he sat back, sated, with a cup of the nut-brown nectar in his hand and enquired, 'How long to Henderson, Nic?'

The answer was, 'Just over two hours at Mach point nine five.' And a little more than one hundred minutes later, the Gulfstream was throttling back towards 500 knots and settling on to the long finals that would bring it to a safe landing on Sand Island in the south-west section of the remote Midway Atoll, a couple of thousand miles east of Tokyo.

Like many of the deserted atoll islands in the vast emptiness out here, Midway, famous as the most decisive naval battleground of the War in the Pacific, had once been a USAF base. It was unmanned now but nevertheless kept stocked with supplies and fuel for emergencies. The last one had been way back in June 2011, but the avgas was still kept fresh and plentiful by the Boeing Corporation. The Greenbaum International Gulfstream touched down there at twelve forty-five Tokyo time, which was sixteen forty-five local.

Nic and the stick-stiff Richard helped the two pilots and one engineer fire up the diesel-fuelled generators that powered the gas pumps, though the flight crew insisted on overseeing the refuelling themselves. So, by eighteen hundred they were in the air again, with the pilot reporting to the nearest flight controller, at Barking Sands Airfield, Kauai, Hawaii, that the avgas supplies on Sand Island needed the Boeing gas supply team's urgent attention. The hostess served an early dinner – or a late lunch, depending on which time zone their stomachs were in. And by the time they had consumed their vichyssoise, chicken chasseur and wild rice accompanied by a medley of green vegetables, followed by *pots de crème au chocolat*, they were on long finals once again.

The airstrip on Tern Island, French Frigate Shoals, was like that on Midway – unmanned but well maintained. At nineteen hundred hours on a tropical evening it was dark, and, had it not been for the crew of the chopper awaiting them there, there would have been no landing lights, and the runway as impossible for them to see as Howland Island had proved for the unfortunate Amelia Earhart. But the crew of the Changhe CA 109 which was waiting for them there had had the opportunity and the forethought to get everything ready.

Richard and Nic transferred to the helicopter and left the Gulfstream's flight crew loading enough avgas to get them down to Hilo International on Hawaii. Then, pausing only for Richard to make a swift survey of the deadly shoals that had nearly stopped the redoubtable Robin in her tracks, they were whisked up into the night sky once again.

The Changhe's accommodation was far less sumptuous than aboard the Greenbaum International Gulfstream, but Richard and Nic were strapped safely into bucket seats and given headsets that dulled the relentless thrumming of the rotors. Luckily neither of them was hungry, and both had relieved themselves before the Gulfstream touched down on French Frigate Shoals.

By nine thirty p.m., the Changhe was settling on to the landing area aft of the massive bridgehouse of the Heritage Mariner supertanker *Prometheus*, which, having emptied its huge tanks of a quarter of a million gallons of fresh water at Tuvalu, was now making its leisurely way north towards Alaska to fill up with oil for the European market. Like all Heritage Mariner supertankers it carried an emergency supply of avgas suitable for use in choppers. There was a quick turnaround on *Prometheus* and the Changhe was off again by ten p.m.

And so, by midnight local time, though it was only coming up for eight p.m. in the heads of its passengers, even as eight bells were sounding for the change of watch from the first to the middle, the Changhe arrived home. And waiting to greet her on the afterdeck of the adapted corvette *Poseidon* as she carried the submersibles *Neptune* and *Salacia* at flank speed into the all-too actual Pacific Garbage Patch, were Captain Mongol Chang and her first officer, Lieutenant Straightline Jiang.

'*Ho*,' she said in characteristically gruff greeting as they both climbed – equally stiffly – down on to the deck. 'I hope you will not bring me any monster jellyfishes or Moby-Dick whales this time!'

English Defence

I t was only an overdose of the pills which Nic had got from the Tokyo hospital that allowed Richard six hours' solid sleep. He took a handful while concluding a swift briefing with Captain Chang. And then another as he stood increasingly dopily through a couple of abortive attempts to contact *Katapult,* whose red dot seemed so tantalizingly close ahead of them. Then he went into his bunk at one a.m., lay down as though poleaxed and woke at seven the next morning.

He knew at once that something was not quite right. He eased himself on to the thrumming, choppily heaving deck and was shocked and relieved both at the same time to note that he had collapsed into bed without getting undressed. Even his shoes were still in place. But at least the fact that he was still dressed meant he could get on to the bridge more quickly than would otherwise have been possible. Pausing only to freshen up, check his reflection, brush his hair and rinse his mouth, he rushed up two decks. Rushed, he observed wryly, like a centenarian who has lost his Zimmer frame.

When he did make it up there, he found himself standing stiffly between the silent forms of Captain Chang and her first lieutenant, staring ahead over the garish brightness of the two submersibles on the foredeck. The morning had dawned overcast a couple of hours earlier, and the leaden colour of the sky was reflected by the surface of the ocean, in sharp contrast to the brightness of *Neptune* and *Salacia*.

As far as the eye could see, the legendary blue of the Pacific was hidden beneath a layer of plastic. The majority of the rubbish seemed to be clear bottles of every conceivable size from 330-millilitre water bottles through two-litre stalwarts the same size as Tanaka's good ship *Cheerio,* to family-sized containers capable of holding a gallon or maybe two. There were personal items: trainers, flip-flops, footballs. Then there were the ubiquitous bags – from small ones that had once contained crisps or chips to big silver-throated multipacks. Shopping bags without number, from a worldwide range of stores and business outlets. There were black bags that had once held garbage – and some of them still appeared to do so. Green bags full of garden rubbish. And, floating in among the billions of bags, there were commercial containers. There were square ones – everything from Tupperware sandwich boxes to plastic dustbins – to massive water tanks such as could be found in any Western attic. There were barrel-shaped ones varying in size from fizzy drink cans to oil drums to the occasional hot water central heating cylinder.

And that was before he began to add in the kinds of flotsam that he was already familiar with from his adventures with the jellyfish. Floats and nets from day fishermen's tackle to huge commercial trawler gear. Fish crates, life jackets, Day-Glo working jackets that looked at first glance like the torsos of corpses, thick red rubber gloves, yellow boots, tyres, ships' fenders of every sort, size and shape. There were even full-sized containers like modest houses floating half submerged out there. And God alone knew what they contained.

Frowning with concern, Richard hobbled over to the starboard bridge wing and opened the bulkhead door that connected to the outside world. At once the bridge was filled with a strange, unearthly rumbling grating sound and a piercing, oily stench. 'Where is *Katapult*?' he croaked, concerned for Robin.

'Dead ahead,' answered Straightline. 'We have had to cut speed but so has she. We'll be up with her by midday.'

'Which is when she will be at the bottle Cheerio's location,' added Captain Chang. 'Though how Captain Mariner will find one bottle in the midst of this . . .'

Nic arrived on the bridge then. 'What the . . .' he said in disgust, looking out at the mess on the water.

'What about the others?' asked Richard, swinging the bridge door closed.

'The same,' said Straightline. 'Mr Greenbaum's daughter in *Flint* seems to be making steady headway towards us. The wind is a light northerly – they can both tack across it even though they are heading in opposite directions. The two vessels are in the teeth of a fierce competition now, but they don't seem to be taking any risks from what I can judge of heading and speed from the locator beacons and the radar.'

'Other than sailing through this crap in the first place,' grated Nic. 'Where's Professor Tanaka?'

'Here,' Straightline gestured to the twin displays that showed the red dots familiar from the laptop screens, and *Poseidon*'s combat-standard radar display. 'We will all get there to the same place at about the same time – the middle of nowhere – and the middle of whatever this excrescence is.'

'That's something I must remember to ask Professor Tanaka when I see him,' said Richard thoughtfully.

Then Nic demanded suddenly, 'Are we all right to be doing this? It looks pretty flaming dangerous out there.'

'It is!' snapped Chang. 'Dangerous for us but also very dangerous for *Katapult* and *Flint*. Much more dangerous for them, in fact. If we cut and run to safer waters, then who will help them if anything goes wrong?' She swung round and looked at her two employers with her fiercest frown. 'And is that not what we are here for? *To help them if anything goes wrong?*'

Over a breakfast of cold noodles, *congee* warm rice porridge and *crullers* deep-fried doughsticks, Richard and Nic began to finalize their plans for the fast-approaching endgame as eight quiet chimes announced the start of the forenoon watch at eight a.m. ship's time. As the bustle of the watch change went on all around them, they fell into an increasingly deep discussion. For they had a fine equation to balance: two yacht captains locked in the final stages of a race that neither was willing to lose – though neither of them knew the true worth of their prize. To make matters worse, communications with the vessels in question was intermittent. And, as wild card against them, *Dagupan Maru* was also closing on the bottle. Also being highly selective with regard to communications. And she was a container vessel more than capable of running them both down, smashing them to kindling and killing everyone aboard. 'I wonder,' mused Richard, mid-conversation, almost an hour later, 'if Sittart could have had anything to do with the car that almost killed us?'

'What put that in your head?' asked Nic quietly.

'I don't know. But there's *something* here. Something not quite right.'

Nic nodded, frowned and shrugged, used to Richard's sudden flashes of insight. Feeling a little like Dr Watson sitting opposite Sherlock Holmes.

But after a moment's silence, their discussion resumed. For they had to assume that someone aboard the sinister container ship – some*one* at the very least – knew very well what a colossal fortune the bottle might represent.

And *then,* like the extra odds always skewed in the house's favour in Las Vegas casinos, there was the fact that Tanaka's predictions turned out to be true beyond anyone's wildest dreams. The weather around the Pacific Rim had clearly speeded up the currents of the North Pacific Gyre so that there was in fact a small but expanding continent of floating garbage, a plastic Sargasso Sea, gathering here. A Sargasso that was not yet solid enough to present a hazard to shipping in terms of blocking progress or hard enough to make collision damage likely – unless someone was unlucky enough to run into one of the containers – but which was sure to be full of other, as yet uncalculated, dangers.

After breakfast, the two men returned to the bridge and stood

side by side with the captain and her navigator for a while, as
three quiet chimes Warned that it was nine thirty a.m. aboard
Poseidon, only two-and-a-half hours from their projected rendezvous. The four of them stood watching as the vessel pushed its
way with increasing caution through the slowly thickening trash.
Richard's unease continued to mount and he found himself
limping out on to the outer bridge wing where he could come
closer to the strange conditions they were sailing through, as
though experiencing them with all five senses would also bring
him closer to understanding the danger.

As Nic, less seawise than his battered friend, went below
and started looking into business of his own, Richard leaned
against the forward rail of the bridge wing, his whole aching
body seeming to yearn forward as though some part of him
could fly far ahead of *Poseidon* and come aboard *Katapult* to
Robin. But it wasn't long before his fatigue-enhanced fanciful-
ness gave way to the need for urgent physical action and he
hurried below again, as fast as his bruised and battered body
would allow.

On A deck, he found Nic deep in conversation with Ironwrist
Wan and Fatfist Wu, controllers of the submersibles on the foredeck. And it didn't take long for the four of them to agree that
action – any action – would be better than this relentless waiting,
made infinitely worse by the amount of decisive energy that it
had taken to get two of them here in the first place. And that
decision seemed to lift a weight from each man's shoulders. For,
given where they were, there was only one course of action open
to each of them.

But before either Richard or Nic could take anything like the
action that they agreed, they were called back up on to the bridge
by a peremptory summons broadcast by Captain Chang. 'What
is it?' demanded Richard as he limped through from the lift abaft
the bridge. Captain Chang did not answer. She simply gestured.
And there, heaving over the port-quarter horizon was the massive
bulk of *Dagupan Maru*, black against the wide grey sky.

Richard grabbed the binoculars from their holster on the
console beneath the clearview and was limping out on to the
port bridge wing even before Nic arrived on the bridge itself
behind him. This was the first time he had seen the freighter

with his own eyes. And her picture on the laptop files that Jim sent from London Centre – let alone the photo of her name on the drifter's camera phone – came nowhere near to doing her justice.

Dagupan Maru was a bloody big brute of a vessel, he thought. Not quite the size of his three-hundred-metre, quarter-of-a-million-ton supertankers like *Prometheus*, but bigger than any other vessels in the Heritage Mariner fleet. She looked every one of her two hundred metres in length, each of her twenty-five metres beam. And her deadweight tonnage could even be more than *Prometheus*'s, let alone *Poseidon*'s. Her command bridge, six decks above her weather deck, watched the watery world ahead of her over the tops of four blunt cranes that seemed like roughly squared oak tree trunks, the arms of their gantries squared away fore and aft in a line above the centre of her deck. There was a forest of satellite, GPS and communications equipment on top of her bridge house which served to make her radio silence more sinister still. There was a tall mast at her forepeak, festooned with radar equipment. And, focusing in on the massive flare of her bow at the foot of this foremast – a broad bow which seemed to him to be little more than a brutal black wall smashing arrogantly through the relative scum of waste – he could all too easily see how its larger sister had ridden down an eight-man Transpac without noticing the impact. How it could equally easily grind down *Katapult*, or *Flint* – or both. She was certainly not bothering with *Poseidon*'s increasingly careful approach. She must be running at full speed, Richard calculated, relying on the huge ram of her bulbous bow to get her safely through the rubbish. But even taking Chang's caution into account, *Poseidon* could outsail *Dagupan Maru* any day of the week.

'Shit,' came Nic's voice at his shoulder. 'So that's her, is it? She's sure an ugly-looking brute. Sparks is trying to contact her but she's not answering.'

But no sooner had Nic said this than Sparks, the radio officer, was on the bridge wing beside them. 'I have *Katapult*,' he said. 'Captain Mariner's on.'

'Richard,' said Robin's voice in the radio headphones an instant later. 'Where are you?'

'Only a couple of hours away, closing up behind you in *Poseidon*,' he replied.

'*What?* Why ever are you doing that?' she demanded.

'In case this garbage gets to be anything like as dangerous as it looks.'

'You're fussing over nothing! We've got this far without needing any help and we've no intention of starting to ask for any now. This is a race, not a regatta! We're being careful. The radio's been playing up and the sonar's on the blink but the radar's fine and we're tracking the bottle and *Flint* clearly enough. We see *Poseidon*'s echo and identification numbers clearly enough, now you mention it, though I can't get over the fact that you're aboard her! And anyway, if anything goes wrong, there's a bloody great freighter just pulling over the northern horizon. I haven't managed to raise them yet but I'm sure they'd be happy to help.'

'Well, my love, about *that* . . .'

Richard was in the middle of his explanation – though he hadn't got to the bit about the lottery ticket yet – when the four bells gently announced that it was ten a.m. ship's time midway through the forenoon watch, and the most unexpected thing happened. Suddenly Nic's cell phone started ringing. He got it out, shaking his head with surprise. And froze.

'Son of a bitch,' he said. 'It's Liberty!' Then suddenly he was locked in a conversation with his daughter that was in many respects the same as the one Richard was having with his wife.

Neither man had made any real progress with the fiercely competitive women, when their attention was called to the next stage in the chess game that seemed suddenly to be evolving with disturbing rapidity out across the dead sea ahead of them. For, no sooner had *Dagupan Maru* settled into their field of vision than a helicopter lifted off it, leaping up from behind the solid wall of the bridge house and skimming forward with disturbing speed.

Richard broke contact with Robin and crossed to the bridge wing once again, grabbing the binoculars as he went. Then he was out in the stinking morning with the glasses glued to his eyes, scanning the skies for a close-up of the machine. As soon as he focused on it, he started swearing under his breath, for before he could even register the make or model, he saw that it had been fitted with floats. 'Nic,' he called, without taking the glasses from his eyes, 'get Ironwrist and Fatfist to fix floats to *Poseidon*'s chopper . . .'

'Already done! That was one of the things we were discussing when you joined us on A deck. The pilot's ready too. You want to go up and see what's going on out there?'

'Yes,' Richard growled. 'And soon. I hate being caught on the back foot . . .'

He turned and as he went back through the bridge, he asked, 'Straightline, can you guide us to Tanaka's bottle if we go up in the chopper?'

'Yes, Captain. I can get you to the location, but from the look of things it would be too risky for you to land and pick it up.'

'OK. We'll see when we get there . . .'

Ten minutes later, *Poseidon*'s Changhe lifted off with floats attached in case a landing on the water was possible and both Richard and Nic aboard. Richard was happy to occupy the co-pilot's seat and direct the pilot according to Straightline's advice from *Poseidon*'s bridge.

As soon as *Dagupan Maru*'s chopper saw the Changhe, it speeded up and so both aircraft sped low across the littered water. Richard's rotors nearly took the tip off *Katapult*'s mast as he raced due east and she tacked northward one, maybe two, tacks away from her goal. And for a moment, Richard thought he could hear Robin's howl of protest at this underhanded cheating.

The two helicopters arrived at the same point at almost the same moment, saw the same thing and made the same decision – as though they had a choice. For both Chang and Straightline were correct. The sea beneath them was thick with thousands of plastic bottles. Only a very detailed search at sea level would show precisely which one was Tanaka's Cheerio bottle. But such a search was forbidden to the helicopters by the heaving thickness of dangerous rubbish that the armada of bottles surrounded. There were more containers, clashing together like bergs on the restless Arctic Ocean. Oil drums half the size of tree trunks rolled restlessly in the choppy water. Swathes of commercial netting swirled, waiting to wrap themselves round the choppers' floats and drag them down. There was no clear water here – none in fact closer than either *Katapult* which they had just overflown or *Flint* which they could see approaching on a southerly tack.

And yet neither chopper wanted to be the first to leave. They circled round the place, watching each other like duellists, as soon as they realized landing was out of the question. And Richard, the earphones clamped over his ears, looked straight into the cabin opposite and saw his opposite number quite clearly. And it took him a moment to register, with a frisson of icy shock, that the man in the *Dagupan Maru*'s helicopter was not wearing headphones like his own. That the black boxes on those distant ears were permanent fixtures.

That the unaccountably shocked and angry face opposite did not belong to Professor Reona Tanaka. It belonged to Professor Satang S. Sittart.

Endgame

'**R**ight!' snapped Richard. 'We go back. Now. If Sittart's involved personally and directly then that changes the game. Gets rid of the rule book, for a start. And makes our car accident, Nic, look a lot less accidental. But Sittart's not going to risk drowning himself – even for a fortune in lottery winnings! He might be ruthless, sadistic; murderous, even. But he's not barking mad!'

The Changhe lifted, turned, began to race back the way she had come. Sittart's chopper did the same. As they sped towards their next move in this strange, deadly chess game, Richard continued planning aloud. 'But he'll have other tricks up his sleeve. Lucky that chopper of his doesn't look powerful enough to carry anything heavy, or he'd be dropping one of *Dagupan Maru*'s lifeboats right on top of the bottle next. But he can't. He could drop a swimmer or a diver I suppose but he'd have a hell of a job retrieving them – even if they could survive in that mess for long enough to find the bottle. So if he wants to go in at sea level he'll have to wait till the freighter's closer and lower a boat from there. And lifeboats aren't noted for their speed. Which explains why the freighter's running at the top of the green. Straightline, do you think we could risk one of *Poseidon*'s Zodiacs? They're faster than lifeboats.'

'I wouldn't like to put an inflatable into that,' cut in Captain Chang decisively. 'Even the Kevlar-reinforced sides would stand very little chance. I would hesitate to permit *you* to try it – and I would forbid *my crew* outright.'

'Right,' said Richard. 'That settles that! Flank speed for the moment, please, Captain and get ready to try Plan B as soon as we land.'

'Flank speed?' spat Chang across the airwaves. 'Not through this, Captain Mariner. I go *safe* speed, thank you very much. Still plenty fast though!'

'No,' said Richard gruffly twenty minutes later, sounding a lot like Captain Chang. 'Even if you have got her prepped and ready, it's too risky for you to take her out, Nic, even after Liberty. We stick with what we discussed at breakfast and on the flight back in. I don't mind running the risk of dropping *Neptune* overboard without slowing down but if you go out in *Salacia*, we'll have to heave to. And you know we can't afford the time. Not only that, but *Salacia* is our camouflage. She's positioned between *Neptune* and *Dagupan Maru*. She'll mask what we're doing and give us an element of surprise. But if we deploy her, that will simply give our hand away. Besides,' he continued, moderating his tone, 'you know we'll be more flexible if we're all still aboard. Far more use to both of our girls if push comes to shove . . .'

Nic turned mutinously and strode across the foredeck until the port-quarter safety rail stopped him. He stared out into the gusty grey morning as though he could see *Flint* in the distance racing towards them along her southerly tack. But all Richard could see over his friend's shoulder was the restless ocean with *Dagupan Maru* still well to the north smashing relentlessly southward, and *Katapult* running up towards her, ready to change tack – perhaps for the last time before she reached the bottle. The wind battered fitfully under the upturned hull of *Poseidon*'s port-side Zodiac and howled in the equipment supporting *Salacia* above Nic's head. The starboard gantry above Richard groaned as it jumped into motion, swinging *Neptune* out over the littered surface. Then Nic turned back. 'When you're right, you're right,' he said, decisively. 'Let's get to work.'

He joined Richard at the starboard rail, and they felt the deck angle slightly as *Neptune* swung out over the water. Then the pair of them watched with sharp-eyed concentration for a relatively clear bit of ocean. Richard didn't mind taking the risk of dropping *Neptune* while her mother ship was still running, but he was not about to drop the precious remote vehicle on to a solid container or into a cat's cradle of tangled netting.

Then, 'There!' called Nic, and Richard saw what he was pointing to: a patch of water that seemed to be soiled with nothing more substantial than a rainbow skim of oil. Richard raised his hand and the team in charge of the gantry tensed at his signal. 'Three . . . Two . . . One . . .' he growled, then slammed his arm down. And started swearing at the sudden pain that seared through his shoulder. *Neptune* dropped.

Richard hurried down to the control room in *Poseidon*'s bulbous bow where Ironwrist sat waiting for him to fill the second operator's chair. The Chinese controller was flooding the submersible's tanks at the same time as running through the speediest of start-up routines.

Richard took over as soon as he arrived, pushing the throttles to maximum even as the lights came on and the video-feeds from the on-board cameras went live. The first thing the submersible saw was the stern of her mothership departing in a swirl of bubbles as *Poseidon* raced on forward. Richard and Ironwrist angled *Neptune*'s crablike body like the well-practised team they were, following *Poseidon* as faithfully as a duckling chasing its mother, checking for a safe depth without losing too much forward motion, but staying on the surface for the moment. At full speed, *Neptune* could manage ten knots, a fantastic pace for a submersible, and one that Richard had found useful in the past. Ten knots was about half the velocity the cautious captain was currently allowing *Poseidon* to do. And just comparable with the ten knots Sittart's freighter was capable of. But they needed more of an edge than that.

'Monitors on,' said Nic's voice in Richard's headphones, confirming that they had visual on the bridge.

'Looks like we're clear from about three metres down,' said Richard, checking the range of readouts on the screens in front of him while pushing *Neptune* forward in *Poseidon*'s churning wake, relying on the adapted frigate's hull to keep things clear ahead for the moment. 'There'll be one or two containers and maybe some drifts of netting sitting that deep, but not much.

'Now, let's get to work. Straightline, you keep me updated on the location of the bottle and I'll get that precisely factored in to *Neptune*'s GPS guidance. Nic, you keep me up to speed with both what you can see on the red-dot display and out of the clearview. I suspect we're getting close to the point where eyes in your head will be more useful than eyes in the sky. Or eyes under the water, for the moment. Going for a basic series of remote arm and gripper tests as long as they don't slow us down any. Fatfist, are you ready with the after line?'

'*Ready*,' came the crisp reply.

'*Engage*,' ordered Richard. And three decks above his head, the whole length of the sleek hull astern, Fatfist Wu fired the magnetic bolt on the end of the long line that would join *Neptune* to *Poseidon* until Richard chose to break contact and set his little command free to do her underwater work. The bolt flew like a harpoon from an old-fashioned whaling gun and hit squarely on the magnetic link pad on *Neptune*'s broad yellow bow where it held as though superglued in place. At once, *Neptune* was jerked forward through the water at twenty knots as *Poseidon* pulled her forward. And at last, having calculated the safe depth for their vessel, Richard and Ironwrist angled the planes and finished flooding the tanks while Fatfist played the ungainly remote vehicle like a fish on the end of the towline. 'It should be me up there,' mourned Ironwrist. 'I'm the big fisherman aboard *Poseidon*!'

'No can do,' said Richard, rising slowly and giving the readouts one last scan. 'I need both of you exactly where you are. I'll be back when it's time to cut her loose. Until then, you're in full charge of the *Neptune*, Captain Wan!'

Richard's next port of call was the afterdeck where he checked that the Changhe was being refuelled and that Fatfist was doing a good enough job of keeping *Neptune* safely in place three metres below *Poseidon*'s screws, thirty more behind her square stern. He rested his hand on the thrumming tow rope and looked narrow-eyed into the water it was cutting like a cheese wire. Then he returned to the bridge and joined Nic and Chang watching narrow-eyed as the red dots on Straightline's display converged, and the vessels they represented began to come together.

Both *Flint* and *Katapult* were on the radio now that range was short and line-of-sight signals easily received; Liberty and Robin offered running commentaries on progress as they made their final tacks and began their closing runs in across the suddenly sporadic northerly from the north-east and the south-west, both fiercely fixated still on being the first to recover the bottle, neither of them welcoming the distraction of incoming contact. Richard and Nic talked to them when permitted, but their advice like their eyes focused on the looming bulk of *Dagupan Maru*. The nearer it came, the more threatening it seemed. Richard had taken for granted that the massive freighter could run over *Katapult* or *Flint* with ease, but now he was beginning to wonder whether those brutal bows could smash even *Poseidon* to kindling.

As he wondered, so Nature began to take a hand in the already tense situation. The clouds thinned and the sky began to clear with unsettling rapidity while the wind, already fitful, became sporadic, falling through three on the Beaufort scale disturbingly quickly. Then two. Amid howls of frustration from both Liberty and Robin, an almost dead calm descended. Air stilled. Clouds vanished. The sun came out hot and heavy.

The yachts were slowed to a dead stop, their sails drooping emptily, flapping fitfully as the wind deserted both of them. But, while they lost their forward motion and settled to a standstill like two more bits of flotsam in the huge Sargasso of plastic, the powered vessels continued to surge ahead. *Dagupan Maru* and *Poseidon* began to close together on the central dot that gave the position of Tanaka's Cheerio bottle.

Robin broke first, but only by moments – probably because she had *Dagupan Maru* closing relentlessly from the north and *Poseidon* powering in from the west while the wind had utterly abandoned her. '*Katapult*'s in motion,' observed Straightline suddenly and Richard crossed to the console. 'She's started her motor,' he deduced. 'And there goes *Flint*.'

'You can hardly blame them,' said Nic defensively. 'They've come so far and now . . .' His voice trailed off and he looked out of the clearview at the burnished blue sky, the white disc of the sun, the utter calm of the littered water – stirred now only by the long deep-ocean rollers and the relentless approach of the two motor vessels. Beginning to steam a little in the humid heat. 'I'd fire up the on-board motor and cruise for the last couple of miles.'

'Me too,' admitted Richard. 'What's the old saying? "If at first you don't succeed, *cheat*!" That's one of my favourites. Captain Chang, can you swing *Poseidon* to the south? It looks as though there's clearer water there; we can maybe push our speed up a notch or two. Then we've maybe got enough sea room to swing round on to a northerly bearing. I'd rather be head to head with Sittart than have him coming at my beam like a Roman galley at ramming speed.'

'*Shi*,' nodded Chang. 'It is so.' *Poseidon* swept south, accelerating into an area of clear water and racing up towards her at full speed then swung on to a northerly bearing, so that the disposition of the five dots on Straightline's schematic looked roughly cruciform. *Dagupan Maru* and *Poseidon* were facing each other and closing on a north-south heading. The two yachts were coming in north and south of the east-west axis, depending on the last tack they had taken before the wind deserted them. And the red dot of Reona Tanaka's bottle sat squarely in the middle.

'Nic,' said Richard, 'come with me. It's time we got an overview of this situation. Bring the binoculars.'

Side by side they hurried along the length of the adapted frigate until they were standing on the afterdeck between the helicopter and the line holding *Neptune* in place. 'You go up and I go down,' said Richard. 'One way or another we need to know every move they make from here on in. Whether they know it or not – whether they like it or not – the girls are depending on us now.'

Nic nodded decisively and climbed aboard the Changhe

holding the binoculars in one white-knuckled hand. He pulled on the headset and settled the stalk of the mic. 'Ready,' he said and his voice echoed through the loud-hailing system, then he cinched his seat belt tight and raised his empty fist.

As Nic went up in the chopper with the binoculars to take the high ground, Richard went below. He first checked on Ironwrist in the control room, then he returned to the bridge where he could watch what was going on. No sooner had he arrived than Straightline said, '*Dagupan Maru*'s slowing . . .'

Richard could see that the telltale white line of the freighter's bow wave was thinning. 'He's up to something,' he said.

And Nic's voice came through on the radio. 'He's dropping lifeboats. I count three. All packed with men and they all look armed to the teeth!'

'That's one for *Katapult*, one for *Flint* and one to recover the bottle,' snapped Richard. 'Warn the women, Nic.' He clapped his hands and rubbed the palms together. 'Let's get busy,' he muttered, speaking almost exclusively to himself. 'I'm off below,' he said more loudly to Straightline. 'I'll want pretty precise bearings that will get me to the lifeboat that's after *Flint* first,' he ordered brusquely. 'Then we'll take it from there.'

A couple of moments later he settled in beside Ironwrist. 'I think I'd better do this bit,' he said. 'It could get nasty and it could get legal later.'

'OK,' said Ironwrist, as though he knew exactly what the mad gwailo giant was talking about. But to be fair, he had been one of the first to call him the *Goodluck Giant* – and he had never had any cause to change the nickname.

Neptune was three metres below the littered surface of the battleground, powering forward at her full ten knots. With Straightline calling course and bearings from a combination of GPS readings, red-dot sightings and simple observation, the remote submersible headed unerringly towards the becalmed and helpless *Flint*. Nic supplemented Straightline's directions because, from the high ground of the chopper, he could see what those on the water could not – and he got occasional glimpses of the daffodil-yellow vessel as she raced though the water ten feet beneath the thick-piled garbage. Richard was surprised by how quickly the GPS showed his remote vehicle was close to Liberty's command. Then, again taking his directions from Straightline and Nic, he headed towards the nearest lifeboat. As he pushed *Neptune* towards her limit he caught himself wondering whether he should get Nic to call some kind of warning on the chopper's loud hailer. But then the distraught father made up his mind for him. '*Richard!* They've opened fire! Shit, Richard, they're shooting! At both Liberty and me! The bastards didn't even give a warning . . .'

'You OK?' asked Richard, his focus exclusively on what *Neptune* could see.

'Yeah. And the girls seem OK too. But *Jesus* . . .'

'Hardball it is, then,' said Richard. 'Tell them to forget the bottle, Nic. Head for *Poseidon* now! No argument. No excuses! And tell *Katapult* the same.'

Even as Nic's orders to *Flint* came through on Richard's headset, the picture on *Neptune*'s screen showed the keel of the lifeboat coming into view, punching through a solid ceiling of rubbish that looked thick enough to conceal the submersible from above. Richard angled the vessel down a little, then swung her round until she was following just behind the lifeboat's propeller. Holding his breath with the tension he unfolded one of *Neptune*'s mechanical arms and pulled out one of the magnetic explosive charges she used for deep-water demolition work. It took less than a moment to attach it to the metal blade of the lifeboat's rudder. Then he said to Ironwrist, 'Dive, dive, dive!' and hit the remote detonator button.

The explosion was supposed to disable the vessel but instead it blew the entire stern off the lifeboat and sent the warlike crewmen straight into the water. 'My God! That was more than I expected!' said Richard. 'Still, with any luck it should distract their mates for as long as it takes to pick them up . . .'

'I don't think so,' came Nic's distant voice. 'Neither of the other boats has turned off course. Liberty! For heaven's sake do what I say. Head straight for *Poseidon*! Now!'

'*A friend in need is a friend indeed,*' observed Richard cynically. 'Is *Katapult* coming in?'

'No,' said Nic. 'She's still going for the bloody bottle.'

'Yes,' confirmed Captain Chang. 'Captain Mariner says if you watch her back for five more minutes . . .'

'It won't be as easy this time. They'll know I'm out here somewhere . . . I'll bet they're keeping careful watch now. Anything else I should know?'

'Wind's picking up again,' Straightline said. 'It's from the south this time.'

'That'll slow *Katapult* big time,' said Richard grimly. 'Especially if it picks up. She must be heading directly into it. She can't start sailing and tacking across it again. She'll just have to go full throttle, hell for leather, and hope . . .'

'The other lifeboats are closing up with her though,' warned Nic. 'With those three hulls of hers she's got three times more exposure to the rubbish than the lifeboats have. I'd say at least one lifeboat's going to catch her before she gets to the bottle, let alone before she gets to *Poseidon*.'

'*Bloody woman*!' swore Richard. 'Straightline! Get me to the nearest lifeboat and I'll try kicking ass again . . .'

'You'd better hurry,' warned Nic. 'They've opened fire again . . .'

'*Christ!*' blasphemed Richard. 'How's *Flint*?'

'Coming in pretty quickly now, thank God. She'll be alongside *Poseidon* in five minutes,' Nic called.

'Right. So, where's the nearest lifeboat to *Katapult*?'

'Dead ahead, Captain Mariner,' answered Straightline. 'If you keep going on that course . . .'

Richard could see the turbulence generated by the lifeboat's propeller in the distance. He pushed *Neptune* to maximum revs and was pulling up towards it in a matter of minutes. He checked all around him on the remote vehicle's sensors. The ceiling above him was still thick with plastic debris and even though the lifeboat was making enough way to create a considerable wake, he calculated that, as with the first, he would be able to sneak up behind it and blow the stern off. 'Update me, Straightline,' he ordered as he came closer.

'*Flint* is almost alongside *Poseidon*,' Straightline answered. '*Katapult* is still after the bottle and the two lifeboats are closing with her.'

'I have one in my sights,' said Richard. 'Closing now.' He brought *Neptune* up under the stern of the second lifeboat and placed the second mine. Mildly surprised at getting away with the same trick twice, he detonated the charge. A moment later, the second lifeboat was sinking like the first and all of its crew were in the water. Then, emboldened by the success of his strategy so far, he went after the third boat. The one still relentlessly closing in on *Katapult*.

Using Straightline's directions, he swept beneath *Katapult*'s triple hull and closed with the last lifeboat, swinging under her stern. But this time, as he reached out with his last charge, *Neptune*'s articulated arm was roughly caught by a brutal hook. The whole vessel was jerked up to the surface and Richard found himself looking at a face familiar from the mugshots Jim Bourne had sent of *Dagupan Maru's* officers. This one was called Sakai Inazo. He was first officer. Even as Richard recognized him, Sakai started shooting at *Neptune*, point-blank. Richard lurched back in his seat as though the bullets could hurt him. And then he leaped to his feet with shock. The screen before him exploded into dazzling brightness and for an instant he thought the shots must have smashed *Neptune*'s video. Then he saw the figures from her onboard temperature gauges and realized the truth, even before he recognized that Sakai's burly figure was wreathed in red and yellow flames. He was halfway out of the door when the alarms started and Chang's voice bellowed, 'Captain Mariner to the bridge! Captain Mariner to the bridge!'

On A deck he met Nic and Liberty, also rushing upwards. The gaping bulkhead door behind them showed *Flint* etched against a wall of fire. 'Everyone off *Flint*?' he gasped.

Liberty nodded, her eyes huge. 'Just . . .'

'Then it's *Katapult* next . . .' he grated. And realized they couldn't hear him; he could hardly hear himself because of the simply appalling noise coming in from outside.

The three of them burst on to the bridge, adding some disorder to the ordered pandemonium there. Captain Chang was rapping out orders at the top of her voice and everyone there was bustling to their emergency stations as *Poseidon*, partway through her fastest and tightest emergency turn, tore away southwards. And away from *Flint*. The abrupt manoeuvre had simply snapped *Flint*'s mooring line. *Poseidon* was racing on to a southerly heading at the kind of speed the captain had refused to countenance less than half an hour ago.

The entire ocean to the north of them seemed to be on fire. From east to west, almost as far as the eye could see, the surface of the water was a sheet of flame. And only the southerly wind was keeping *Poseidon* safe. For it was blowing the wildfire up towards *Dagupan Maru* in a wall that reached more than fifty feet high in places and was already pouring thick black fumes hundreds of feet further up into the wide blue sky.

But Richard wasn't worried about the Japanese freighter. He had much more immediate concerns. For there, just ahead of the wall of flame, just behind *Poseidon*'s racing stern, came *Katapult*. Sails in, poles bare, pushing forward into the southerly gale as fast as her onboard motor could move her. Richard hesitated for a nanosecond, his mind racing. 'Cut speed,' he called to Chang. 'Give her a chance to catch up . . .'

'Why risk my command?' snapped Chang ruthlessly. 'It is *lost cause*.'

'I think I can get a line to her,' answered Richard desperately. 'We can tow her out.'

Chang hesitated. Her face twisted with disbelief. Then they both were distracted by a cry from Liberty. Pushed by the strengthening southerly, *Flint* was drifting into the fire wall, and even as they watched, the flames seemed to leap out and claim her. The sturdy composite hull seemed to wilt. The tall mast toppled and she exploded into a ball of flame.

'Very well,' snapped Chang. 'I give you five minutes. Take headset. Stay in contact for my orders. Remember, Captain. You are owner. I am *commander*!'

Richard and Nic ran side by side on to the poop deck, past the Changhe with its floats still attached and down to the ship's square stern. Even as they were racing aft through her bridge house, they had felt the way come off her as the motors powered down. And now, they saw all too clearly the risk that Captain Chang had agreed to run for them. The heat was astonishing. The noise disorientating. The wall of fire simply petrifying. And there, between the high stern of the adapted corvette and the terrifying flames, came *Katapult*, doggedly, refusing to give up. Her decks steaming, her tall mast seeming to writhe and waver as the heat fought the brutal headwind and sought to claim her at last. And there, like some kind of figurehead at her forepeak stood the flame-haired figure of Florence Weary. 'Captain Mariner!' barked a peremptory voice in Richard's ear. 'You running out of time!'

And he wasn't the only one.

Suddenly the radio operator came on to the captain's waveband and into Richard's headset. 'Captain! I have a helicopter asking permission to land. It's from *Dagupan Maru*. There's a man and two women aboard as well as the pilot.'

'*No!* We are wasting enough time already. I would have to throw our own chopper overboard to give him room. Tell him he cannot come aboard.'

And that was that, thought Richard as he grabbed the handles of the gun Fatfist had used to fire the magnetic bolt at *Neptune* and took aim. *Sod off, Sittart*. Then he dismissed all thoughts of the professor and focused on the job in hand. Dismissed also all thoughts of Robin and her crew – thoughts that would simply incapacitate him if he indulged in them now.

He knew there was nothing metallic aboard *Katapult* for the magnetic bolt to fasten on to. But Flo was no fool. If she saw a line coming aboard she would certainly secure it to something. The wind pounded him distractingly on the back like a drunk in a bar. Somewhere deep in his subconscious he calculated that the breeze blowing up from the south must be strengthening pretty rapidly as the updraft of the colossal fire sucked yet more air in to feed the furnace at its heart. Would that work to *Katapult*'s advantage? Or add to the likelihood of her destruction? Robin's life hung in that terrible balance . . .

'Captain Mariner . . .' came Chang's voice. '*Time's up!*'

And he fired.

The bolt flew straight and true, the line arching behind it, streaking off the spool beside the gun. It slammed into *Katapult*'s central deck and Flo dived desperately after it. Richard felt *Poseidon*'s deck shiver as the engines raced up towards full power once again. Flo was on her knees, securing the line to the starboard cleat and Richard let the line continue to run as the corvette gathered way. Playing the beautiful multihull like Ironwrist playing a fish. As soon as Flo rolled clear, he eased the brake on to the line, watching it come taut and quiver with the strain. The three forepeaks behind him rose and three white bow waves added their complications to *Poseidon*'s racing wake.

Away to the north, behind the scarifying wall of flame, something exploded like an atomic bomb, sending a mushroom cloud to tower high against the smoke clouded sky. That would be *Dagupan Maru*, he thought numbly. Her hold packed full of thousands of tons of priceless timber and the temperature around it reaching 350 degrees Celsius, hot enough for spontaneous combustion. The power of the explosion was so colossal that it seemed to suck the flames northwards towards the massive vacuum so much instantaneous devastation must have caused. A wind thundered northward, to fill the vast vacancy at the heart of the explosion even as a blast wall ran counter to it, making the flames gutter and die for a moment. Richard was thrown back and forward like a puppet. So were *Poseidon* and *Katapult*.

Then the pounding on his shoulder stopped being the wind. It was Nic. He let go of the gun handles, looked dazedly down at his blistered palms; up at his beaming friend; out at the brave vessel that held his wife still safe.

'*Katapult* secured, Captain Chang!' he bellowed into the headset.

'Good job!' she answered. 'We go full ahead now.'

The captain must have switched on to a general band then, for Richard suddenly found himself in the middle of a conversation between *Poseidon*'s radio operator and Robin. '. . . reporting all aboard *Katapult* well . . .' came her familiar voice. 'A little scorched, and smelling more like Sunday roast than sailors, but we're fine. Glad to hear Liberty and the girls are safe and that Ironwrist thinks he can get *Neptune* back in one piece. Sorry about *Flint* though . . .'

'Robin?' he said hesitantly, suddenly choked and shaking.

'Hello, sailor,' she answered, her voice softening. 'Good thing you were here after all, eh?'

'Looks like it,' he answered, suddenly feeling very sore and shaky. Looking for a place to sit down.

'We'd never have won without you,' she persisted.

'Won?' he asked, simply astonished. 'What do you mean you *won*?'

'We have the professor's bottle, of course,' she chuckled. 'Not that it was worth all this trouble in the end. *What price glory*, eh?'

Now Richard really did need to sit down. 'Robin, do you know what that thing's *worth*?' he gasped.

'I dunno,' she answered dismissively. 'A battered old second-hand plastic drink bottle? Not a lot, I'd say . . .

'Now what on earth's amusing you, Richard? What are you laughing at? Come on, you bloody man, share the joke, why don't you?'